The House of Fame

ALSO BY OLIVER HARRIS

The Hollow Man

Deep Shelter

Oliver Harris

THE
HOUSE
OF
FAME

JONATHAN CAPE
LONDON

3 5 7 9 10 8 6 4 2

Jonathan Cape, an imprint of Vintage,
20 Vauxhall Bridge Road,
London SW1V 2SA

Jonathan Cape is part of the Penguin Random House group of companies
whose addresses can be found at global.penguinrandomhouse.com

Copyright © Oliver Harris 2016

First published by Jonathan Cape in 2016

www.vintage-books.co.uk

A CIP catalogue record for this book is available from the British Library

ISBN 9780224101875

Typeset in India by Thomson Digital Pvt Ltd, Noida, Delhi
Printed and bound in Great Britain by Clays Ltd, St Ives plc

Penguin Random House is committed to a sustainable future for our
business, our readers and our planet. This book is made from Forest
Stewardship Council® certified paper.

The time is coming when man will give birth to no more stars.

Friedrich Nietzsche

1

THEY'D CUT THE ELECTRICITY. Mid-morning the sun hit the CID office, sliced by the window's metal screen into planes of tobacco smoke and dust. By 3 p.m. it reached the back of the building: Belsey liked to open the doors on the first-floor corridor so light stretched from the kitchen to the interview rooms. Long lozenges of gold slipped across the chipped walls, made the place feel less abandoned. It created a sundial around him. He sat on the floor and watched it all. Caught in the bars of light, the dust seemed frenzied, directionless. His smoke rolled through it. He used the clocks as ashtrays.

Hampstead police station had closed three weeks ago, one of six across London disposed of in cost-cutting measures. Most staff had been reassigned at the end of last year. Belsey had expected to go to Holborn, but nothing happened. The DI at Holborn said they'd tried to get him only to be told he was blocked. Then, ten days after the station closed, he was informed he'd been officially suspended pending a hearing over allegations of gross misconduct. No details. A few hours after that, he got a call from a man who wouldn't give his name but told him he was under surveillance: the Independent Police Complaints Commission were collecting ammo, approaching everyone from

Belsey's exes to his past informers, putting obs on his car, his local, his current landlord. They were bracing themselves for a shit-storm. *Stay safe*, the caller said, and hung up. An hour later Belsey withdrew the contents of his current account, bought a gas stove, three bottles of Havana Club and a book – *Teach Yourself Spanish*. He broke into his old place of work, changed the locks. It was, he felt, the last place they'd look for him.

Eleven days ago.

It had been an odd stretch of time. Sometimes he found himself following patterns of an old routine, standing in the CID kitchen at 10.30 making a tea; lying on the floor of the old meeting room watching the wiring exposed by missing ceiling panels. He'd wander the station. The building dated to 1913, a labyrinthine relic with adjoining courthouse and cells. Most of it had been disused for decades. But in the process of clearing out, older areas had been unlocked: the abandoned station had grown, extending itself back into the past. Belsey walked through the magistrate's court to an Edwardian custody suite, past old fuse switches to cells that had become carpeted in handwritten reports from the 1950s and '60s: loose, yellowed papers, notebooks with cracked leather covers like shells. They had spilled from rat-chewed cardboard boxes, an infestation, filled with the handwriting of dead policemen. Sometimes he'd skim through old cases to keep his mind occupied. There were unnerving moments, once or twice a day, when it felt as if he was meant to be here after all, assigned for reasons that had faded. The thick old glass made the place feel submarine. His kingdom until ten minutes ago, when someone had started knocking on the front door.

The steady insistence of the knocks was troubling. Ceremonious. A ceremony he was failing to perform: the coming of reality. He knew that this last misdemeanour, like the rest, had been a taunt, the gambler's desire to suspend the moment of reckoning, to conjure options from nothing. The knocking was at the main entrance, directly beneath the CID office. Belsey looked down through the shutters but the angle was too tight. The sign down there was clear enough: HAMPSTEAD POLICE STATION IS NOW CLOSED. YOUR NEAREST STATION IS KENTISH TOWN. No one knew where he'd chosen to lie low. But the knocking felt like the return of something he'd forgotten: a debt, an arrangement, a plan of action.

Belsey walked down to the wood-panelled shadows of the old magistrate's court. He took a clean shirt from the line of phone cable he had strung above the pews. He picked up a heavy overcoat with metal buttons and white thread where the sergeant's stripes had been. The pockets contained his phone charger, passport, bank card and £220 in cash. Next to the coat was a foot of copper piping he'd picked up from the basement just in case. He put the coat on, slipped the piping up the sleeve, ran a hand over his eleven-day beard and took a breath. He unlocked the door at the back of the court and stepped out.

The day seemed unnaturally bright. Forty-eight hours since he'd been directly beneath the sky. Belsey climbed over the fence and dropped, silently, to the pavement. He walked to the corner and watched: a woman with shoulder-length white hair glancing up at the shuttered windows. Torn, mauve jacket. Feet in socks and sandals. Belsey stepped out.

'Are you OK?' he asked.

'I need the police,' she said.

'This station's closed. Want me to call them for you?'

'Closed?'

'Since last month.'

Belsey looked around. Hampstead's boutiques had their awnings unrolled, couture on display. Nothing had changed. It was the afternoon, but not school run yet. The lull between lunch and rush hour.

'Are you a policeman?' the woman asked. She had pale eyes with fear frozen into them.

'Not really,' Belsey said. 'Nearest police station is Kentish Town. Lots of police there.' He gestured towards the phone box. 'I can dial the number; you can tell the police what happened.'

'I was told to come *here*.'

'Well, someone made a mistake.'

She nodded, as if she'd suspected as much all along. 'Would I find Detective Nick Belsey at Kentish Town?' she asked.

Belsey stopped. His mind tracked through possible explanations.

'Why do you want Nick Belsey?'

'I was told he could help.'

'With what?'

'My son. He's disappeared.'

'Who told you to come here?'

'A man – he phoned the house.'

'Who was he?'

'I can't remember his name. I wrote it down. It's not on me.'

She looked desperate. The day turned a little colder.

'Your son went missing and a man called and said you should come here?'

'Yes.'

'What else did he say?'

'Just that I should try to find Mark, urgently.'

'Mark's your son?'

'Yes.'

'What's his surname?'

'Doughty.'

It was no one Belsey knew. 'How long's he been missing?'

'Almost two days.'

'How old is he?'

4

'Forty-one.'

This didn't seem to lower the urgency – she reached for the railings to support herself, looked unsteady. Belsey helped her down to sit on the front steps. He took a seat beside her.

'I'm Nick Belsey,' he said.

She glanced at him with her scared eyes, chest rising and falling. He wasn't sure she'd taken it in.

'I know you must be very busy,' she said, when she had her breath.

'What's your name?'

'Maureen.'

'Try and breathe, Maureen. Nice and calmly.'

Belsey leaned back, shut his eyes, felt the sun on his face. Life sought you out. The sun rose, people knocked. He let the piping slip out of his sleeve and placed it on the step. There were plenty of old acquaintances who might recommend him, plenty oblivious to his predicament. What difference did any of it make? He imagined a distress flare penetrating the roof of his mouth and igniting in his brain.

When he opened his eyes Maureen Doughty was studying his face. He smiled, got to his feet and helped her up. 'What day is it?' he asked.

'Monday.'

'Monday,' he repeated. They stood there for a moment, Belsey with a hand beneath her arm, Maureen watching each car that passed, as if it might contain her son. He didn't want to be outside. He wanted to return to the dust and continue entertaining the idea that he had options. She clutched the railings again. 'Let's get you home,' Belsey said.

2

THEY CAUGHT THE 46 BUS. Belsey ignored the stares of his fellow citizens: on his coat, his beard. At Queen's Crescent, Maureen pressed the bell and they disembarked. She led the way to a ground-floor flat in one of the low council blocks behind the high street.

The key shook in her hand as she unlocked the front door.

They stepped over carrier bags into the hall. The house smelt of damp and soil. It was cold. Off the hall was a living room cluttered with pot plants and bound piles of Christian pamphlets. A bed had been made up on a floral sofa. Belsey hadn't been in someone's home for a while. Not an aspect of the job he missed: the underwear on the clothes horse, the halos of grease up the wall behind the armchairs. Pill bottles crowded the coffee table like pieces for a game: donepezil, which meant Alzheimer's or dementia; ketoprofen, for arthritis; heavy-duty painkillers.

Nothing happened when he tried the light switches. In the kitchen, the microwave display was off; same with the radio. Stacks of plates crusted with old food, a back door into a cramped concrete courtyard. Someone had kicked in the cat flap leaving an empty frame of plastic. The glass was cracked.

Maureen filled the kettle.

'You've got no power, Maureen. It won't work.'

'Oh yes.' She stood with the kettle for a moment, then poured the water into the sink.

'How long's the electricity been off?'

'I'm not sure. Mark does it.'

Belsey checked the fuse box. Then he found the meter flashing in a cupboard by the front door. She needed to top up a power key.

'This is him,' she called from the living room. He returned to find her tapping a framed photo on the living room's chest of drawers. It was a school photo. Mark Doughty's twelve-year-old face had been propped between a school prize and a prayer card. She picked it up and gave it to Belsey. Mark had been a striking child, paper-white skin, eyes small and bright, hair neatly combed. In the uniform of a local private school. A scholarship boy, Belsey imagined, who never quite fitted in.

'He's a bit older than this now, isn't he?' Belsey said.

'Yes.'

'Do you have any more recent photos, Maureen?'

'I'm not sure.' She looked troubled by this and began casting about the room. The fear in her eyes was permanent, he saw. But she wasn't mad. He knew from experience how hard it was to gauge sanity. Beyond a modest dose of fear and disorientation she seemed sharp enough.

'Does Mark work at all?'

'He can't work. He looks after me.' She eased herself down onto the sofa.

'Have you told any other police?'

'They say there's nothing they can do. He hasn't been missing long enough.'

'What happens when you try to call him?'

'It's the recorded message.'

7

There was a small room on the ground floor that she used as a bedroom. Belsey climbed the stairs. At the end of the landing was a very pink bathroom, beside a spare room with a washing machine and cupboards of her old clothes. Also off the landing, a closed door. Locked.

'Is this where Mark sleeps?' he called down. 'The locked door?'

'Yes.'

He crouched and checked the keyhole. No key in the lock; darkness on the other side.

'Do you have a key?'

'No.'

Was Mark Doughty in there? he wondered. Was she sure he wasn't? Two days. No flies, only a slight smell that seemed general to the place. Belsey took a wire coat hanger from the wardrobe in the utility room, uncoiled it, bent the end until he had a loop. It was an easy lock. He felt the click, paused, turned the handle slowly and walked through.

'Christ.'

The room was an explosion. Books and clothes covered the floor. Cans of energy drink and takeaway packaging. Magazine pages taped up across walls and cupboard doors.

Belsey stepped over the mounds of stale clothes and opened the curtains. He turned and admired the décor again. Celebrities – singers, actresses: glossy pages of eyes and teeth and brightly coloured dresses like frigid pornography. Gowns spilled over red carpets, bikinis emerged from turquoise water. The A-list gazed out over a double bed with a coverless duvet, opened packets of biscuits, disposable razors. Mugs had grown mould, shelves were crowded with tattered books that looked like they'd been rescued from a skip. A cupboard with its mirrored door off its hinges added another plane of reflected chaos. There was a smell of urine and unwashed denim.

Rooms like this never boded well, places that had witnessed too much unspent life, had taken on the burden of living themselves; growing septic, choking.

No PC visible, but print-outs, from an internet café or library. Belsey sifted through a few sheets on a desk beneath the window. They were shuffled with other cuttings. Mark Doughty, it seemed, collected interviews, adverts, gossip columns. He cut out diet ideas and had printed an online personality test: 'What's stopping you living the life you want to lead? Try this simple survey.'

After twenty years in the police force, Belsey had concluded that not everyone should live the life they wanted to lead.

On the bedside table was a perfume box: *Bride: The New Fragrance by Amber Knight*. It shimmered in reflective pink. The bottle stood proudly beside it, clear glass in the shape of a diamond. He couldn't smell any perfume. This bedside nook was a shrine, he realised. On the wall behind the table, all the decorations related to Amber Knight: carefully preserved interviews, photo spreads. Teen Amber, precocious and oblivious. Twenty-one-year-old Amber, dress slashed down to her belly button, seductive eyes heavy with false lashes. Then sophisticated Amber, a year or so later, pale in a silver sheath dress on a red carpet: 'Stunning in Dior at last night's Woman of the Year Awards, chart-topping British singer and now Hollywood actress Amber Knight . . .'

As an obsession, Belsey respected Mark's choice. She was alluring, working a well-tested combination of innocence and newly awoken sexual hunger. And there was something that put her a cut above; eyes that established a pact with you personally, sidestepping the photographer and the sheen of the magazine.

'You got in.' Maureen stood uncertainly in the bedroom doorway. She stared at the walls as if she hadn't seen them for a while.

'He liked Amber Knight,' Belsey said, for want of anything better to say. 'Lots of her.'

'Oh yes.'

'He's got the perfume and everything.'

'He wasn't queer.'

'No.'

She glanced around once more then retreated downstairs. Belsey stepped over the clothes to a dresser: on the top were empty canisters of Lynx, a pouch of tobacco, candle stubs and a pub ashtray filled with the ends of rolled cigarettes. In the drawer of the dresser he found library cards for three boroughs and a dog-eared King's University ID from 2001. Mark had knifed up the laminate and manually adjusted the date. A student discount was nothing to lose. Mark Doughty stared out, late twenties, early thirties, postgraduate or mature student. The years since school hadn't added much colour to his cheeks. They'd added wisps of brown beard and lent a certain mug-shot defiance to his eyes: long hair thinning, tucked behind his ears. The clever scholarship twelve-year-old had gone awry. He looked addict-thin. Belsey found a roach in the ashtray, split it with his nail. He sifted the tobacco for powders. Hard to tell. The pouch of tobacco was fresh enough; it contained Rizlas, no other drug. Belsey pocketed it and walked back to the landing. He heard Maureen Doughty talking. Belsey thought she was on the phone, then heard her addressing the Lord. He stood at the top of the stairs and felt a place thick with incestuous madness.

When he went down she was on the sofa, curled over her clasped hands, eyes closed.

'The man who called – his name. You wrote it down.'

'Yes. I wrote it down.' She stopped praying, searched amongst the pill bottles on the coffee table and found a leaflet for the Catholic Medical Association. 'Here. Look.' On the back, in shaky writing, was the name 'Lee' followed by a mobile number Belsey knew off by heart.

'Lee Chester.'

'He didn't give his full name. Do you know him?'

Every police officer in north London knew Lee Chester. He was senior management in the capital's flow of proscribed narcotics.

'What did Lee say? Exactly?'

'Just that you might help.'

'He didn't say Mark owes money? Anything like that?'

'I'm not sure.'

'Did he threaten you?'

'No.'

'But he didn't just call, did he, Maureen? The back door – that was him.'

She wouldn't look up.

Belsey went out to the concrete courtyard and dialled Lee's number.

'Nicky, mate.' Belsey could hear a car engine, traffic.

'Guess who I'm with.'

'Did she come to you? I didn't think she would.'

'It's not very nice to scare old ladies, Lee. How much does he owe you?'

'About a grand. Is he there?'

'No.' Belsey looked back at the maisonette, up to the window of the bedroom. He sat down on a broken section of wall. 'What does he score?'

'All sorts.'

'Where does he get the money?'

'A life of crime, I imagine. Fuck knows. Whatever it is, he needs to do some more of it fast.'

'So you told his mother to hire a private investigator?'

'You're not a private investigator.'

'That's a good point, Lee. Let's bear it in mind next time. It can be what we take from this whole miserable experience.'

'You've got connections.'

'Right now my best connection's sitting on a piss-stained sofa praying to Jesus.'

'Who else am I going to send her to?'

'Anyone.'

'I'm not writing it off, Nick. People think I'm a muppet for dealing with him already.'

'You kicked the back door in.'

'I'm not like that, Nick.'

'Yes you are.'

Belsey hung up and went back in. There was no food in the cupboards. On the sofa, Maureen stared dumbly at an empty bottle of pregabalin, massaging her swollen hands. He found the repeat scripts on the counter behind the prayer card, took the power key from the meter.

'I'll be straight back.'

He left the house, turned onto Queen's Crescent. The road was a curve of shops, cutting through the estate. It filled up twice a week with stalls selling cheap clothes and household cleaning products. Without the market it felt deflated. Poundland, Magic Hair Salon, a scruffy pub, a lot of identical grocery stores, owners standing in their doorways, looking out.

Belsey found one that charged power keys and put ten pounds on Maureen Doughty's key. The shopkeeper was unshaven, in a leather jacket, keeping an eye on a TV above the door showing news in Turkish.

'Do you know a man called Mark Doughty?' Belsey asked. 'He's local, maybe charges his power key here. Son of Maureen Doughty.'

The shopkeeper shook his head. Belsey walked out. The afternoon was sinking towards its end. A man in a wheelchair sat on the corner of Malden Road sipping Tennent's, another dutifully moving between phone boxes checking the coin slots. Three kids drifted past on bikes with the solemn air of a security patrol.

Belsey sat in Bubbles Launderette and rolled a cigarette with Mark Doughty's tobacco. He watched the pub across the road, the Sir Robert Peel. He wondered what spirit of mischief inspired this corner of London to name a pub in honour of the founder of the modern police force. The launderette clock said five past four. Belsey counted his money. A clever man would buy seeds, fill the drawers of his old desk with compost, survive alone. Belsey walked into the pub.

The place was cool and dark. An old man sat in the far corner, eyes closed, a beer mat protecting his pint from flies. A landlord whose polo shirt didn't fully cover his stomach nodded to Belsey.

'A Guinness, please.'

The man pulled the pint and let it settle.

'Does a guy called Mark Doughty ever drink here?' Belsey asked.

'No idea, son.' He took Belsey's money and passed the drink over. Belsey remained standing at the bar. Seventy-two hours without proper sleep: his body was finely balanced. He sipped and let the alcohol ride to his brain. He drank to Sir Robert Peel. Fuck the police, as the saying goes.

An inquiry into him was one thing, suspension another. Suspension, to his mind, meant a foregone conclusion. It meant they either thought he could prejudice the investigation or it would look bad having the subject of a gross-misconduct inquiry turning up for work. The whole thing was being managed by a new commander, Clive Randall, who Belsey had never met – who refused to meet Belsey now or speak to him on the phone. He heard the voice that had tipped him off, as he had done often over the past week. Someone who had cared about him once or was worried about how much he might reveal. It felt important, partly because it was the last significant human contact he'd had before today, partly because Belsey's interpretation of his past hinged on the voice's concern. All judgements were contained in that one.

A pair of community support officers ambled past the pub, met his eyes before he could look away, kept walking. He waited for them to turn the corner before finishing his pint and stepping out.

He bought tea, milk, some bread and eggs, then went into Fine Pharmacy. Between the racks of slimming pills and incontinence pads, a man with his hood up was drinking methadone. Behind the counter, a locked glass case displayed razor blades and fragrances: Eternity, Chanel, Dior. No Bride by Amber Knight.

Belsey handed Maureen Doughty's prescriptions to a small woman in a white coat. She glanced at the paperwork, eyed his beard and creased shirt.

'Usually it's the son,' she said.

'You know him?'

'Not really.'

'He's gone missing.'

'OK.'

'Since Saturday. I'm trying to find him.'

'I only know him to see. Who are you?'

'A friend of the family.'

The chemist checked the prescriptions, assessed him again then fetched the drugs. She bagged them up and gave Belsey instructions about when and how often they needed to be taken. He thanked her and took a final look at the perfumes.

'There's a new perfume. I think it's called Bride. By Amber Knight.'

'Yes.'

'Do you stock it?'

'No.'

'OK. I'll try elsewhere. Thank you.'

He was past the toothpastes when the woman said: 'You won't find it anywhere.'

Belsey turned back.

'Why not?'

'It's not out.'

'Not out?'

'It's not available. Not yet. It hasn't been released.'

'When's it released?'

'Next week.'

'You're sure?'

'Yes.'

He stepped out with the paper bag and wondered what he'd seen in Mark Doughty's room.

Maureen Doughty answered the door and looked surprised to see him again. Belsey gave her the bag of medication and charged the electricity. Then he went to Mark's bedroom and switched on the light. He picked up the perfume bottle. It was a good weight. He put it back and lifted the box. This also struck him as authentic: UK barcode, the name in raised lettering against the pearly background.

He looked around the room again, crouched, peered under the bed – and saw the toe of a stocking.

It trailed from a rucksack. Belsey pulled the bag out. It contained women's clothing: vest, leggings, skirt, underwear. There was a pair of silk Alexander McQueen pyjamas, a Chanel clutch, a Gucci scarf. He emptied it all onto the floor. The knickers were all small; the bras all 34B. They were in good condition but not shop-new; no price tags, freshly laundered, high quality.

The only other thing under the bed was a blue carrier bag containing nylon gloves, a torch and two screwdrivers. A housebreaker's kit.

Belsey searched through the pile of clothes again. Hidden amongst the underwear were a tub of Crème de la Mer face cream and a photograph of Amber Knight with her family. At the very bottom of the rucksack was her passport.

He took the passport into the centre of the room, held it beneath the naked bulb. It looked genuine. He wouldn't have recognised her in the photo: hair scraped back, light make-up, scoop-necked top. But it was her: Amber Sophia Knight. Date of Birth: 2 June 1991. Validated seven months ago.

She had a stalker with very intimate access. Belsey took out his phone and tried to find where exactly Amber Knight was living these days. An article came up with pictures of Amber house-hunting for a central London base.

Until recently she'd been living with her mum near Epping, in the village of Theydon Bois, where she'd grown up. Her mother ensured she 'kept her feet on the ground': '"We chat, we bake, we watch TV."' In February last year the appeal of standing on the ground must have worn off. Along with the appeal of being managed by her mother, who she ditched. Amber bought a £13 million mansion on Wadham Gardens in Primrose Hill. She put in a £1.5 million basement extension and re-landscaped the garden. The result was somewhere she could call 'her first proper home'. She was twenty-three years old. Her first proper home was ten minutes' walk from Mark Doughty's.

Belsey studied the passport again. He sifted through a few more clippings. Underneath pages of *Grazia* and *Heat* was a more sober document from a site called the Home Chemist: 'Three poisons you can make in your kitchen'. It listed recipes for ricin, cyanide and the botulinum toxin.

He picked up the university ID from the dresser, met Mark Doughty's troubled gaze, then slipped it into his wallet. He took Amber Knight's passport and went downstairs.

Maureen Doughty was standing nervously in the living room, like someone awaiting test results.

'I found this,' Belsey said.

'What is it?'

'It appears to be Amber Knight's passport.'

'Amber Knight?'

'Know her?'

'I don't know anything about that.'

'Has Mark ever been in trouble with the police, Maureen?'

'No.'

'Did he ever say anything about things he wanted to do? Maybe bad things?'

She hesitated.

'He wanted to be famous.'

'Excellent,' Belsey sighed. 'Maureen, what did he study at the uni?'

'Chemistry. He started, twice. But he doesn't finish things. He was always very brilliant, Mark. But he has difficulty concentrating.'

'Has he brought any chemicals into the house, ever?'

Maureen Doughty shook her head despondently. She came over, took Belsey's left hand in both her own. 'He's my only child. I don't know what I'd do without him.'

3

THE SHORTEST ROUTE TO AMBER Knight's house was across Chalk
Farm Road. The busy thoroughfare was all that divided Maureen
Doughty's estate from one of the most desirable enclaves of an expensive
city. But Amber's neighbourhood, Primrose Hill, was isolated enough
to keep its rich inhabitants happy, protected by rail tracks to the west,
Regent's Canal to the east, and a general air of affluence more effective
than a moat. It was an island and another world.

Belsey crossed the bridge over the tracks and wondered where he
was headed and why.

Last time he lived somewhere with a TV Amber Knight was still a
teenager. He remembered seeing her on a chat show and she came
across as young, self-possessed, ambitious. On a date a year ago he
saw her in her first film role: a nurse in a time of war, with decisions
to make. She was a good actress as well. He could name two hit singles
in the last year and picture the videos to go with them. Her personal
life was vaguer, gleaned from tabloid pages he hadn't dwelled on. Men
happened; she'd briefly been in LA with an actor, then in London with
a footballer, he remembered that. He had a sense that she currently
considered herself a businesswoman, branching out, taking control.

He didn't wish a slow death from botulism upon anyone, and all she'd done was be beautiful and talented. Mark Doughty concerned him. Everyone's sick and evil; humanity's redeeming feature was its laziness – most people kept their malevolence in fantasies. Then there are the industrious ones, those who get off their arses and prepare. From what he could tell, Mark Doughty was nothing if not industrious.

If he could get into her underwear drawer, he could get into her stomach, her lungs, her nervous system. That was how stalkers worked, imposing intimacy, turning up uninvited in nightmares.

Belsey turned onto Regent's Park Road. Primrose Hill twinkled in the sun. Cherry blossom, hanging baskets, new cars gleaming. Pale bricks held the soft light. Children with ski tans walked beside Asian nannies. The local adults wore gilets, tailored jackets, knee-high boots. The high street curved unhurriedly towards the park, pastel-coloured, independently owned: delis, pet accessories, cupcakes. Belsey stopped at a rack outside a newsagent's and browsed two tabloids. Nothing about an Amber stalker or a break-in at her home. But there she was on the gossip pages. All the talk centred on her upcoming wedding to a millionaire property developer: rumours about her dress, her diet, her tears.

Kentish Town – that was the closest police station to Primrose Hill. Belsey called an old drinking buddy.

'Jim, it's Nick. Nick Belsey.'

Jim hung up.

Same with Matt Yarwood at Holborn, Sheila French at West End Central. Guilt was contagious, every police officer knew that. Belsey put his phone away. A wine shop across the road advertised its own book club: *Our sommelier will match wines to the books. First glass free.* He went in, bought a miniature of vodka and drank it in the shop. Back outside, he took the passport from his pocket and checked it again. He felt the same buzz of excitement, a bit of fame in his possession.

The address was one street away from the park. The properties themselves hid behind high brick walls and mature trees. No mistaking Amber Knight's wall though: four schoolgirls sat on the pavement beside a very large, very solid-looking wooden gate. They clutched T-shirts and CDs. The gate had security cameras angled down on either side. Across the road were two men, one in a Mini with the door open, one leaning against a low garden wall, both in heavy coats. The man on his feet had a camera around his neck and a bag of photographic lenses.

The photographers looked wary as Belsey approached. He showed Mark's uni ID.

'Seen this guy around at all?'

They were happy enough to look at the picture, reluctant to divulge information. The standing one shrugged.

'Amber in?'

'Maybe.'

'Has there been any trouble recently? Police about?'

'Why?'

They were cagey. In their line of work you had to earn your tip-offs. They had him down as an amateur hack.

Belsey crossed the road. He bummed a cigarette off the schoolgirls, squatted down and got a light.

'Do you know if Amber's in at the moment?'

'Yes.'

'She's filming.'

'We saw her car go through.'

Belsey went to the gate and buzzed the intercom. No one answered. Belsey waited sixty seconds then walked to the park.

He sat on a bench beside a mother and daughter. The mother was on her phone, talking about a problem with a French tutor. Belsey called Charlotte Kelson at the *Mail on Sunday*.

'Well, Nick Belsey. What a pleasant surprise. Are you OK?'

'Why wouldn't I be?'

'I heard things have got a bit complicated.'

'Things have never been simpler.'

'Where are you?'

'Primrose Hill. I'm actually phoning about Amber Knight.'

Kelson laughed. 'Going to the wedding?'

'Probably not. Have you heard anything about a stalker getting into her home?'

'No. Sounds like you've got a story. You know a guy last week got twenty grand for a copy of the guest list.'

'Twenty grand?'

'For a sheet of paper.'

'When's the wedding?'

'Saturday.'

'And her perfume, Bride, that's connected to the wedding.'

'Well done, Nick. You've still got it.'

'OK.'

'I reckon you could get thirty grand for a picture of the wedding dress. It's meant to have half a million quid's worth of Swarovski crystals on it. Forty-plus for anything juicy.'

'What does juicy mean?'

'Well, something like trouble with a stalker, Nick. Come to me. I'll let you buy me dinner.'

They hung up. Belsey checked gossip sites on his phone in case any less official corner of celebrity news had a lead. Amber was rumoured to be on a liquids-only diet. She swore by Revlon's Autumn

Spice scented nail enamel. She kept a picture of her ex by her bed. She was secretly quite shy.

There were a lot of pictures of her holding cocktails in exclusive London situations, not looking shy. Nobu, Scott's, the Berkeley. In a city to which the world aspires, someone has to look like they're having fun. Amber was the gold standard underwriting it all. Her favourite designer was Valentino. She had been named Gillette's Legs of the Year. She loved Vitamin Water's new range of spring flavours, and used a Sony Cyber-shot camera to capture special moments.

Last year, after splitting from her parental manager, she'd moved to another company. All enquiries directed to Karen at Milkshake Management. Belsey found a number for the company and dialled.

'Milkshake,' a woman answered, brightly.

'This is Nick Belsey, Kentish Town CID. I've been asked to get in touch about Amber Knight. Is Karen there?'

'Karen's not in today.'

'OK. Anyone I can speak to today?'

There was some hesitation.

'Who is this?'

'Detective Inspector Nick Belsey. It's quite urgent. I have Amber's passport here. I think she might be in danger. Is there a PA or anything?'

'You have her passport?'

'I found her passport at the home of someone I believe broke into Amber's house.'

'Really?'

'Yes.'

'Hang on.' The woman disappeared, came back thirty seconds later. 'You can try Gabby. Gabby's at the house.' She recited a mobile number. 'She's the PA. She deals with security.'

It took Gabby a minute to answer the phone.

'Who is this?'

'My name's Nick Belsey. I was told to call you about Amber's security.'

'Nick Belsey?' Her accent was an icy transatlantic.

'I have some concerns about—'

'Hold on.' It sounded noisy behind her: there was a dog barking, men's voices, echoes across a large space. She exchanged words with someone before addressing Belsey again. 'You were meant to call us yesterday.'

Belsey considered this.

'It's been hectic,' he said.

'I explained to whoever it is at your office that this was urgent.'

'Has something happened?'

'I think it was a Chris I was dealing with.'

'Sure. This is Nick now. Chris is away.'

'For god's sake. Where are you? Can you come in?'

'Can I come in?'

'Now is all I've got. And it will have to be quick.'

He suppressed an urge to laugh.

'I'm in Primrose Hill at the moment, actually.'

'Give me a call when you're outside.'

She hung up. Belsey moved the phone from his ear and stared at a lot of people jogging in a line. The world had become stranger since he withdrew his involvement. Gravity was lighter, oxygen thinner. The woman on the bench beside him hadn't paused. 'Natasha used them with the twins and said they were superb, but all she's learned in three weeks is how to order a bloody ice cream.'

Belsey walked back to Amber Knight's road. He checked his reflection in the wing mirror of a Lambretta and shook his head in wonder. What the fuck was he doing? Past the paparazzi, the schoolgirls. He dialled Gabby again.

'I'm outside.'

'Make sure the gate shuts behind you.'

The gate buzzed open. A schoolgirl ran up and handed Belsey a pink envelope.

'Can you give this to Amber?'

'Sure.'

He walked through. A camera clicked behind him. The gate shut.

Amber had bought a beautiful home. A double-fronted house looking like nothing in two hundred years had left a mark. White gravel stretched to the front door with neat lawn either side. Two Porsches, yellow and silver, had been moved onto the grass to accommodate a black van. The front door of the house itself was open a crack, cable running out to a generator on the lawn. Belsey pushed it and stepped into a hallway with huge mirrors and polished floorboards. A grey pug ran out of a room to the right and pawed at his legs. Someone said: 'Cut.'

Through the doors he could see a small film crew, a man with a camera on his shoulder, a boom, lights, other people with headphones, radio mics. The room was double height with a white piano on a rug, glass stairs twisting up to a mezzanine level, a swing seat hanging from the ceiling. It stretched to the back of the house, to more glass: a wall of it looking onto a garden. As well as the film crew there was an entourage of smarter men and women with IDs hanging around their necks. On the sofa, head tilted to receive a make-up brush: there was Amber.

The star was more brightly lit than the anonymous people around her, but she looked real enough. Odd with reality, in fact. She wore a white sweater, jeans with a rip exposing tanned thigh. Her hair was up. She was no more than ten metres from him.

That had been easy enough.

She was alive at least. No sign of any chemical poisoning. Belsey turned back to the hallway, put the fan's envelope on a ledge at the side. Someone said: 'Excuse me.' He turned to see a young woman with a headset and clipboard emerging from the living room.

'Have you signed a release form?'

'A release form?'

'Have you been in it before?'

'No.'

She thrust a clipboard with a release form in his direction, pen resting on the dotted line. He checked the sheet: Halcyon Entertainment. *One Perfect Day.* 'I hereby irrevocably consent to the inclusion in this documentary of my appearance and words . . .'

'I'd rather my face wasn't shown.'

She peered at him, struggling to get her head around this.

'Seriously?'

'I'm on the run.'

The woman shrugged and took the clipboard back as if he was an arsehole. Her radio crackled. Belsey watched her return to the room, head over to a man with a utility belt who was peeling tape from the floor.

He walked towards the back of the house, past a huge chrome and copper kitchen, a room with a small catwalk and mirrored walls adjoining what looked like a fully functional salon with sinks for hair-washing and a nail bar. Five model heads sported wigs in different styles. Wide, carpeted stairs took him up to a first floor with a lot of rooms that looked like waiting areas for Thai restaurants – tasteful combinations of cream, dark wood and slate. Belsey peeked through doorways until he found a woman going through a chest of drawers. He watched her sifting papers for a moment before she sensed him, stiffened, then placed the papers back very carefully before turning.

'Hey,' she smiled. She was short, in patent leather heels, long dark hair, bright red lips and thick mascara.

'Hey.'

'I haven't seen you around before.' The woman thrust a hand out. 'Terri.'

'Nick. I'm looking for Gabby, Amber's PA.'

'She's definitely around somewhere.' Terri studied him, hungrily. Now Belsey saw the notebook and Dictaphone on the coffee table. 'So how do you know Amber?'

'I'm security. Just started.'

'Ah. Security. Well, welcome to the madhouse.' She winked. 'You've got a job on your hands.'

'Why's that?'

'Oh, you know. Everything. I'll let Gabby fill you in.'

She gave him a business card and smiled again. The card identified her as Terri Baker, the *Mirror*'s show-business correspondent.

'Do you have a card?' she asked.

'Not on me.'

'We're all one big team here,' Terri said. 'I'm sure we'll see each other around.'

'I'm sure.'

Belsey returned to the corridor, went up another floor. There was a room with massage tables and one with a dance floor beneath a mirror ball, framed magazine covers on the wall, windows leading onto a large balcony. Belsey crossed the unlit dance floor to the balcony. It was busy out there, he saw as he got close. On the other side of the window two men with secateurs and watering cans tended a lush set of window boxes. Beyond them, a miraculous half-acre of garden lay green and empty. Intruders like side doors, back doors, access from gardens. And here it was: a set of steps leading down from the balcony terrace to the garden. A half-acre – that was a lot of perimeter to protect.

He returned to the landing and followed it to a pink marble bathroom as big as the Hampstead CID office. A jacuzzi took up a whole corner, next to twin sinks crowded with lotions, ornaments, awards. Adjoining the bathroom was an austere bedroom with a lot of white fabrics, white walls, hyacinths and scented candles. It had a flat-screen TV facing the bed. No picture of her ex by her bed, as rumour had suggested. One framed photo of a teenage Amber with a much older man who looked like he was her father.

Belsey opened drawers, found lingerie. The sizes matched Mark Doughty's haul. A woman passed the doorway, glanced in, stopped.

'Excuse me. Who are you?'

She was short, in her early thirties, with a severe black fringe. She clutched a bulging file. The voice was instantly recognisable.

'Gabby.' Belsey shut the drawer. 'Nick Belsey. The security guy.'

'What are you doing in here?'

'Exactly. This is a shambles.'

She stared at him. She looked angry, but also like she didn't have many facial expressions to choose from.

'I don't have long,' she said. 'Follow me.'

No handshake.

She led him back down the corridor, talking to the space in front of her.

'Do you need coffee? Water?'

'I'll be fine.'

They reached an office that didn't look like it had been fully occupied yet: neat piles of paper on the floor, bare shelves, an incongruous leather-topped desk, empty but for a MacBook. She dropped the file on the desk.

'Take a seat. I didn't realise Karen was on it.' She took one of the piles of paper from the floor and spread it over the desk. 'Where do you want to start?'

Belsey sat down and placed Amber's passport on the table, but Gabby was focused on her paperwork.

'We need a full twenty-four-seven team back on. There were originally three guys on rotation here. Amber might need some persuading, of course.' She ran her finger down bullet points. 'We need a review of her phone and emails and how secure that is. We've had someone trying to hack in, journalists snooping. All that needs to be sorted out.'

'Does that include the one downstairs?'

'Terri? Terri's OK. Terri's on-side.'

Her phone rang. She checked, then muted it. 'The thing right now is I need you to help keep costs down as much as possible. Obviously, this is sensitive . . .'

Belsey slid the passport towards her. Gabby checked it this time, frowned.

'I've been looking for this. Where did you get it?'

'It was in the bedroom of a man called Mark Doughty, about ten minutes' walk from here.' She showed no recognition of the name. Belsey moved the paperwork to the side and placed Mark's ID on the desk. 'Recognise him?'

Gabby took a good look.

'Yes,' she nodded. 'I've seen him. That's him.'

'Go on.'

'He's been around a few times. I've seen him at events.'

'Ever in here? In the house?'

'God no.'

'He had some clothes that look like they belong to Amber as well.'

Things were dawning slowly and unpleasantly on her. 'Is that where they've been going? Oh wow. Yes, some clothes have been going missing.'

'You've told the police?'

'No.'

'Let them know. I think Mark Doughty may be dangerous, but there's a limit to what I can do. Check any security footage you have. If you see him entering the property pass it to the police. And tell Amber.'

'What are you saying about me?'

They both turned. Amber stood in the doorway, cradling the pug. Belsey hadn't been prepared for the effect of proximity. She was just a person, of course, but a person in a lot of dreams across the globe, on billboards, magazine covers, the sides of buses. And here was the original, with eyes that didn't look at him. Belsey tried to imagine someone being in your house and not bothering to look at them.

Gabby got to her feet. 'Amber, you remember we had concerns about a fan.' She held out the ID.

Amber walked over. 'That's the guy.'

'You think?'

'Definitely.'

'I think so too,' Gabby said.

'Jesus. He's freaky,' Amber said. 'Who are you?' She hit Belsey with eye contact for the first time.

'This is our new security guy,' Gabby cut in. 'He's the best in the business. And totally checked out.'

'Good. Pleased to meet you.' She freed a hand to shake. Her hand was warm, the shake indistinct.

So he'd touched Amber Knight.

'What are you going to do about this?' She nodded at the ID. Her eyes had a curious intensity.

'I don't know.'

'You don't know?'

'We've got a strategy,' Gabby said. 'Don't worry.'

'Will you keep me informed this time?'

'Of course.'

Amber looked at the ID again, then at Belsey. 'I guess I'll be seeing you around.' She gave a sweet and unconvincing smile. Then she was gone.

Gabby exhaled. 'In future, please – she needs reassurance.'

'She needs good security,' Belsey said. 'What happened to the old team?'

'It didn't work out. Don't worry about that.'

'You fired them?'

'Amber fired them.'

'Why?'

'She thought they were spying on her.' Gabby checked the landing, closed the door. She sat down again. 'There's a situation here. A lot of nerves, a lot of high spirits. We have the wedding in less than a week, with a lot riding on it. This is a very important few days. Amber has a schedule.' She found a spreadsheet amongst the lists of security concerns. 'What I'd appreciate is, if she goes anywhere that isn't prearranged – I mean, by Karen or by myself – you let me know.'

Belsey glanced across the spreadsheet. The whole set-up shifted a little, the sense of what security meant here. Half an hour ago he couldn't get through the door, now he was being asked to babysit.

'Why?'

'Just do it. Right now, we're on a mission: get Amber to the church on time. Or to the Dorchester, at least. That's where the thing's happening. We had a little intervention last week – to calm her down – and I don't know if that's helped. We can't afford more bullshit. Tell me if she goes anywhere – and if she tries to get any money. Have you saved my number?' Her phone rang again. She checked the screen.

'I've got it.' Belsey pocketed the schedule. 'I'm going to need a cash float for expenses . . .'

'Right. I reckon that's possible. So long as you understand, at this moment in time, money's tight.'

'I'm sure.'

'Cash float.' She scribbled this on papers as she rose, phone still ringing in her hand. 'I'm going to have to take this.'

'And give Chris a call,' Belsey said. 'Just in case I'm redeployed at the last minute.'

'Stay there.'

She stepped out of the room, talking about a delivery of display stands. Belsey waited a moment then picked up Mark's ID and walked onto the landing. Gabby was down the corridor, pulling another door closed behind her. Privacy. The house felt more constricting now. He returned to the party room, with the balcony overlooking the garden. The gardeners had gone. He stepped onto the terrace, past the window boxes to the steps and down.

There was decking at the bottom, with an inbuilt barbeque and hot tub. He was on the other side of the sliding glass wall, looking into the living room, which had emptied, the abandoned flight cases of the film crew stark against the white décor. Someone had knocked out a lot of bricks to create this ten-metre-wide sliding door. But then the garden was worth seeing in panorama. Plum trees, a rock garden with its own waterfall, a stack of sun loungers. He crossed a Japanese-style bridge over a pond to the perimeter wall. The original wall had been supplemented with the razor wire of twenty-first-century security. He followed it to the furthest corner, to an incongruous shed.

The shed was locked. A dusty window afforded a glimpse of hi-spec gardening tools. Belsey looked up. There was something on the roof, material of some kind. He got a foot on the ledge of the window and hauled himself up. Folded on the tar paper was a pink, tasselled bath mat. Damp. Belsey unfolded it and saw diagonal grooves pressed into the underside. He compared them to the razor wire, now just a couple of feet away, and concluded it would make good protection for someone climbing over. It didn't match the décor of Amber's new home. But it would have gone nicely in Maureen Doughty's bathroom.

He couldn't see any security cameras. Belsey looked back towards the house. The sightline was obscured by the cluster of fruit trees. From the top of the wall he could see the neighbour's garden. It was equally large, but overgrown. The house it belonged to looked uninhabited: no lights on, a general air of neglect. Nestled within ragged hydrangeas at the foot of the wall was a retractable ladder.

Belsey draped the mat over the razors. The wall was wide enough to make the step-over easy. He dropped down into the hydrangeas. The ladder was untarnished, in good condition compared to the garden around it. He leaned it against the wall and saw how that would work.

Nearer the darkened house, things got bleaker. A swimming pool sat empty but for dead leaves. No garden furniture. He followed a side path to the front of the house and saw the estate agent's board. A chain had been fastened across the grand iron gates to the driveway but there was a smaller gate to the side, human-sized, and it opened stiffly towards him when he pulled.

It opened onto a back road. No photographers here. It was quiet, residential.

Belsey returned to the ladder, climbed up, stepped across to the shed, then down to the lawn. He imagined being Mark Doughty, dropping into Amber's world. The trees gave perfect cover as you descended. The curve of the garden meant you were out of view of the house.

He walked back towards the house, across the decking to the wall of glass. No security lights came on. The sliding window moved slickly aside, weighted so that you hardly had to touch it. He stepped into the living room.

He could hear the crew upstairs, knocking equipment into place. Belsey heard a mobile ringtone, then silence. He sat on the stool by the piano, lifted the lid and pressed a key. He took a photo of the room on his phone. What did he want? Thirty grand for a picture of the wedding dress? He had no desire to interfere with someone's wedding. Maybe he was just stalking.

He got up and opened a door at the far end of the room and gazed upon two or three hundred boxes of Bride.

They were stacked in a rough pyramid, the lower tiers formed by plastic-wrapped blocks of six. Beside the pyramid was a pile of silk pouches, silver ribbon printed with Amber's name, her fiancé's name – Guy – the date of the wedding. The perfect bag for the perfect gift – *One Perfect Day*. Perfect except for Mark Doughty helping himself to a pre-launch freebie.

Beyond the stack of perfume was a small door. Belsey walked in.

What had once been a drawing room of some kind now served as a crowded museum of strangers' affections, the final resting place for the debris of fame: boxes of chocolates, bouquets of dead flowers, racks of clothes with the labels on. There were several cases of unopened samples including tanning creams, protein shakes, gourmet diet meals and a revolutionary cordless epilator. At the back, past crates of Evian and a rowing machine, were six grey postbags all bulging with envelopes crudely slit open, letters still inside. '*I am 15 years old. I am from Tallinn. Maybe you know where that is. I am having a hard time in life and there's no one else I can share this with.*' Belsey sat on the floor and sifted through a few handfuls. No Mark Doughty. He got a lot of other Amber obsession. There were drawings, photographs, poetry.

You probably don't remember me. I had the copy of Heatwave *that you signed. I was so faint from queuing all night that I didn't have a chance to say what the album means to me . . .*

Next time you are in Japan please visit my town. Me and my sister love you. I want to be a singer . . .

Can you write my daughter a letter? Last June she was diagnosed with lupus. She is in hospital now and it would make her very happy . . .

He heard boots on the stripped floorboards of the living room. A lot of people, moving fast, coming towards him. Belsey eased the door closed. Then he heard Amber's voice.

'So here they are. My babies,' she said. 'This is what they'll look like.'

There was some discussion.

'Let's try one with you picking it up,' a man said.

They were filming right outside the door.

Belsey waited. After ten minutes they began setting up another shot.

He sat down on a box of nutritional supplements. It was a curious feeling, hiding in Amber Knight's house. The world's media was focused on the place and he was secret within it, sheltering in the eye of the storm. He picked up a bottle of CocoVodka with a note attached: '*Amber, we think you'll love this new concept . . .*'

He opened a sachet of the nutritional supplement and poured it into the new coconut-flavoured vodka sensation. He unwrapped a gluten-free energy bar, sat with his back against the door, read the fan mail and drank.

4

THERE WAS SOMETHING CALMING ABOUT hearing the crew clear up, the entourage rush about, the whole operation wind down. Belsey waited until it was silent, then waited for the silence to deepen. He wanted a clear exit out. No Amber, no release forms. He rested his eyes and dozed for a bit.

By the time he tried the door his phone said 7.30 p.m. The ground-floor lights were off. Grey twilight shrouded the swing seat and the piano. The house felt empty. Belsey crossed the living room then stopped, listening to the floors upstairs.

No one.

He imagined Amber out on the town, fulfilling her responsibilities to glamour. Eating sushi, drinking champagne. He couldn't imagine her arriving back any time soon.

He walked upstairs, found the kingsize bathroom, urinated, washed his hands and face. There was a small, golden gramophone amongst the body lotions: AMBER KNIGHT: BEST POP VOCAL ALBUM. He lifted it, put it back.

He sat on the edge of the bath.

He really hoped Mark Doughty wasn't killing anyone. Out there in the lonely world, with his aspirations to fame and his latent chemistry degree. He'd email his security advice to Milkshake Management. Maybe he'd put an anonymous call in to Kentish Town CID. Not that it would be taken very seriously. He didn't expect to be thanked.

Amber's voice broke the silence.

'No, that's not what she said to me. She said it was Conor she was worried about – what might happen to him. She's just not dealing with it . . .'

She was walking across the living room. In a second she would see the light from the bathroom at the top of the stairs.

'Ask her. I don't know.' It was a phone conversation. She was alone. 'Yes. Tonight. I've got to go now . . . Yes, OK.' There was a big sigh, then footsteps into the hallway. Belsey eased himself to his feet and went out onto the landing. The steps stopped.

'Hello?' Amber called, voice uncertain.

Belsey considered escape.

'Hello?' Amber called up again.

'Hey,' Belsey called brightly. 'It's me, Nick, the security guy. Just finishing off.'

He saw her anxious face, peering from halfway up the stairs. She wore a cropped T-shirt and leggings. She still had her hair and make-up from the filming.

'What are you doing?'

'Just some final checks.' He walked meaningfully towards a window and took hold of its handle.

'When did you get these window locks installed?' Belsey asked.

'What do you mean?'

'Are they connected to the main alarm system?'

'I don't know. I thought you'd gone.'

'I didn't want to leave these unchecked.'

He rattled the handle. She stared at him – a little like he was mad, but not scared or disbelieving any more.

'OK.'

She went back downstairs. He took a breath. Felt momentarily the dizzy thrill of being alone with Amber Knight in her darkened mansion. Went down.

Amber sat cross-legged on the living-room sofa, staring at her phone. She had a wine glass and a half-full bottle of Stolichnaya on the table in front of her.

'Sorry about that,' Belsey said. 'I'm off now. Good to meet you.'

She looked up.

'Where are you going?' She didn't sound angry. Sad, maybe. What a lot of house to be alone in. There was something melancholy about all that glass, looking onto darkness. He wondered if she'd locked it. Wondered how full the bottle had been.

'Honestly? I've no idea where I'm going.'

'How long are you paid for?'

'What do you mean?'

Amber took a deep breath. 'I need a favour. I sent them all away. I couldn't take it. And now I'm stuck.'

'You're stuck.'

'I need to get out. Badly. I mean, I need to not be here. Not be sitting here alone. There's a thing, in town. I thought I wasn't going to have any security. I didn't think I was going to go.'

'Right.'

'And, you know, I'm worried about this stalker,' she added.

'I think you're right to worry.'

'I can pay overtime,' Amber said. And she suddenly looked tearful, as if something had broken. 'I just don't want to be here.'

'You're asking me to accompany you?'

'Literally for two hours, there and back. And I'd make it worth your while.'

Her expression was blank again now – another rapid change.

Belsey tried to think of any reason he shouldn't. He made a show of checking his phone, as if it connected to a life.

'Sure,' he said, nodding. 'That's possible.'

'You could do that?'

'For two hours, why not? What's the event?'

'It's a launch, an after-party thing – for Beluggi. I mean, they're old but they're doing bags now. It won't be very special. Fashion people, cocktails. It's being run by a friend of mine. I'm meant to be an ambassador, you see.'

'I see. Well, it sounds fine.'

'Thank you. Thank you so much.' Amber ran a knuckle beneath her eyes. 'I'll get dressed and order us a car. Wait there.'

Belsey took a seat on the sofa. She needed a chaperon. An entourage. Was that it? He got up, checked all the doors and windows were locked – for real this time. He saw someone in the garden, the reflected ghost of himself. He tucked his shirt in.

Amber has a schedule. What I'd appreciate is, if she goes anywhere that isn't pre-arranged – I mean, by Karen or myself – you let me know.

He took the schedule out of his back pocket. No mention of tonight's party. He was still mulling this when Amber came downstairs in a very short, tight blue dress.

'Is it OK?'

'Yeah, it's definitely OK.'

She spun. It was backless. 'Are you sure?'

'I'm sure.'

Amber glanced at her phone. 'He's here. Let's go.' She grabbed a black leather jacket. 'What's your name again?' she said.

'Nick.'

'Nick, I really appreciate this. You're a life-saver.'

5

A MERCEDES E-CLASS WAITED ON the pristine gravel of Amber's drive. Tinted windows. A silver-haired man stood beside it in uniform, *Shield Executive Cars* stitched across the breast pocket. He opened a passenger door for Amber, eyed Belsey cautiously.

'Sit in the back with me,' Amber said.

They slid in.

'Are there still people outside?' Amber asked the driver.

'One or two.'

Amber bent over her knees, assuming the crash position. The driver leaned out, pressed a button and the gates opened. Belsey sunk down into his seat. He heard camera clicks as they turned fast into the road. At the next corner, Amber straightened and turned to peer through the rear windscreen. The driver adjusted his mirrors, glanced back. They weren't being followed.

The car relaxed. Belsey pushed back into the cool leather seat. He cut a look at his companion. Up close, in the unexpected light of a Mercedes interior, her face was smaller than he'd thought, the features larger on it. Maybe it was just that she looked real. Her eyes were almond-shaped and emotionally opaque. Hooded, it seemed, though they were wide open. Her hair contained every shade from burnt caramel to pale blonde.

She looked focused, almost nervous; legs crossed, a silver clutch on her bare thighs, phone dangling a Chanel charm. Her engagement ring bore a rock of yellow diamond the size of a grape. He couldn't tell if their silence was awkward. Presumably security guards didn't initiate conversation. Amber stared out of the window as they left Camden. Then she turned and studied Belsey.

'Where did you get that ID card? Of the stalker?'

'His bedroom.'

'His bedroom? Where does he live?'

'Herbert Street. It's towards Kentish Town.'

'Did you meet him?'

'No. He's gone missing.'

'Oh great.' She swung her phone up. 'Herbert Street,' she said, typing it in. Her nails were silver, tiny crystals set into the varnish. 'Jesus, that's right by me. Are you sure?'

'Pretty sure.'

Amber leaned back, groaned. She disappeared into her own head again. A moment later she snapped out of it: 'This is good of you,' she said. She patted Belsey's thigh. She left her hand there when she'd finished patting, looking away from him, back out the window.

'No problem,' Belsey said.

Her hand slipped from his thigh and lay upturned on the seat between them. He opened a window.

'Maybe keep the window closed,' Amber said. He did as he was told. Amber hit a button and the air con sighed into life.

'So where's your fiancé?' Belsey asked.

'Guy's finishing a hotel,' she said to the tinted glass. 'He's in New York for a few days. There's nothing he can do.'

'That's a shame.'

But he'd lost her again. Regent's Park sped by. Belsey watched her reflection in the glass. Prescription meds, he speculated. Lucid but detached. Good state of mind to cruise through London in a blacked-out Merc. Let's see where this goes. In a car, going to a club. Hardly out of his comfort zone. The worst that could happen to him was already happening, far away in his own life. It wasn't happening here and wasn't going to be made any more unpleasant by a night out.

Amber checked her phone again, then threw it onto the seat.

'Never let a company sponsor your wedding.'

'There are several reasons why that's unlikely to be a problem.'

'It's crazy,' she said, her eyes back on the passing streets. She pronounced each word slowly to the glass: 'It's all so fucking crazy.' She turned to him. 'Did you see Terri Baker today?'

'Yes.'

'What was she doing?'

'Rifling your drawers.'

'Can you keep her away from the house?'

'I doubt it. Your PA says Terri's on-side.'

'Yeah? What else did she say?'

'Not much.'

'What did she say about me?'

Belsey hesitated. 'It's obviously an exciting time, with everything going on. You know – the perfume, the wedding. She wants you to be all right.'

Amber nodded, unconvinced. They passed Great Portland Street. Belsey saw police he recognised, West End night patrol, picking up coffees from Subway. He felt a dark joy uncurl in his stomach like adrenalin. The Merc was outrunning his sense of disbelief. They glided across Oxford Circus, cool as a state funeral, then cut into Mayfair. Amber watched the streets grow narrow and exclusive.

'What do you think life is for?' she asked. She didn't look at Belsey. It was only when he'd been contemplating the answer for a few seconds that she turned. Her face was calm, quite beautiful.

'I don't know.' Which was the honest answer. She looked away again. A few seconds later the car began to slow.

Amber flipped a panel in the back of the driver's seat and checked her face in a mirror. Outside, street level had become embassies, boutiques, luxury hotels. Belsey wondered if he should sharpen his look. Before the thought was completed they were pulling up on a small street at the back of Shepherd Market. No obvious club – just a red rope, a small tree in a pot, and two tall men in long grey coats.

'Where are we?' Belsey asked.

'Loulou's.'

He'd never heard of it. The rope was unclipped before they were out of the car.

'Evening, Ms Knight. Sir.'

The security nodded, smart and serious. Amber took Belsey's arm as they passed through a doorway with steep steps leading down. They appeared briefly in the mirrored walls as they descended, an odd couple. But not without allure. Then someone pulled back velvet curtains and they stepped into the party.

Even with the laughter and music, you could sense awareness rippling through the crowd. The club was full and dark; a burnished, intimate darkness beneath ornate ceilings. A man with a grey moustache appeared from amongst the other guests, kissed Amber and shook Belsey's hand as if genuinely delighted to see him. The crowd parted and they were ushered through to a secluded area at the back.

'Amber!' people cried. A mini VIP party was underway. There were a lot more kisses and handshakes, women in designer dresses and men in partially buttoned shirts.

'This is Nick,' Amber said.

'I'm just security,' Belsey kept saying. It became a double-act: *This is Nick. I'm just security.* He suspected a convincing security guard wouldn't be doing what he was doing, which seemed to be gratefully receiving a mojito to start with.

'I didn't order it,' he told the girl who gave it to him.

'Do you want it?' she laughed, and continued on her way. That was simple. Magical even.

'I don't usually drink on duty,' he told someone.

'Go on.'

He clinked glasses. He kept to the edges and managed to avoid the official photographer. The ice buckets also kept to the edges. Some had Bollinger champagne, some had Cîroc vodka with shot glasses in the ice. VIPs got their own little dance floor or they could venture out and dance with other people; global rich kids, white leather, pale blazers, gold heels.

Amber worked the crowd. Belsey left her to it. He met identical twins who had set up a production company and were in talks with Amber's people, then someone who described herself as a fashion muse and thought this was even funnier than he did. Belsey wandered out of the VIP area. The main bar was a masterpiece, an art-deco explosion of brass and alligator skin. Belsey ordered a large Courvoisier and tried to pay. The barman wouldn't accept his money. He took his cognac through various plush rooms, past chaises-longues and taxidermy. A giraffe's head and neck emerged from the floor beside the stairs. Beyond it was an ornate salon, all crystals and purple wallpaper. He nodded at people, passed through another doorway into a sunken courtyard. A small, buzzy crowd of smokers had congregated amongst stone urns and a fountain lit with green spotlights. Someone came up to him.

'You're a friend of Amber's.'

'Sort of. New friend. Hanger-on.'

'I recognise you.'

'Really?'

Then he was in the group.

'This is Nick. He's a musician.'

'Am I?'

'Delighted to meet you, Nick. I love the jacket.'

He relaxed into the role. He seemed to be able to hold his own amongst these people, who didn't seem much less desperate or fraudulent than himself. They laughed at his jokes, talked speculatively about projects.

Someone brought more cocktails on a tray. 'This is Eugenie, she's from Switzerland, and this is Alastair.'

Before he knew it, he'd found a clump of dog-eared business cards at the back of his wallet and was giving them out.

'It says Metropolitan Police, but don't pay any attention to that. It's my mobile number at the bottom. Nick Belsey.'

'Metropolitan Police!' He relished sullying the brand a final time, and felt light-hearted seeing the cards going.

'I'm in the station. But there's no station. That's my mobile number. That's all you need. I'm freelance.'

Freelance wasn't a bad idea, he thought. They must all have stalkers, and he was doing a pretty good job of keeping everyone alive so far. He knew what private security charged. Someone gave him a glass snuff-bullet full of cocaine. He went to the toilets. The walls were covered in oil paintings. There were two men in suits who turned out to be the bodyguards of someone in a cubicle. The guards left. He chatted to a yacht broker for a while before Belsey realised the guy was trying to pick him up. By the time he returned to the courtyard he didn't recognise anyone.

Then he met Chloe. As he remembered it she was standing alone, as if waiting for him. So it was easy to fall into conversation. She was very young, a brunette in a strapless black dress that left a lot of skin flushed with oblivious beauty; a nervous, virginal air involving single-sex education; wide blue eyes.

'You're the guy with Amber Knight.'

'I came here with her. We're not together. Obviously.'

'You're a musician.'

'Not a very good one.'

They introduced themselves. Chloe's expression flashed rapidly between polite smiles and something more inquisitorial. Both were charming in their own way. She had a turquoise pendant on her necklace that chimed nicely with her eyes. 'I didn't think Amber was coming tonight.'

'She decided she wanted to. Do you know her?'

'Not personally.'

'Are you here with anyone special?'

'Just a friend.'

'I don't really know Amber at all,' Belsey clarified. 'I was in her house under false pretences and I just tagged along. I shouldn't really be here.'

'Ha. What were you doing at her house?'

'I was trying to save her from a stalker.'

There was another moment of uncertainty. He sensed a lot of thought going on behind those eyes. She was trying to find something out. Maybe just where he was coming from. Maybe whether he was good stock, or something. Pumped with cognac, Belsey took the ID out.

'This is the guy I was looking for.'

Chloe took the card. She stared at it. It was a moment before she said: 'This is the guy stalking Amber?'

'That's right.'

Her expression had grown dark. It occurred to Belsey that there may well be other people on the scene who'd had run-ins with Mark Doughty. There was nothing to say this young woman wasn't also on Mark's walls.

'Who exactly are you?' she asked, looking up at Belsey now.

'Nick,' he was saying, when another woman arrived with drinks and saw the student card in Chloe's hand. 'Are you IDing him?' she laughed. She was six foot something in a silver top and leather hot pants, Russian or Eastern European, with genes like a violent blessing. Definite model. 'I think he's old enough, Chloe.' She turned to Belsey. 'No offence.'

'This is Tatiana,' Chloe said, returning the ID with a shiver, as if shaking off a bad dream. A different, more bubbly personality emerged. 'Tatiana, this is Nick.'

'Pleased to meet you,' Tatiana said.

'Nick's offering protection,' Chloe said. 'Against stalkers.'

'That's very heroic.'

'I'm guessing you guys are famous,' Belsey said. Both girls laughed.

'Why?' Chloe asked.

'Did you ever see a programme called *Fortune's Heirs*?' Tatiana asked.

'I haven't had a TV for a while.'

'You didn't miss anything,' Chloe said. 'I was in it. It sucked. Tatiana's a model; she's staying with me while she's in London.'

'And you?' Belsey said. 'Do you model?'

'No.'

'She's a princess,' Tatiana laughed. 'She's technically royalty.'

'Half the people here are *technically* royalty,' Chloe said. 'I work for Beluggi. We're the ones throwing the party.'

They chatted about this, about fashion and what a great place Loulou's was. Belsey gave them his last two business cards, and after a few minutes Tatiana sensed what was going on and left them alone. They smoked a cigarette together. He was focused enough to ask for Chloe's number, intrigued by her restlessness. She gave it to him.

'Do you dance?' she asked.

They joined the dance floor. Belsey wondered vaguely where Amber was. Another round of drinks appeared. At one point he was trying to say something to Chloe over the music and it became a clumsy kiss. She tasted sweet, of whatever was in the cocktails, peach or apricot. When he went to get more drinks he promised he'd be back; he got the feeling she wanted to stay close to him. Then he got in a debate with the bartender about the best way to fix a Manhattan and never saw her again.

People were dancing on tables now, coked-up blondes letting their dresses ride, men in Armani kissing their legs. At some point he got tight with a crew who had cigars and said they were over from LA. They were in black tie, bow ties loose around their necks.

Are you a whisky man? A man who knows his malts? Want to play a game?

He won the game. Talk turned to ambitions. They were Hollywood people.

'Just fly me out there,' Belsey said. 'Set me loose.' He was serious. Hollywood lay seven hours' drive from Mexico. He could see to his own career progression, down to the border, fast.

Someone wanted to play poker. Someone wanted to charter a flight to Lake Como.

We'd be there for sunrise.

Then Amber Knight was beside him, hand on his arm. She had her jacket and bag. She looked wired.

'Where've you been?' she said.

'All over. Have you been having fun?'

'Can we go?'

'Sure.'

'OK. Let's do this.'

Belsey took a second to digest this, grinding gears as he switched from one improbable scenario to another. He even found the clarity of mind to worry about paparazzi. He'd only been intimate with fame for a couple of hours but he knew the difference between arriving together and leaving together.

'Do we call a cab?' he said.

Amber checked her phone, said something about the paps knowing her account cars.

They didn't leave the way they'd come in. Instead, they headed for a door beside the bar. Belsey kept a last guilty lookout for Chloe. No sign. They went up a flight of stairs to an empty restaurant, then back down to a fire door at the rear of the building. Amber pushed the emergency bar.

'Check the street,' she said.

He checked. A different Mercedes was waiting, engine running, door open. Nothing else around.

'Coast's clear.'

They jumped in.

'Let's go,' Amber said, slamming the door, thrusting her head into Belsey's crotch. Belsey lowered himself over her body, pressing his nose to her ribcage as they tore off. He wasn't sure what to do with his arms. In the end he put them over her. By the time he looked up they were making good progress through central London. No paps behind. He eased his arms away from Amber's body. She sat up.

She fanned herself with her hand. Still in the dark hours of night: 12.55 on the dashboard clock. Whirling joyfully deeper into the absurdity of his situation.

'I like that place,' Belsey said.

'Yeah?'

'I had fun.'

'Good.'

They continued north along a cold and empty Baker Street. Amber became more apprehensive the further they travelled from the club, away from her tribe, a fragment of glitz cast alone into the early morning.

'I can get out whenever,' Belsey said.

'See me home.'

'Sure.'

They crested St John's Wood in silence. Then Amber said, 'Stop the car.' The driver glanced at her in the rear-view mirror. She leaned forward. 'Drop us here,' she said.

The car pulled over. They were by Regent's Park, on a straight, empty avenue with moonlit parkland either side.

'Is this right, ma'am?' the driver asked.

'Yes.'

Amber climbed out. Belsey followed.

'It's a short walk from here,' she said. 'Do you have money to pay him?'

Belsey peeled thirty quid from his roll. He heard the final 'Thank you, sir, ma'am.' Then they were alone in a neatly mown silence.

Amber stretched. Alone against the scenery in her dress and heels; it looked like a fashion shoot. There were no cars. To the south, the peaked nets of London Zoo rose up amongst dark trees.

'Follow me,' Amber said.

She led him across a small bridge over Regent's Canal, then down a muddy track to the waterside. The canal stretched between steep banks, sporadic lamplight giving a dull orange glare to the water. Seclusion. Amber took her shoes off and walked to the edge. Belsey opted for a graffitied bench. He found Mark Doughty's papers and tobacco. A moment later he heard a splash and looked up to see Amber tossing pebbles into the water like an eight-year-old.

This was her freedom – maybe that was it. Nocturnal. This was where she reclaimed a few minutes of the twenty-four for herself. Still, not a great place to loiter. He checked his phone – dead. He smoked and kept an eye on the path. They were alone.

'Is this somewhere you come a lot?'

'No.'

'It's peaceful.'

'I've come here twice.'

'OK.'

She turned to face him. 'Did you tell Gabby we were going out tonight?'

'No.'

She nodded, turned back to the water, skin ghostly white. It must be strange, being so valuable. Too big to fail. With a whole team around you, an industry in your name. He thought about that intervention Gabby had mentioned – their attempt to 'calm her down'. But about what? Belsey had never been convinced by the concept: the very people you're drugging yourself to forget, brought together, unexpected and looking at you, like a bad dream. The whole set-up resembled a coup, Gabby and whoever else securing Amber in the way you'd protect an oilfield. Maybe the coup had happened and she was already in exile, wandering by the canal, just herself and one loyal retainer.

'Last time I was here there was a man sleeping in a sleeping bag. Just there.' Amber pointed across to the far bank. 'I know it's ridiculous, but I thought: that's a nice place to sleep. To wake up and see the sky. To go to sleep beneath the stars.'

'Not bad. When it's dry.'

Another moment passed. For the sake of conversation, and because she was on his mind, Belsey said: 'Do you know a girl called Chloe? She was at the club, works for Beluggi.'

'Chloe? No, I don't think so. Why?'

'She seemed to recognise the ID of your stalker.'

Amber turned. 'Really?' She considered this. 'What do you think he wants?' she asked, eventually.

'To be noticed, I imagine. By you.'

'Well, that's worked. Is he dangerous, though? Do you think he wants to kill me?'

'No,' Belsey lied.

'Would it be so bad if he did?'

'I suppose someone could sponsor the funeral.'

She didn't laugh.

'Have you ever seen a dead body?' Amber asked.

'Only about thirty times.'

'Really?'

'I used to be a police officer. People encourage us to see them.'

'What did you think?'

'When I saw one? Usually I thought how easy it was to die, how surprising it was that it didn't happen more often.'

She contemplated this.

'Do people always look different when they're dead?'

'Not always.'

Amber peered at the water's surface. Belsey wondered about its depth. Say she jumped – would he take his shoes off before going in after her? Remove his phone from his pocket? He thought of the call-outs he'd attended involving potential suicides, the tenth-floor ledge, the locked bathroom, feeling foolish turning up as a representative of the law. Not the people you really need in that situation, him and an array of firefighters and paramedics turned border guards. He'd had the standard training on these scenarios, but never figured out what to say. He looked at her. Amber was twenty-three years old. At twenty-three you think a lot's over. You're part right. And yet the fun's hardly begun. Seen it all, but not seen how it repeats ad infinitum.

What do you think life is for?

'We should start getting back,' he said. There was no answer. 'Things are always better in the morning.'

'Really?'

'No. But I'm getting cold.'

'You've got no idea,' she said. 'About the situation I'm dealing with right now.'

Belsey sighed. He stood up and went to join her beside the water.

'Amber, in less than a fortnight I'm going to be charged with misconduct in the course of duty. A few weeks after that I'll receive a seven- or eight-year custodial sentence. Prison for ex-police officers isn't a happy place. So we're both dealing with situations right now. You know what I mean? Don't underestimate the shit other people deal with.'

'Is that true?'

'Unfortunately.'

'I'm sorry.'

'There's nothing to be sorry about. It's life. Maybe that's what it's for: fucking up.' He flicked his cigarette into the canal. Amber felt for his hand. She wove her fingers into his own, let her head roll back. He could feel her pulse throbbing.

'Can you see that? The whitest one?'

Belsey looked up at the stars. More came into focus every second. 'I think so. Just.'

'That's Venus. Did you know that on Venus it snows metal?'

'Really?'

'It's so hot the metal comes out of the ground like water.'

'That's amazing.'

'Isn't it. Do you think I'm crazy?'

'I think you live a crazy life,' Belsey said. 'Maybe you're not crazy enough for it.' But what he was thinking about was Mark Doughty's bedroom. He wanted to bring them together, Amber and Mark, have them chat. Here he was instead. He'd crashed someone's wet dream.

'Let's get you home.'

They walked back to the road. She took her shoes off and carried them as they crossed the empty slopes of Primrose Hill. When they got to her street Belsey went ahead. No photographers. He gave her a thumbs-up. She keyed in the gate code fast. Only when they were inside the house with the door closed did she exhale with relief.

'We made it,' Belsey said, wondering what was meant to happen now.

'I've got to go to the bathroom,' Amber said.

He fixed a drink from a well-stocked cocktail cabinet in the corner of the living room. A moment later he heard crying.

He went upstairs and found Amber on the floor of the bathroom in expensive-looking black underwear, Gillette's legs of the year folded under her, retching into the toilet. Here was the glamour. Belsey crouched down and got her hair out of the way as she vomited again. Policing London you learned to analyse vomit more than blood splatter or ballistics. Amber's was yellow. There was a lot of bile. No blood in it, little food. Not a huge amount of alcohol from the smell of it. Make-up had rubbed off her arms and he could see scars, two or three years old, across her wrists.

'Have you taken anything?'

'No.'

'Any stomach pain?'

'No. I'm fine. Give me a moment.'

Belsey gave her a moment. When he next went looking for her she was in bed with headphones on. Her clothes lay strewn over the bedroom floor.

'Are you sure you're OK?'

She nodded, very slowly. Breathing steadily, it seemed. She was fine. Relatively speaking.

Belsey returned to the party room and sat down. He plugged his phone in to charge. Amber's laptop was open on the floor. He didn't want to pry. But he checked the screen. '*Become the most attractive version of yourself and be magnetic in personal and business relationships. What's stopping you living the life you want to lead? Try this simple survey.*'

A free personality test. The one he'd seen at Mark's. And it looked like Amber had tweeted it, beamed it into the radar of another discontented soul. 'Love this!' '*Find professional success and fulfilling relationships by simply knowing yourself better. Discover your true personality. Question 1: What is life for?*'

So it was Positively Happy Surveys that had put her in such a philosophical frame of mind this evening. The question looked less overwhelming in this context. You had to grade answers out of five. They included 'making money', 'learning', 'family' and 'having fun'.

He closed the laptop. Strange life, he thought. In an odd way, Amber's high-altitude existence resembled his last couple of weeks: a life without the everyday questions that come with normality, just the unanswerable ones. Like it's always the middle of the night.

He took his drink out to the balcony and looked for Venus. He felt, in the last flickers of well-being, as if he'd circumnavigated the globe and understood it all. The night air was crisp, sky clear. To the north he could see the sullen towers of Mark Doughty's estate. Belsey raised his drink towards them and knocked it back.

6

VOICES WOKE HIM, SHOUTED INSTRUCTIONS from the floor below. He was on a leather sofa in the party room, beneath a wall of gold discs. His shirt and jacket had served as a blanket. His shoes and trousers were on the floor beneath the mirror ball.

It sounded like the film crew were back. Belsey assumed the business-like sounds downstairs meant no one had stumbled upon Amber blue and cold. He felt surprisingly OK. He got up, stretched. Interesting evening: an insight into the world of Amber Knight. Ruined, as every other world. Still, in a selfish way, it had been therapeutic and, alongside the usual morning despair, he felt something unsettling. Hope. Hope enflamed by the recent proximity of lucky people. Hope somehow born of seeing Amber Knight vomiting bile.

Belsey found his phone still plugged in. He turned it on. It told him it was quarter to eight and he had five missed calls. Which wasn't so unusual since he'd been on the run. He didn't usually check them. But he didn't usually have one from a number he'd saved as 'Princess'. That was a teenage kick. He'd forgotten the feeling – a call from someone you wanted to hear from. Someone other than Her Majesty's Inspectorate of Constabulary, who never put out. Chloe was a bit of the fairy tale he'd quite like to sustain. He'd give it an hour then try calling her. Then figure out how to effect a transition into his actual life, which didn't bear thinking about. Invite her back to the abandoned police station: blow her aristocratic mind?

Four other calls: numbers he knew and numbers he didn't. Three messages.

Belsey listened to a message.

'Nick. Hope I'm through to your phone. This is Andy Price from AP Total Media. Someone gave me your number. I'd like to buy you a drink and we can talk about where things go from here. I've got some very interested people waiting.'

Where things go from here. He checked the next message.

'Nicky, mate. It's Gez. Is that really you? What are you up to, you crazy bastard?'

He felt the first ripple of concern and went online. He ran a search on Amber Knight. First hit was the *Mail*, a story posted two hours ago: '*Mystery friend escorts Amber as she parties five days before wedding.*' They had a picture from the start of the night, front of Loulou's. There they were, in that no-man's-land between Mercedes and red rope. Amber looked good. He looked like the kind of security that had been working in the desert with mujahedin. Beneath their photograph were other 'couples' arriving at last night's 'star-studded Bulaggi Blanca after-party'.

He got dressed fast. The film crew were on the stairs. Belsey could hear Gabby's nasal instructions from somewhere down there. He stepped silently past the room that looked like a hairdresser's and saw Amber sitting in one of the chairs, watching a wall-mounted TV as a woman wound rollers into her hair.

Belsey kept his head down, moving swiftly and purposefully out of her life. There would be the usual photographers out the front: he used the stalker exit, through the garden and over the wall.

Fuck that, Belsey thought, continuing fast towards Camden. He was hungry. He walked into a café on the High Street then changed his mind and ducked down a side road to a smaller establishment with fewer windows. He ordered eggs, bacon and coffee, took a seat at the back. His phone rang. This time he answered it.

'Hello?'

'Nick! Andy Price here. Left you a voice message.'

'How did you get my number?'

'I got passed it. Someone said they met you last night.'

'Have you given my number to anyone else?'

'No, Nick. I'm a professional – and I'm here to help.'

'I'm not looking for publicity right now.'

'Sometimes publicity comes looking for you.' He laughed, coughed.

'It's not a game I'm playing.'

'Sure. Terri Baker says she met you at the house yester—'

Belsey hung up. There were many things he needed; a career in show business wasn't high on the list. He sipped his coffee, searched himself online. Nothing, he was relieved to see. He searched Loulou's, got a photograph of an attractive young woman it took him a second to recognise as Chloe. She was outdoors somewhere, in sunshine, smiling. She looked even prettier than he remembered. On the BBC News page. *Woman found stabbed to death in Mayfair.*

Belsey stared at the screen. The story had gone up fifty minutes ago.

The woman found stabbed to death in a residential street in Mayfair, central London, has been named as 22-year-old Chloe Burlington, daughter of Sir Malcolm Burlington. An ambulance was called but the victim was pronounced dead at the scene.

Her body was discovered by a local resident in the early hours of the morning, just moments from the private members' club

Loulou's, popular with A-list celebrities and royalty. It is believed the victim had been attending an event at the club.

Belsey got up, switched the café's TV on.

'Excuse me,' the owner said.

'I need to check something.' The screen showed a BBC reporter on Piccadilly looking serious. Behind her, a thin line of police tape interrupted Down Street, heading up towards Loulou's. *'That's all the information they've released. We're expecting a more comprehensive update at around eleven, when the Chief Inspector will be hosting a press conference.'*

The ticker at the bottom of the screen scrolled past: '22-year-old socialite in fatal stabbing.'

The obese café owner craned his neck to see the screen, appeared indifferent. The TV cut back to the studio and a weather forecast.

Belsey clicked through to Sky News. Same police tape from a more acute angle. No additional information. He put a tenner on the counter, walked to the high street and caught a cab.

'Piccadilly.'

He barely saw the city pass. They followed the route he and Amber had driven last night, which seemed to emphasise something bizarre about chance and something that wasn't chance. He was conscious, in a vague, professional sense, of an element of shock, in the way you have glimmers of self-awareness on a drunken night. He saw her looking at him, remembered the warmth of her mouth, and tried to understand that she was dead.

He got out his phone. The call he'd missed from her came at 12.19. That can't have been long before she was killed. What had she wanted to say? He thought about Chloe's expression when she saw Mark Doughty's ID. Staring at it, her face darkening somehow. Staring at Belsey as if he'd brought her bad news. And then clinging to him. He called Maureen Doughty as they drove.

'Maureen, it's Nick Belsey, from yesterday.'

'Have you found anything out?'

'I'm not sure. I want you to call me if you hear from him. That's important, Maureen. If Mark calls or visits, you contact me immediately, OK?'

He reached Piccadilly at 8.35 a.m. Traffic was snarled by the number of emergency service vehicles parked along both sides of the road.

'Nightmare,' the driver said. 'It's going to be like this all morning.' Belsey paid and got out. A long line of media sat alongside Green Park, from the Ritz down to Hyde Park Corner: broadcasting vans, random cars illegally parked. Police vehicles filled the other side of the road, in front of the Park Lane Hotel and the Japanese embassy. They'd kept Piccadilly itself open to traffic but taped off the alleyways north into Mayfair. These were occupied by Scene of Crime vans.

He headed for the tape. It was a cold, bright day. Wind whipped down Piccadilly towards the Wellington Arch. The brass horses on top of the monument reared up, hooves kicking at a hard, white sky. Three constables guarded the tape, fielding questions from tourists. Sneaking through wasn't viable.

Belsey walked to the Park Lane Hotel, skipped up the steps.

'Is this where I check in?' he asked a doorman in top hat and tails.

'Straight through, sir. On your right.' He held the door open. Belsey walked briskly past the reception desk, down a corridor to the back of the hotel. Fire doors led onto Brick Street.

He followed alleyways towards the crime scene. The area was a warren that had served individuals seeking expensive discretion throughout history – he remembered reading about its high-class whores. The small, winding streets must have given good cover to the eighteenth-century punters. They'd gone now, brothels converted into expensive restaurants and skincare clinics. It was a ghost town this morning. Security grilles over shop windows. The whole area had been sealed off, right up to Curzon Street. No fewer than five pairs of plain-clothes officers worked Down Street and Hertford Street, knocking on doors, trying to summon up a witness. Senior police stood in scattered huddles at the junction of the two roads. Scene of Crime officers in white boiler suits came and went from Stanhope Row.

Belsey turned the corner onto Market Mews and saw the forensics tent. It filled the road, sudden and incongruous as an air bag. An inner cordon of police tape surrounded it. More SOCOs came and went from the tent. Several performed careful operations in front, charting the tarmac: photographing, measuring, combing and collecting.

It was a couple of hundred metres west of Loulou's. Not a very visible couple of hundred metres if you decided to walk it at night. Market Mews was barely the width of a car, cobbled, blind, reached via the backs of restaurants and hotel loading bays. Wrong direction for transport or shops. A dog-leg turn into it, so that most of the road was totally hidden from the world. There was no reason you'd end up there after leaving the club.

He approached a pair of DCs doing door-to-door enquiries.

'Excuse me, who can I speak to about the investigation?' They looked at him suspiciously.

'Who are you?'

'I'm based locally. I have information.'

'What information?'

'Information about the victim. About Chloe Burlington. About a possible suspect.'

The pair looked around for a senior officer. Either they sensed significance or trouble. The older one led him towards the broad back of a grey-haired man scribbling notes, resting papers on the bonnet of a car.

'Sir.'

The officer turned, saw Belsey. His eyes widened. Belsey's heart sank.

'Geoff.'

'Nick. Of all people.'

Not the homicide officer Belsey would have chosen to run into. Anywhere, ever. DCI Geoff 'Bullseye' McGovern. His first mentor in CID. First and last.

'What are you doing here?' McGovern asked.

'He says he might have information,' the constable said.

'Really?' A cruel smile played at the corners of the Inspector's mouth. 'How thoughtful of you to come down. Let me get you a coffee.' He led Belsey away from the other officers, stopped when they were around the corner. 'What the fuck are you up to, Nick?'

'I was there last night. At the club.' Belsey found Mark Doughty's ID in his wallet. 'I think this is the guy who did it.'

'Yeah?'

McGovern glanced at the ID then back at Belsey. Belsey studied his former boss. Six foot, heavy-set. He'd lost weight but not in the way that made you look healthy. His greying hair was cropped close, high forehead still ready to break your nose.

'I met her,' Belsey said. 'I spoke to her.'

'Are you winding me up?'

'No.'

McGovern looked disgusted by the whole scenario. He turned away and continued down Brick Street. Belsey followed. Nine years, he thought. Nine years since they'd last seen each other. But then time was a weak thing compared to hate. Still, McGovern was a good detective on his day. And hate was a connection of sorts. Hate, and the miracle of having survived.

Belsey caught up with the DI as he ducked under the tape, back onto Piccadilly. The media scrum across the road was growing. Belsey kept his head down. McGovern stopped at a shiny new BMW and beeped the locks. Certainly not a Met car. Belsey wondered if he was still on the take. McGovern chucked paperwork onto the passenger seat, took a bottle of hand sanitiser from the dashboard.

'Give me ten minutes,' Belsey said. 'For old times' sake.'

McGovern had the good grace to laugh. In the full light, Belsey saw the scar, a neat arc of white that began at the corner of the Inspector's mouth and led down beneath the jaw; the curve of a broken pint glass, stopping an inch from the artery. I almost did it, Belsey thought. I almost killed the bastard.

McGovern closed the car door.

'Ten minutes,' he said. 'For old times' sake.'

Piccolo Sandwich Bar was a 1950s relic: vinyl seats, photos of Sinatra and three generations of taciturn men in stained white aprons. Belsey and McGovern queued in silence. Breakfast with Bullseye. It used to be a ritual – the post-crime-scene fry-up. He remembered McGovern ordering him a full English on his first call-out with Borough CID, one involving a month-old corpse they'd unwrapped from a carpet in a recycling depot. *Don't skimp on the extras, Nicky. This one's on me. Tuck in.*

McGovern ordered tea, black. He took a banana from a dish on the counter. Type 2 diabetes, Belsey guessed. A man on doctor's orders. Not wife's orders; no remarriage according to his ring finger. McGovern took his tea to a stool by the front window, perching like someone who didn't intend to get comfortable. There was a stiffness to the way he held himself which could have been age or his senior rank, or a wariness particular to this encounter.

Belsey ordered a double espresso and joined him. McGovern reached inside his jacket and, for a second, Belsey half expected the old 30ml of Smirnoff to appear. He took out saccharins. They sipped and watched the street, both being careful, as if a wrong movement could open a floodgate of toxic memory. Old times. For Belsey, they coalesced to a single vision of the Crown, their last Christmas Eve, every bottle smashed, alcohol pouring onto the floor behind the bar. McGovern looking for a weapon with which to retaliate. Quite a mentor. He was dry now, Belsey could tell: fury had retreated to the last stronghold of the eyes. With his saccharin and banana, his awkward bulk and strangler's hands. No longer larger than life. No longer Bullseye, with psychological flaws that set the tone for an entire CID unit.

'Eight minutes.' McGovern checked his watch. Belsey placed Mark's ID on the ledge.

'Mark Doughty. Forty-one years old. He lives at 37 Herbert Street, in Kentish Town. He has a thing about celebrities, socialites, party girls. I found instructions on making poison in his bedroom. I also found Amber Knight's passport and underwear.'

'Amber Knight.'

'Mark Doughty scores drugs off a dealer called Lee Chester. That's how I heard about him. He owes Lee money and he's on the run, not seen since Saturday.'

'And what do you think he's got to do with it?'

'I showed Chloe Burlington this ID last night and she seemed to recognise him. She then tried to call me, just after midnight. What time was she killed?'

McGovern picked up the ID and almost let himself appear interested. He set it back down.

'Not long after. Has he got previous?'

'I haven't checked.'

McGovern stared at the greasy brown surface of his tea.

'You knew her well?'

'I met her last night,' Belsey said.

'What time?'

'About half-ten, maybe eleven. It's hard to say.'

'When did you last see her?'

'Approximately half an hour after I met her. She had a friend, a model called Tatiana. I didn't see her speak to anyone else.'

'What time did you leave?'

'A bit after midnight.'

'Alone?'

'With Amber Knight.'

McGovern nodded.

'Of course you did, Nick. And where did you go with Amber fucking Knight?'

'Back to hers. She thinks I'm a security guard.'

'But it's this Mark guy I should be worried about.'

'That's right.'

McGovern sipped, winced, set his mug down.

'Was she sexually assaulted?' Belsey asked.

'Not that we can tell.'

'Stuff taken?'

'We can't find her phone.'

'Whereabouts was she stabbed?'

'Throat.'

'Just the once?'

'Yeah. There's also a skull fracture and a broken right cheekbone. Looks like she might have fallen or been thrown up against the wall, maybe punched – huge smack on the head anyway. The throat might have been a *coup de grâce*. I'm not sure whoever did it meant it to end that way.'

'How did she get there? Did she leave the club alone?'

'I don't know.'

'Checked with paps?'

'We're checking with everyone, aren't we. So far no one's sure when she left. And the paps were all moved on by the bouncers around half-eleven.'

'Why did she walk in that direction?' Belsey said. 'If she was alone. Why did she not get straight into a cab?'

'Maybe she wasn't alone. Or maybe she met up with someone after leaving. Keeping it discreet.'

For the first time McGovern tore his gaze from Piccadilly and looked straight at Belsey.

'Any idea who, Nick? Because, you see, your business card was on the ground. A foot or so from the body. Your old business card, as far as I understand.'

And it was then Belsey realised McGovern had sat between himself and the door. There were three squad cars parked across the road from the café. He saw, again, McGovern's expression when he'd turned from his notes on the car bonnet. Surprised: pleasantly surprised. Like something had fallen into his lap.

'Was her bag there?' Belsey asked. 'It could have fallen from the bag.'

'You gave her an old business card?'

'It has my mobile number on. Her bag was there, right?'

McGovern nodded.

'Was it open?'

'Yes.'

'But nothing else taken, apart from the phone?'

'Doesn't look like it.'

'Traced the phone?'

'Signal cuts just east of Avenue Road, about an hour later.'

'That's in the direction of Mark Doughty's home.'

McGovern nodded again, slowly. He picked up the ID.

'Can I take this?'

'I was hoping you would. Who's heading the investigation?' Belsey asked.

'A guy called Steve Tanner. West End Central.'

'Know him?'

'He's all right.' McGovern put the tea down, finished his banana and folded the peel beside his mug. 'They've tried to get in touch with you.'

'There's a lot of messages I haven't listened to yet.'

'They'll keep trying, I'm sure.'

McGovern pocketed the ID. He pushed his mug away, stared out of the window at the plush trees.

'I bumped into Mick Donovan down in Elephant the other week.'

'Long time. How's he keeping?'

'He told me about this misconduct investigation into you. Is it happening?'

'I reckon.'

'Know anything else about it?'

'No.'

'It'll get historical though.'

'You think they'll drag you in? You're employee of the fucking year, Geoff. No one wants to stir up that much.'

'People who don't know anything sometimes do.'

'It's not in my hands, is it.'

'This is.'

'What are you saying?'

'I mean there's going to be a shitload of attention on you now. Because of this.'

'So it seems.'

'I can steer it away.'

'Christ, Geoff. Don't make this worse than it already is.'

'I think you need a favour here. Maybe you don't realise how badly. What I need is you to be very fucking careful if the IPCC are going to start poking around in the past. If it's getting archaeological you need to tell them where to dig.'

So this was it – manoeuvres, self-protection. Welcome back to the old school. Belsey remembered what was most disturbing about McGovern: the sense that he was driven by something too febrile, too gleeful, to call a sense of justice. It was a love of power or, more accurately, the games involved; of violence. A sadist who thought that winning meant you were on the right side. Belsey used to work in a station full of them.

'You could have played it clever, Nick. You know police is a family. No one wants to turn against their own.'

'You once told me a family's just the people statistically most likely to kill you.'

McGovern allowed himself his second smile of the day. The squad cars peeled off into the traffic. He'd been paranoid. McGovern had been clever, using whatever props came to hand. Belsey remembered that lesson.

'I can keep you out of this,' McGovern said.

'I don't need you to keep me out of this.'

The Detective Inspector shrugged. 'Don't say I didn't try.' He dabbed the corners of his mouth, folded the napkin on the counter and stood up. 'Her dad owns half of Oxford Street. Imagine that.'

'Oxford Street's a dive.'

'People saw you leave the club with her.'

'No they didn't.'

McGovern nodded thoughtfully. He walked out. Belsey watched him belch, then turn right towards his BMW.

Mind games. Feeling out the levers to work you. It had been a while.

Chloe Burlington. Slipped through that back door out of existence, invisible and everywhere, affording no readmission. Pushed through. He felt the guilt of proximity. Of having unwittingly accompanied someone there and not crossed over with them. The guilt of not having done something, of not pursuing a course of action he couldn't quite imagine.

His business card beside her body. If McGovern wasn't entirely bullshitting. Why? It said police on it. People thought that meant you could take care of things, look after them. She called at 12.19 a.m. No signal in the club itself. In the courtyard maybe. Or after leaving. He didn't use his own voice on his voicemail. She would have got through to an automated message, and declined to leave one of her own.

Belsey downed his cold espresso and walked out. No one tried to arrest him.

7

HE BOUGHT RAZORS AND SHAVING cream from a chemist by Green Park station then took the bus back to north London. Things he wanted to establish: was Mark Doughty actually involved? Could he have known Chloe Burlington was going to be at Loulou's? Did he loiter outside, waiting? Could he lure her away? Force her, or get her to follow him somehow?

A phone number Belsey recognised as West End Central was trying to get through to him. He rejected the call. For the moment. He left a message on Gabby's voicemail: 'I don't mean to panic you but there's a possibility the murder last night connects to Amber's stalker. The police will need any details you have. Make sure you contact them.'

Lee Chester's phone also went to voicemail.

'Call me,' Belsey said.

Hampstead police station looked as silent and neglected as he'd left it. He checked the windows, then climbed into the car park, undid the padlock on the side door and stepped in. Twenty-four hours away had given him some perspective: the drying clothes, empty bottles, improvised meals on old canteen plates. He saw a perverse defiance, as if he'd been trying to prove something. A misguided loyalty. A dog by its owner's grave. He thought of the knocking that started all this. And he understood it now. Maureen Doughty had come to a place of dereliction to find someone who knew the terrain. Someone familiar with the cracks through which people fall. That was his thing.

He tidied up the empties, the cigarette butts. His own crisis, which had been overwhelming twenty-four hours ago, seemed relatively minor now.

The cold taps still ran. Belsey filled a pan in the office kitchen, fixed his last gas canister to the camping stove and turned the flame on high.

He searched through his missed calls again as the water boiled. Finally, inevitably, the unreturnable call at 12.19 a.m. He was surprised by the intensity of the feeling it evoked. He wondered if this was how death felt when you didn't have the rituals of policing to absorb it. Even strangers' deaths. Not quite strangers.

Signal cuts just east of Avenue Road, about an hour later. Suggesting the killer had travelled on foot. Or visited somewhere first. Avenue Road wasn't on the most immediate route back, by foot or public transport.

He would have gone via the West End, was Belsey's guess, into the comforting chaos of Oxford Street rather than through Mayfair to Baker Street, the way he and Amber had driven. There would have been people out and about either way. There were cameras.

Belsey split the water between a cafetière and the bowl he used for shaving. He shaved as the coffee brewed, studying his reflection in the glass of a framed photograph: Hampstead subdivision of the Metropolitan Police, 1932. His eyes switched focus between his face and the rows of stern, moustached officers.

He took the coffee to the old courtroom, sat in the dock and felt justice lingering in the semi-darkness.

He thought about Geoff McGovern.

Bullseye. Belsey had initially thought the nickname related to McGovern's precision, because he got results. It was the Sarge, Neil Atherton, who led Belsey into the interview room after a McGovern interrogation and showed him the dart holes in the wall behind the suspect's chair; Atherton pissing himself. *Interviews are all about the psychology, Nick. Like a game of chess.*

After a few months the word 'mentor' acquired an ominous tone. Things Belsey had learned from Geoffrey McGovern: how to strike fear into fearless men; how to recycle the seized proceeds of crime to run informants off the books; how to use journalists as a combination of investigative tool, source of bribes and moral alibi. McGovern approached work as a spectrum of opportunities, from the restoration of law and order to enhancing his portfolio of income streams. And the two weren't always incompatible. Not when you were getting good intelligence off your chosen dealers, letting them grow their business, creaming off profit to fund your own unorthodox brand of investigation.

Happy days. Happy crew. And the Crown: their pub, at a time when every pub in south-east London had its own flavour of corruption. That was the coppers' pub, a stronghold, and Belsey had destroyed it. *If it's getting archaeological you need to tell them where to dig.* He imagined spades hitting something hard: clearing the top soil to reveal a single night, like a fragment of bone. Christmas Eve, 2002. A raid had gone down, a huge batch of ecstasy seized. Big motors parked outside the pub, men from the Yard, Drugs Squad. Everyone was going to claim their Christmas bonus, Belsey amongst them. There was a cheer as he walked in. He realised what a position he'd come to occupy; saw younger officers watching him; handshakes and backslaps. The air was thick. Someone pulled a cracker. Everyone laughed. They were wearing paper hats. There was a stink of aftershave and sweat. Someone put two hundred quid in Belsey's jacket. He looked around at the smiling faces, saucer-eyed, jaws working.

Jesus Christ.

A pub full of thirty corrupt police officers on ecstasy is a sight you don't forget. Pat Durham, Tommy Reeves, John Rossdale; men unaccustomed to euphoria. A few of the regulars missing. Must be guarding the haul. Divvying it up. Waiting for the heat to pass.

'Fucking A, lads. Where did it go? Where's the rest?'

Rossdale winked, nodded to the storeroom, put a finger to his lips. 'Merry Christmas, Nick.'

'Here?' Belsey grinned in disbelief. 'Are you mad?'

They weren't mad: they were police. They owned the night and day. They were high as kites.

'Where'd you get the tip-off?'

Rossdale leaned in, unsteadily. 'You.'

'What do you mean?'

'The pills are from the Adjaye brothers.'

His informants.

'You've done us a favour.'

'Samuel can't have liked that very much.' Belsey tried to keep his smile, his voice.

'He ran to the Yard,' Durham laughed. 'Tried to turn supergrass. Guess who he went to? Jim fucking Kiver. Chief Superintendent Skiver himself.'

'What did Skiver do?'

'Drove him straight back to us, of course.' A roar of laughter, mouth wide, face contorted as if screaming.

There were specks of blood on the party hats. Belsey clinked glasses with his colleagues, checked their grazed knuckles. Someone forced a pill into his mouth. He left the pub.

Samuel Adjaye lay cuffed on the floor of a cell in Borough police station, seventeen years old, naked but for a Santa Claus hat. The hat had been pulled down over his eyes, his teeth broken. Piss spread around him across the tiles. Belsey got him out of the cuffs, found him some clothes.

'I didn't know about this,' Belsey said.

'Bullshit,' he said through his broken mouth, chin wet with mucus and tears.

'It's true.'

'You said I was protected.'

'How much did they take?' Belsey asked.

'Five hundred grand cash, a thousand pills.'

Belsey got Adjaye into an ambulance. He went to evidence stores and checked the book. According to DS McGovern, they'd seized a total of fifty pills and two grand in cash. That was breathtaking duplicity, even by Borough standards.

Up to the deserted CID office. Belsey took the claw hammer from McGovern's desk drawer, then he put it back, picked up the phone and dialled.

'It's me.'

'Nicky. Merry Christmas.'

'Got a proposal if you're able to move fast. Big haul. Once in a lifetime.'

'How fast?'

'Fast like now. And you'd need kit.'

The memory still made his heart race, as if to compensate for the calmness he felt in the moment. A debt of adrenalin he'd never pay off.

Back to the Crown, men dancing on the pool table, passing around a World's Best Dad mug filled with whisky. *Come on, Nicky.* Then the moment when all the windows fell in. Officers hitting the ground as

74

they heard gunfire. It was beautiful. Half the partygoers didn't even know what was going on before the attackers were leaving again, spilling pills, popping shots from a handgun at the stock behind the bar. Belsey had chosen the right men for the job. As he lay there on the floor he took a moment to appreciate it. To appreciate the end, which, even then, he knew was a rare privilege: to know it when it comes. To feel darkness folding back into the night.

Officers ran to their cars. Everyone pretended they knew who to fuck up, because you had to, but they were just running. No one was going to be caught anywhere near the place. And when everyone had run, it was just Belsey and McGovern. Last out as ever. And it was peaceful, standing there. Knowing they wouldn't see this place again. Knowing it was over and they were about to kill each other. Buzzing.

They didn't manage to kill each other. Belsey was discharged from St Thomas' Hospital after forty-eight hours, arrested, locked up for another two days. McGovern left A&E the following Wednesday, Boxing Day. Eventually Belsey was released from custody, told to go home, stay silent and wait. The days that followed were the strangest in his life. The city entered that limbo between Christmas and New Year and it felt as if the Yard had extended its cover-up operation to the world at large. The streets themselves had taken a vow of silence. On 12 January, Belsey was reassigned to Hampstead police station. He heard McGovern was on his way to Islington CID. As if, beyond the worst of violence and corruption, there was nothing but the upper-middle classes.

Did McGovern think he'd won now, as his career ascended and Belsey's remained earthbound, then subterranean? McGovern's smart move had been to get onto the next rung of the ladder fast. His personal network was broad and there were photographs of him playing golf and attending gala dinners with everyone from the Chief Constable to the Lord Mayor. Last year Belsey heard he'd arrived at Homicide and Serious Crime Command, which had offered refuge to no shortage of sick men. But he and McGovern were always going to be with each other in some way. McGovern, who knew him at his worst. And who, more dangerously, knew what Belsey had seen of his own heart. Not a figure he wanted in an already complex scenario.

He heated water for porridge. Fished half a lime from a mug of dark rum and squeezed the juice in. Keep scurvy at bay, or something. Then he splashed in some rum as well. When he'd eaten, he turned his phone on, went online.

'Stars Shaken by Death of Socialite.' Front page of the *Daily Mail* website.

Chloe Burlington, murdered last night in what is being described as a random attack, was the daughter of Sir Malcolm Burlington, owner of the Derringer Group of companies, and heir to the Beaufort Estate in Somerset. A talented artist and designer who came to London in 2010 to study at Central Saint Martins, Chloe was described by friends today as 'a warm and kind person', 'the life and soul of any party', and 'a girl who had everything before her'. Burlington led a glamorous, jet-set lifestyle, dividing her time between Paris, Geneva and Monte Carlo before establishing herself at Beluggi's London HQ, where colleagues say she was expected to rise fast.

Apparently the height of her fame involved *Fortune's Heirs*, a reality show about beautiful European aristocrats. It didn't seem like the design career had taken off, no matter what her friends said. There were projects in the pipeline. She used to be a party animal. She hosted legendary parties at her father's palace. To a detective's eye, there were gaps in the CV.

The *Mail* ran a screenshot of her Instagram account from the previous evening: the princess with a Beluggi bag. '*Can't wait to celebrate this tonight.'* That post would have given a heads-up on where she was going to whoever cared to know.

He kept searching. There were a couple of photographs online from the time of the TV series. That was two or three years ago. Belsey couldn't see anything to inspire current murderous obsession. He looked through the rest of the ghost Instagram account, life's pleasure outliving its owner like hair and fingernails. And what a life of pleasure, a bright, expensive shell of a life: health food, cocktails, international travel. All that was missing was the advertising copy. Now perfect for ever.

Only, her last posting wasn't about Beluggi: it was a picture of a bridge.

Odd. A photograph of a bridge over clear blue water, taken at an angle, as if from some way down a river bank. The bridge was small, humpbacked, stone, with ornate white railings. Through its arch you could see water continuing, expanding into a lake. Trees either side. Hills in the distance.

Posted 11.58 last night.

Fifteen people had liked it. Belsey scrolled through a handful of her followers. No Mark.

His phone rang: the talent agent, Andy Price, again. Belsey sent it to voicemail and ran a search on the man. Price had a colourful online presence. Aside from being sued by two former clients, including 2013's Miss Blackpool, he seemed entirely charming. The website for AP Total Media Management celebrated 'one of the fastest-growing media consultancies, housing an expanding celebrity client list'. Belsey didn't return the call. He finished his coffee. Then the floor shook.

He went to the window. A black Mitsubishi Shogun had pulled up: tinted windows, chrome alloy wheels, bass pumping. It sat for a moment, just entertaining the neighbourhood, then Lee Chester got out.

Belsey went downstairs fast. Lee was still staring at the notice when he arrived at the front.

'Closed?' he said. 'You mean I won?'

Lee wore a white vest that showed off his chest and its artworks. His head was freshly shaved, left arm wrapped in cling film. Belsey checked the car and saw a man in shades and braids in the passenger seat. The car meant Lee wasn't carrying – for actual drop-offs he used a much less conspicuous Golf GTI – but this wasn't what Belsey needed stationed outside his home.

'Kill the music,' he said.

Lee conveyed the message. His passenger turned the music down.

'You didn't tell me you knew Amber Knight,' he said.

'I didn't.'

'You're a dark horse.'

'Can we get out of sight?'

They climbed into the car. Belsey squeezed in the back, next to gym bags, a weightlifting belt, a lot of empty mineral water bottles. A shelf of subwoofers dug into his neck.

'I told you I knew him,' Lee said to his companion, waving a picture of Belsey and Amber on his phone's screen. His companion considered Belsey from behind his mirrored lenses, nodding. 'You're a dark fucking horse, Nick. What else aren't you telling me?' The dealer grinned, eyes bright with placid wonder. His neck veins pulsed beneath a tattoo of fruit-machine cherries. The new piece, under the cling film, appeared to be St George killing the dragon. Belsey moved a stack of flyers from his seat. Over the last few years, Lee Chester had developed a tactic of surrounding himself with shallow industry – club promotion, property refurbishment. He was charming and professional, but you don't make money out of hard drugs for ten years without occasionally burning people in the face with a clothes iron. Lee's eagerness to hurt competitors legally as well as physically had helped Belsey put away several less diplomatic dealers. It had earned Lee a .22 bullet still lodged in the thigh he liked to show off after a couple of Stellas. He considered himself immortal, which Belsey imagined helped with everything.

'This here's my friend Daniel,' Lee said. 'Does a bit of the old music production. Was hoping you'd meet.'

Daniel nodded in the rear-view. Lee twisted in his seat, arm around the headrest. 'Get Amber to my club and I'll write off whatever Mark owes me. We've got a special night coming up, a relaunch. She'd love it.'

'Why would I care about Mark Doughty's debt?'

'Sounded like you cared.' Lee looked momentarily hurt. Then he smiled again. 'What's she like? Does she party? Does she need my number?'

'Right now, Amber's like someone in danger. Serious danger, from your friend Mark Doughty. I think Mark might have murdered someone last night. I'd like to find him before he kills anyone else.'

'You're joking.'

'No.'

'Fucking hell. Who'd he kill?'

'The girl in Mayfair. It's on the news.'

'Jesus Christ.' He straightened to face the windscreen again and bit a cuticle.

'I need to know who he is,' Belsey said.

'I barely know the guy.'

'He was stalking Amber. He's been in her house. Has he been in trouble with the police before?'

'Probably.'

'Why?'

'He's a weirdo, isn't he. He chats a lot of shit.'

'About what?'

'Everything.'

'When did you last speak to him?'

'Tuesday.'

'Did he say anything that struck you as unusual?'

'He seemed tense.'

'About what?'

'About everything. The world. Forces ganging up on him. He was, you know, paranoid or whatever. He wasn't around that much anyway.'

'What do you mean?'

'Like he was sometimes at his mum's but other times he'd be AWOL, for days on end.'

'Where?'

'I don't know. That's what AWOL means. You're the detective.'

This fitted with what Belsey had seen: the Queen's Crescent flat could easily have been just a crash pad, a hideaway for Mark and his obsessions. The question was, where was this alternative accommodation?

'What's he like?' Belsey asked. Lee gave it consideration now.

'He's one of those people who've been done in by their own head. You know what I mean? Smart guy, but lost it. Lost in there.' Lee tapped his shaven skull.

'What does he score?'

'Everything. Speed, coke, gear, downers.'

'Where does he get the money for that lot?'

'I don't know. But he had money. What's up with you, anyway? You been fired?'

'Suspended.'

'You'll be back.'

'Not this time.'

'You've got to be cleverer than that, Nick.' He straightened to face the windscreen again, sighing. 'You should have done your sergeant's exams, got a proper grip on it.' Lee shook his head. 'Where've you been? Here?'

'Lying low.'

'Lying low!' Lee laughed. He checked his phone again. 'You're low, Nick. Right now you're practically invisible.' He scrolled through a few more shots of the Loulou's crowd. Belsey sensed a useful alibi.

'Have you seen anything claiming me and Amber left that club together?'

'Why?'

'I'm just asking if you've seen anything saying that. It might be helpful.'

'No. Will I?'

'Probably not.'

Belsey's phone started to vibrate: 'Amber PA'. Lee smiled.

'Answer my calls,' Belsey said, getting out of the Shogun. 'Tell me if you hear from Mark, or anyone who's heard from him. And tell me right away.'

Belsey took the call. Gabby was breathless.

'He's been in again,' she said.

'What makes you think that?'

'More stuff's gone missing. Last night.'

'Last night?' Belsey wondered if that was possible: Mark Doughty in the house while he'd slept on the sofa. After the killing? Given the state he'd been in, it wasn't as impossible as Belsey would have liked.

'And what do you want me to do?' he asked.

'Help us,' she pleaded. 'You know about him. I need you to do something.'

'Gabby, I'm not the person you need—'

'Just get here. Amber's terrified and I don't know what's going on or what we can do about this. Just get here and be discreet.'

Belsey groaned. The sensible thing – the only thing – was to start putting some distance between himself and whatever it was that was happening here. But he found himself walking down Pond Street past the back of the Royal Free Hospital, to a crumbling structure that still promised Late Night Dancing and Shisha Garden. Currently it was offering little more than a skip full of rusted catering equipment and a mound of refuse sacks. Belsey slipped through a gate at the side, through a concrete garden filled with old casks and a pool table streaked with bird shit. He took the padlock off a garage.

His Audi 80 was still there: boxy, navy blue, reliable as it was unfashionable. He sat in the car, in the darkness beneath the garage's mouldy canopy, wishing he could stay there for ever. Then he turned the key in the ignition. The engine started. He didn't feel particularly relieved.

8

HE FILLED UP WITH PETROL at the Morrisons in Chalk Farm then
continued into Primrose Hill. The high street was lively: bistros
crowded, couples lunching with shades on. Belsey drove by Amber's
place. It looked quiet enough outside. He parked a few houses away,
called Gabby as he approached the entrance.

She met him inside the gate, led him fast into the house and upstairs.

'You didn't tell me,' she said.

'What?'

'Last night. I said phone me if she goes anywhere.' Gabby glanced
into rooms either side as they hurried along the landing.

'Is Amber OK?'

'It's a while since she's been OK. Karen's furious. And now we've
got this fucking stalker coming in and out. And there's you – which
company did you say you're with? Nobody's got a clue any more.'

'I'm not,' he said. 'I was lying.' But she'd been distracted by the
sound of voices and hadn't heard him. She put a finger to her lips and
beckoned Belsey into the corridor to the office, where she closed the
door.

'So look. He's taken more clothes, her bag. I don't know what else.'

'Did you check the security cameras?'

'I checked. I can't see him. But I'm not the security expert.'

'A guy breaking into a house is fairly obvious.'

'The All Saints jacket she had last night has gone, her Louis Vuitton bag, a pair of Jimmy Choos and the dress from last night too. The dress was on loan. Did you come back with her?'

'Yes.'

'Oh Jesus. Did you *sleep* with her?'

'No.'

She sat down behind the desk. 'Well, thank Christ for small mercies. Did she have the jacket and her handbag and everything with her when you came back?'

'Yes.'

'Then he's come and taken the lot, hasn't he. And god knows what else. She's been searching everywhere. And she's freaked by this Chloe Burlington story.'

'She should be. It might connect. Do you have any idea how he got in?'

'No.'

'The doors and windows were locked overnight,' Belsey said. 'I locked them.'

'So how would he get in?'

Belsey wondered. Big house, plenty of windows, he could have easily missed a few. 'When did you notice that things had been taken?'

'Amber saw first thing, but thought maybe the cleaner had moved it all. But the cleaner only came in at ten and everything was gone by then.'

'Last night, when we got back, she dropped her stuff in the bedroom. He must have been there while she was sleeping.'

'Oh Christ. What do I tell Karen?'

'Can I see her room?'

Gabby checked the landing, ushered him out. They went up to the bedroom and stood in the doorway. The bed was unmade.

He stepped inside and saw, through the doorway into the bathroom, items beside the sink: keys, lip balm, paracetamol, gum. That was the first odd thing. As if whoever had taken the bag had emptied it first.

'Tell me what was missing again.'

'Jacket, bag, shoes, the Donna Karan dress. Probably other stuff we haven't noticed yet.'

'But the only clothing that's definitely missing is what she was wearing last night.'

'Yes.'

'Why?' he said, more to himself than the PA.

Something nagged. He walked a circuit of the room.

'You said she seemed upset by the murder.'

'Wouldn't you be?'

'Did Amber know Chloe?'

'Of course.'

Belsey turned to the PA.

'Are you sure?'

'Definitely. She hasn't mentioned her for a while. But they were friends. Or used to be – I'm sure.'

'Amber said she didn't know her.'

'Really?'

'I asked her last night.'

'Then I guess she doesn't really know her any more. She probably meant that, or something.'

Belsey looked at the room again. He could picture the clothes where they fell after she'd taken them off. There was only one response he knew to a situation where someone had disposed of all the clothing they were wearing on the night someone was killed. But surely that wasn't the appropriate response here.

He tried to remember how she'd seemed after the club. By the canal. Then, with a small chill – a chill he didn't quite trust – he thought of their conversation. *Do people always look different when they're dead?*

'Has Amber been out today?'

'No.'

'Where does rubbish go?'

'The cleaners do it. There are wheelie bins round the back. It gets collected every morning.'

'Has it been collected today?'

'Probably – they usually come first thing. Why?'

'Maybe Amber threw everything out.'

Gabby frowned. 'Why would she do that?'

'I don't know.' Belsey moved past Gabby, back onto the landing. 'Where is Amber now?'

'She's in the middle of a work-out. You can't talk to her. Not when she's working out.'

'I reckon I'll manage.' Belsey tried to remember where the gym was. Gabby followed.

'I'd really rather you didn't.' He turned the corner and walked into a very tall woman dressed head to toe in black.

'*You*,' she said.

'Karen—' Gabby began.

Amber's manager. Red hair scraped back into a bun, newspapers clutched to her chest. To one side of her was a short man in a roll neck, on the other was a lanky security guard with slicked-back hair and a crisp, white G3 Security shirt.

'What's he doing here?' Karen said, glancing furiously between Belsey and Gabby.

'He's here about the intruder,' Gabby said.

'But he's not a security guard.'

'He's definitely not with us,' the guard added helpfully.

'Did you take her belongings?' Karen asked.

'No,' Belsey said. 'Where is she?'

'Get out. You can't be here. Do you know the trouble you've caused?'

The new security decided it was a chance to prove himself. 'Come on, fella. Looks like you're not wanted. Shall we go?'

Belsey let himself be steered towards the stairs. Amber was in the gym room. Belsey saw her as he was hustled past, on a treadmill in front of a mirror, in Lycra, shoulders glistening with sweat. She saw him in the mirror, met his eyes and kept running.

9

HE LEFT THE HOUSE AND walked to the park. According to McGovern, the signal from Chloe Burlington's phone had cut just east of Avenue Road.

Belsey crossed the park to Avenue Road, down to Prince Albert Road. He followed it to where the hired Mercedes had dropped them last night, walked down the embankment to the canal. He stood by the water.

Splash, he thought.

The water was thick, soupy with chemicals and algae. He couldn't see Chloe Burlington's phone down there, or anything else. He watched the scum and felt his mind struggle.

You've got no idea about the situation I'm dealing with right now.

Stabbed once to the throat. Skull smashed. Amber Knight?

No way.

But detective habit kicked in. First thing you did when you got a suspect was put instinct aside and assess facts. It was facts that were needed in a courtroom. And it meant you avoided clumsy assumptions about what was and wasn't possible. Because there was no limit to what was possible.

But there were patterns. And there were practicalities.

They got back to Amber's between 12.30 and 1 a.m.; say they left the club at 12.30 at the latest. They were there for, what, four hours. Less. The first two he had a sense of what was going on. Amber had been around. The last two he had absolutely no idea. His memories of the night clustered around the sober edges. Individual moments flashed out from the fog in between. He remembered the courtyard, the game with malts, the whole Lake Como plan. He remembered waiting at the bar and being handed a glass of champagne, drinking a toast to someone's racehorse.

He last saw Chloe sometime between 11 and 11.30 by his estimation.

The dance floor, the American guys, then Amber back with him. From then on she wasn't out of his sight.

Could Amber have headed out and back in? She had access to the back door. Belsey brought up a map on his phone. The back door led to Trebeck Street. Trebeck Street to Market Mews, where Chloe Burlington met her end, was a brief and potentially unseen walk.

Then what?

He considered a compromise scenario: say Amber had been present as someone else killed Chloe Burlington. For one reason or another she's there, close enough to worry about blood splash. She disposes of Chloe's phone; maybe the knife as well, getting blood inside her clutch.

There was that other issue: Chloe's reaction to Mark Doughty's ID. How did Mark fit into all this? Both women had responded to the ID with intrigue or puzzlement. He saw Amber's reaction, looking from the doorway in Gabby's little office, walking over to study it. He saw Chloe's expression in the light of the courtyard.

Belsey sat on the bench he had sat on last night. The canal in daylight felt less isolated, but still not a popular stretch. Occasional cyclists tore past, joggers, a couple of men with cans of high-strength cider.

Amber hadn't originally intended to go out. That was one of the first things Chloe commented on: asking if he was with her. Then: *I didn't think Amber was coming tonight.*

And it wasn't on the schedule.

At 7 p.m. Chloe puts a picture online, posing with her Beluggi bag; 7.40 p.m. Amber finds Belsey – and Amber goes out.

Did you tell Gabby we were going out tonight?

He interrogated each scene he could remember from last night, as if he could use his memory like a drill, boring down: from her demeanour on the way there to her vomiting once back.

A canal boat passed. People with wine glasses waved at Belsey from the deck. He waved back. His phone rang. This time he answered.

'Is that Nick Belsey?' a man said.

'Speaking.'

'DCI Steve Tanner here. Calling with regards to the fatal stabbing last night in Mayfair. I believe you were at Loulou's nightclub.'

'That's right.'

'We're keen to talk to you.'

'I'm keen to talk to you.'

'Great. Can you come in now? West End Central.'

'Of course.'

'Want me to send a car?'

'It's OK. I know where it is.'

10

HE PARKED ON CURZON STREET. It allowed him another stroll past the police tape. Four p.m. There was a growing pile of flowers at the corner with Shepherd Street, as close to the crime scene as the public could get – bouquets, cards, other votive offerings: a scarf, some lipstick. It provided a backdrop for news reports at least. Two men were speaking to camera, another handful of crews waiting their turn.

Belsey scanned the messages in the cards. He got a lot of polite condolences. No photos, no memories. Maybe her aristocratic acquaintances were too cool for crime scenes. Something to think about when choosing friends.

He crossed two blocks south.

West End Central police station stood at the north end of Savile Row: a surprising, square-shouldered conclusion to the tailors' shops. Belsey took a breath and climbed the steps.

'I'm here to speak to Steve Tanner. Nick Belsey.'

The woman on reception lifted a phone, announced Belsey's arrival and hung up. She buzzed the internal door and told Belsey to take a seat in the waiting area. Belsey walked in and sat down. Then he got up and went through to the corridor.

The incident room was at the back of the ground floor. It was large, open-plan, with hi-tech screens, whiteboards and, between the various displays, a Major Investigation Team of fifteen police and civilians busy at desks and computers. No sign of the office manager. No one by the door.

Belsey walked in.

A board at the back carried a map of Mayfair with fluorescent stickers marking Loulou's and the crime scene. A panel beside it contained a list headed 'Loulou's 11/5/15', subdivided into guests and staff, just over half with phone numbers. Tick boxes recorded whether they'd been interviewed. Some of the guests had stars by their names. Going by the names, it looked like these were the sensitives: Saudis, minor royalty, men and women who came up on diplomatic protection lists. Even murder investigations had a VIP area. Someone had started filling in the times each guest was at the club. There was his own name and phone number, allowed to nestle anonymously amongst the rest for now. No VIP star. They had his time into the club at 8.50. Time out: question mark.

No phone records for Chloe that he could see.

He walked over to another free-standing board, still unnoticed. On its front, facing into the room, was an inventory of clothing and possessions: what Chloe was wearing, what she had with her, finally what was found within ten metres of her body. The list was topped by his business card. She also had her wallet, sixty pounds, various credit cards and a cloakroom ticket.

On the back were the crime-scene photos. Twenty-five arrangements of Mayfair cobblestones, black dress and cold, white skin. Belsey took a second before looking, considered something between a prayer and an apology. Then he started with a close-up of the neck wound: 8.8 centimetres, according to the pathologist's ruler. Clean-edged on both sides. Wide enough to see the muscle tendons of the throat. He checked the hands. The French manicure remained perfect. No dirt or skin or blood under the nails to suggest a fight. Her knees were grazed, which suggested she moved herself after the attack, or tried to move. Finally he looked at the face. Her eyes were open, empty of expression.

He turned to the preliminary report, displayed beside the photos. The blade had punctured the windpipe. Cause of death: catastrophic haemorrhage.

But it wasn't the only injury.

Her hair had been shaved off and the scalp unpeeled to expose a basilar skull fracture, spidery lines where the bone had smashed – she'd fallen or been thrown against a wall, McGovern thought. The position of the injury, in the centre of the back of the skull, suggested the latter. So did bruising on the shoulder prominences, as if she'd been forced up against bricks. In addition, the right cheekbone was broken. A punch, driving her head back?

No semen. No vaginal abrasions. The report estimated the window of time in which she was killed as 12 to 1 a.m.

Belsey turned back to the stab wound. A *coup de grâce*, he thought. Maybe. Certainly administered easily enough. Sometimes you could see the level of calm or frenzy in a wound. This one looked cool as anything.

Someone touched his shoulder.

'Nick. Steve Tanner. I was worried you might have got lost.'

Tanner had a square head, thick silver hair combed back into a brush. He shook Belsey's hand.

'Just being nosy,' Belsey said.

Tanner glanced across the photos. 'Did you know the girl?'

'For ten minutes.'

'I'm sorry.' He frowned appropriately. 'Geoff McGovern says we're lucky to have you as a witness. A top detective right there. I'm glad you could come in.'

'It's no problem.'

'We're upstairs. More private.'

He led Belsey to the stairs.

'Geoff says you used to work together.'

'Long time ago.'

'Not one of his golf buddies, then.'

'Not quite.'

'In here.'

He directed Belsey into a windowless room next to the CID office. One table, four chairs and a water-cooler. A senior detective he recognised, Jean Courtney, was waiting.

'So you are here,' she said. 'We were getting worried.'

Courtney didn't shake his hand. She gestured to a seat. She was the go-to homicide DCI, a hard-eyed woman with short brown hair. Together, they looked like a couple you might meet on holiday and avoid. You could imagine Tanner trying to sell you a used car. It was hard to imagine Courtney doing anything other than nailing you for murder.

'Counting on you, Nick,' Courtney said. 'You were there. You could be valuable.'

'I hope so.'

'Her old man's on his way over,' Tanner said. 'Private jet and all that. Lots of friends in high places. You're in the game, you know what it's like.'

'Big pressure.'

'So let's get a few times down. When do you reckon you last saw Chloe?'

'Around eleven p.m.'

'See her leave?'

'No.'

Tanner scribbled this on the sheet in front of him. It seemed to take a lot of concentration.

'You got there about ten to nine?'

'That's right.'

'We've got shots of that.' He glanced up, smiled. 'You've shaved, I see.'

'Yes.'

Tanner spent a moment admiring the sheen of Belsey's jaw. He regretted shaving: changes of appearance rang alarm bells.

'What time did you leave the club?'

'A bit after midnight.'

'We can't see you on the cameras when you leave.'

'I left by the back. I was with Amber Knight.'

Tanner smiled. 'Very nice. Tell me about this back entrance.'

'It's a fire exit. Stairs lead down from a restaurant above the club.'

'How did you find that?'

'Amber showed me.'

'She a friend then?'

'No. But I think she might have been a friend of Chloe's. Have you spoken to her yet?'

'Not yet. Spoke to her people.' Tanner did quote marks with his fingers. 'Can't wait to meet her though. Daughter's a fan. What's she going to say?'

'I don't know. I'd be interested to hear.'

A crooked smile from Tanner. Courtney's expression hadn't changed once. She studied Belsey without blinking.

'How did Chloe seem when you last saw her?'

'OK.'

'Drunk?'

'No.'

'Anyone giving her trouble?'

'Not that I saw.'

Tanner thrust himself back in his seat, fists still clenched on the table.

'Loulou's,' he said, with wonder in his voice. 'Not the old Dog and Duck, is it. You a regular?'

'It was my first time.'

'What's it for a pint in there, eh?'

'I don't think they do pints.'

'Really? Taste of the high life.'

'Exactly.'

'And you turn up there with Amber Knight on your arm. I should get myself suspended, Nick. Seems a blast.'

It was their first acknowledgement of his status. They'd been waiting. Soon they'd be onto his lack of a fixed abode.

'It's not all glamour,' Belsey said.

'Then, am I right, you were at the crime scene this morning?' Tanner pressed on, leaving the suspension to one side.

'I heard about it on the news. I came to see what was going on.'

'And you told Detective Inspector McGovern of your suspicions.' Tanner checked a sheet beneath the one he was writing on. Paper-clipped to it was Mark Doughty's student ID, which he unclipped and studied. 'This the guy?'

'He has a thing about celebrities. I think you should try to find him. I'm no longer sure how he fits in.'

'No longer sure.'

'No.'

'OK. Did you exchange numbers with Chloe, Nick?'

'I gave her the business card that was by her body.'

Tanner winced. 'Geoff told you about that?'

'Yes.'

'A few people got one, it seems.'

'I was drumming up business.'

'Where do you usually keep them?'

'In my wallet.'

'Can you show us?'

Belsey showed them his wallet. 'They're all gone.'

'I've got to ask this, Nick. How much had you drunk, personally?'

'Personally? Lots.'

'What kind of thing?'

'Different drinks. Champagne, cognac.'

'Remember who you were talking to between eleven and twelve?'

'Some of them. Look, I wouldn't put too many resources into me.'

'You pose a bit of a problem, Nick, that's all.'

'We had some confusion over your address,' Courtney said. 'We checked 26 Royal College Street. That's the last address we have for you. Landlord says you just upped sticks twelve days ago.'

'That's right.'

'So where've you been since?'

'Sleeping rough.'

'Really. People have been trying to get hold of you. But you're off the radar.'

Belsey suppressed a sigh. If there was one thing police hated it was the lack of an address. As if a home was all that kept people from erupting into criminality.

'So, no fixed abode,' Courtney said, writing this down.

'Not at the moment.'

Tanner joined his stumpy fingers and leaned forwards again.

'This investigation nonsense going on about you, Nick. I've only heard bits and pieces but it sounds like typical crap. Officer who's done so much for the force. Long service. Think you trained with a mate of mine, Phil Godfrey.'

'What are you trying to get at?'

'I'm trying to ascertain your state of mind in recent days.'

'It says on the board downstairs that Chloe had a cloakroom ticket on her when she was killed,' Belsey said. 'Was there a coat at the club?'

'Why?'

'That's strange, isn't it? Leaving a club without collecting your coat. In a hurry, or intending to return. She walks away from taxis, buses, shops, away from everything – into the backstreets. Maybe she was going to meet someone. Someone she knew.'

They continued to stare at him, but looked more thoughtful now. Belsey didn't rush it.

'She knew you by the sounds of it,' Tanner said.

'No she didn't.'

'Things were getting a bit heavy between you, by all accounts. How did that turn out in the end?'

'She left and got killed.'

'They haven't lived, have they, posh birds,' Tanner continued, undaunted. 'Don't understand respect.'

'Christ. Am I the best you've got? You really think I killed her?'

'Did I say that?'

'Everyone's lived as much as anyone else. That's what I've been thinking about. How do you quantify it?'

'Don't change the subject.'

'I'm elaborating on it.'

'You're bullshitting.'

'Of course they understand respect,' Belsey said. 'That's all they understand.'

Tanner and Courtney considered this.

'Maybe that's what got her into trouble.'

'Respect?'

'I met her last night. You want to find someone she trusted. Someone who can say "Meet me a block away" and she goes. Away from people and cameras. Without her coat.'

The detectives didn't take their eyes off him. Belsey pressed on.

'Why take her phone? Police can still pull records of any calls. So what was on it? Photos?'

'I don't get you, Nick.'

'I realise that.'

'What is it you're not telling us?'

How to conduct a murder investigation, Belsey thought. He tried to check his anger.

'There's a lot I'm not telling you. I'm not convinced you'd listen to me anyway. And I'm off the payroll right now, so fuck that.'

He stood up.

'Sit down,' Tanner said. 'Don't mess us about.'

'Don't mess me about.'

'No one pays you for co-operating with the police, Nick. You know that. Withholding information constitutes a serious crime.'

'Then I don't have a clue.'

They kept their exasperation silent.

'Speak to Amber Knight,' Belsey said.

'You think Amber did it?' Tanner's grin returned.

'I'm going to the bathroom,' Belsey said. Things you can't really do unless an individual's been formally charged: stop them going to the bathroom, accompany them to the bathroom, watch them leave the bathroom and leg it. At the very least, it has the effect of putting interviewing officers on the back foot.

'Don't go too far,' Tanner said, uncertainly.

'I'm not going anywhere.'

Belsey stepped out into the corridor and checked the door to the stairs. He heard Tanner and Courtney shift their chairs and begin a consultation. They had a quick decision to make. He'd given them no fixed address. He had a history of absconding. Even if they knew the whole thing was crap, an arrest in time for the six o'clock news would be nice. He would have done it in their position: wrong-foot the real killer, calm public nerves.

The door to the stairs was unguarded. Belsey was heading for it when it opened. A blonde woman appeared, gripping a Starbucks cup. She was followed by a woman constable who guided her to the chairs in the corridor.

'They'll be with you in a second. Need anything?'

The woman sat down, shook her head, watched the PC depart. She lifted her Prada shades. It took Belsey a second to recognise her.

'Tatiana,' he said.

Tatiana looked at him, blankly. 'Are you Detective Tanner?'

'I'm Nick. From last night. I was at Loulou's.'

He saw her trying to work out what this meant.

'Oh.'

She seemed numbed; his guess was a combination of shock and Valium.

'Have they spoken to you too?' she asked. Her speech was muddy. Belsey glanced back at the interview room.

'I'm actually a police officer. I'm working with Detective Tanner. Last night I was undercover.' He paused as the information dripped into her consciousness. 'This is where I work. I can't believe what happened to Chloe. It's awful. But we're going to find the person who did it.'

'You're a police officer?'

'Yes.'

She looked confused.

'Do you remember her leaving the club?' he asked.

'No. I didn't know where she'd gone.'

'Did Chloe know Amber Knight?'

'Amber Knight? Yes. Why?'

'Did she say anything last night – about Amber?'

'No.'

'Anything else? Anything that seemed unusual?'

'Yes, some things. The necklace—'

There was a screech of chairs in the office.

'Come with me,' Belsey said.

11

THEY GOT THROUGH THE DOOR to the stairs and left the station fast.

'Where am I going?'

He led her to his car. She stared at the Audi with a slightly disorientated doubt. Belsey opened the door for her.

'Get in,' Belsey said. They climbed in. He started the car and pulled into Mayfair traffic for the sake of moving, unsure where to go. 'What necklace?' he said.

'She gave me this.' Tatiana searched in her bag. She brought out the necklace Chloe had been wearing.

'She gave it to you?'

'Yes.'

'When?'

'Last night.'

'Why?'

'I don't know. She knew I liked it. She said she wanted me to have it.'

'How did she seem?'

'I don't know. We were drinking. I thought she was joking. She said when I looked at it I could think of her.'

He stopped by Grosvenor Square, took the necklace from her. Held the turquoise pendant and remembered it lying against Chloe's collarbone. It was a large droplet, misshapen. A teardrop, perhaps. Glass. The chain was gold.

'She posted this picture to Instagram. Last night.' Belsey showed her the bridge. 'Know where this is?'

'No. Maybe from a holiday.'

'Has she been anywhere recently?'

'She's always travelling. What's going on?'

'I don't know. Tatiana, last night she said you were staying with her, right?'

'Yeah.'

'You stay there last night?'

'I went back because, when I couldn't find her, I thought she must have gone home. I thought maybe she was with you or something.'

'So you have a key?'

'Yes.'

'When you got home, was anything different? Anything out of the ordinary?'

'No. Not that I saw. It was tidy.'

'Tidy?'

'Yes.'

Belsey returned the necklace. 'What's the address?'

'Beaufort Gardens. In Knightsbridge.'

Tatiana tapped Rescue Remedy into her mouth as he started the car again. She rolled the window down, found a tissue and dabbed her eyes behind the shades. Belsey swung back towards Marble Arch, heading west. Tatiana's phone rang. He could hear Tanner's voice on the other end.

'Yes,' Tatiana said. 'I'm with a police officer now . . .'

'I'll deal with it,' Belsey said. He took the phone and hung up. 'Don't answer it if he calls again,' he said, handing it back. 'This is more important. Last night, you said you were over for a shoot.'

'Yes. I live in New York. I had some work here – and to see friends.'

'When did you get to London?'

'Thursday.'

'And you've been staying at Chloe's throughout?'

Tatiana nodded.

'How did she seem?'

'She's always . . . she gets anxious. Up and down, you know? I mean, she was fine. Then, on the weekend, she was more serious. But that was just her. That was Chloe.'

'What exactly was she doing?'

'She was quiet. Checking her phone. Stuff like that. We were going to get brunch on Sunday, but then she didn't want to.'

'And she was OK Thursday, when you arrived?'

'Yes.'

'Anything that might have happened in between?'

'I don't know. Yesterday, I think there was something about a lawyer.'

'Like what?'

'She went out, said something about that. Needing a lawyer, wanting to speak to a lawyer.'

'What do you think she needed a lawyer for?'

'Maybe business stuff. Or to do with property. I don't know.'

'Do you think she visited a lawyer?'

'I guess. I have no idea. It was nothing to do with me.'

Not for the first time in his career he wished his star witness wasn't knee-deep in diazepam.

'Had Chloe been anywhere over the weekend that might be connected to her starting to worry?'

'She was out Saturday night.'

'Where?'

'She didn't say. It was a last-minute thing. I was going on a date anyway.'

'Did you see her when she came back?'

'Not until the next morning.'

He drove west, past Hyde Park Corner. Into the part of London that felt least like home.

'And you don't remember her leaving Loulou's last night?'

'No. She disappeared. I spent about an hour looking for her. She left her coat. I waited until the very end. She wasn't answering her phone. So I figured she'd gone home. She gave me the necklace. I went to the bar. I was dancing. Then she was gone.'

'And apart from me, you didn't see her talking to anyone?'

'No. It's down here.' She directed him down Brompton Road, past Harrods, to a pristine residential square.

Chloe's apartment block was new: dark grey marble and long windows. The ground-floor reception looked like a private art gallery, with spotlights on small sculptures and an incongruous tapestry behind the security desk. A smart concierge got up from his seat when he saw Tatiana, buttoning his jacket; sombre, eastern European.

'This is a police detective,' she said. The man nodded at Belsey. He took a sheet of paper from the desk and handed it over.

'Here. If it is helpful.' It contained names and contact numbers for building managers and night security. 'All will help with any questions.'

'Thank you.'

'If there's anything further we can do . . .' He spread his hands. Death's own concierge. Belsey thanked him again. They crossed the reception into a lift with a small bench and a pot plant in it.

'How long has she lived here?' he asked.

'A year or so. Her father owns it. He owns the building.'

The lift opened on the eighth floor. The corridor stretched ahead of them. Someone had put a lot of money into making the place feel as soulless as a hotel, in the green-grey of international luxury. Belsey imagined other daughters of aristocrats imprisoned behind the polished doors. Tatiana unlocked number 26 and they walked in.

It was a loft-style penthouse, with London providing most of the decoration. Windows looked over Hyde Park in one direction, down towards the V&A in the other. The flat itself appeared to be posed for a catalogue shoot: brick-effect walls, metal stairs, a right-angle of grey sofa in the centre with wire-mesh chairs, magazines and art books on a coffee table. Chloe had collected a lot of white ceramic vases, but not whatever was meant to go in them. There was a slate kitchen with breakfast island at the back. All tasteful. Untroubled by its owner's absence, as if grateful for one less piece of clutter.

'Is it true I have to stay in the country?' Tatiana asked. She collapsed back on the sofa.

'Maybe. Were you two close?'

'We partied. We had some good times together. I didn't know her that well.'

'Last night she told me she didn't know Amber. Why might that be?'

Tatiana sighed, somewhere between exhausted and bored now. 'They had a strange relationship. They hung out a bit. Then she went funny about her. Didn't speak about her any more. Maybe they fell out. I think Chloe was a bit obsessed.'

'Obsessed?'

'For a while. She'd get the same stuff. Like, go to the same nutritionist, follow the same exercise routine. Stuff like that.'

'How did they meet?'

'I don't know. I know they hung out at some TV awards. And she said she'd seen Amber at the spa a few times.'

'Which spa?'

'I don't know its name. It's the one behind Christabel's in Marylebone. The bar, Christabel's. Maybe that one. She was there yesterday.'

'Chloe went there yesterday?'

'I think so. She had her nails done. I don't know where. Maybe there.'

Belsey saw her nails in the crime-scene shots. Immaculate. He looked out of the window, towards the park. Humanity crawled across the Royal Borough. A hard view to live up to. He couldn't quite match the cold flat to the Instagram account. The problem with the perfect life, he guessed, is it's bullshit. You get in and shut the door and it's gone. He imagined days of expensive loneliness, parties that emptied, people breezing in and out of your show pad.

'You said she tidied this place. Was it messy usually?'

'Not messy. There were some clothes, a few papers.'

'What kind of papers?'

'Just sheets of paper. Like, notes.'

'About what?'

'Ideas. Projects. I don't know.'

Belsey kept his hands in his pockets as he explored. Leaving a print in Chloe Burlington's home wasn't particularly desirable. He found the guest bedroom off the living room, Tatiana's outfit from last night shimmering on the floor, cosmetics across a dresser.

He walked back to the living room, up the stairs to what he took to be the main bedroom. White linen had been tucked tightly over the kingsize bed. A pair of over-the-ear headphones wound in their lead lay on the right-hand pillow. Framed photos of Chloe and her family crowded the cabinets and dressing table. He couldn't see any papers. No laptop either. On the far side of the bed he found two Hermès suitcases on their side. He took a tissue from a box beside the bed, opened them. They'd been hurriedly packed. Clothes, make-up bag, shoes.

He called Tatiana to the bedroom and showed her the suitcases.

'Was Chloe going away?'

'No.' She frowned at the cases. 'She didn't say anything.'

Belsey went back out to the mezzanine railings overlooking the main living area and kitchen. He looked down to the sofa, up to the ceiling. A smoke alarm had been wrapped in cling film.

He went down to the kitchen. The chrome vent above the cooker was out. He wrapped the tissue around his hand, pressed a button and it retracted. He opened the fridge. It contained eye cream, sparkling mineral water, two yoghurts.

'Did Chloe like cooking?'

'I've never seen her cook.'

He extracted the vent again, listened to the almost imperceptible whirr of the fan. He took a tea towel and used it to open the oven.

'She wasn't very good at it,' he said. He removed an oven dish. Blackened scraps of paper and matchsticks lay half an inch deep. Belsey placed it on the side. He checked the sink, ran a finger around the plug hole. Took the strainer off it and picked out shreds of damp, scorched paper.

Tatiana walked over.

'What's she done?'

'I don't know. Can I see the necklace again?'

Tatiana brought it from her bag. 'I hardly knew her,' she said, holding it for a last time. Studying it for evidence of a relationship she'd missed.

'Can I take it?'

'Sure.' She handed it over and seemed glad to be rid of the thing.

12

IT WAS HARD TO FIND a pawnshop in Kensington. In the end he
drove to his usual, behind Victoria station: WE BUY GOLD. There were
two doors, one into a bright jewellery store, all glass and mirrors, the
other into its shadow twin, a dingy room housing two worn sofas and
a counter divided by bullet-proof glass. Belsey rang a bell on the counter.
The manager shuffled out, laid tired eyes on him.

'Nick.'

'Mr Kundaje. Would you take a look at this?'

Belsey passed the necklace through. The pawnbroker took his
glasses off, lifted a jeweller's loupe.

'Sorry,' he said. 'Not for me.' He passed it back.

'What would you put it at? Just as an estimate?'

'It's Christmas cracker. It's glass, gold plate. Find a nice lady to give
it to.'

'Seen one like it before?'

'No.'

Belsey returned to his car. He hung the necklace on the rear-view
mirror and watched it swing. He thought about someone panicking,

maybe looking for a lawyer, throwing clothes in a case. He ignored West End Central calling his mobile.

He thought about two people who deny knowing each other.

He slipped the necklace back into his pocket and drove to Marylebone, looking for the spa they had shared. Somewhere you could establish a relationship behind closed doors. Belsey felt the ice of Marylebone as he turned onto Harley Street: the London that doesn't belong to London; shops and restaurants that back onto St Tropez and Dubai. Nothing moved too fast. Money hung in the air like pollen.

The bar Tatiana had mentioned, Christabel's, was on Weymouth Street. He knew it from tabloids: not quite Loulou's, but adequate for those who wanted to recreate the effect. Behind it was Weymouth Mews. The spa was easy enough to find. It was called the Retreat Boutique & Wellness Spa and it occupied three adjoining mews houses, all painted white.

Glass doors led into a warmly lit reception with abundant plants and a miniature waterfall bubbling down plastic rocks next to a stack of fluffy towels. The air was scented with aromatherapy oils. Even the plants looked rich with wellness. The white-coated receptionist would have been at home on a perfume counter.

'Good afternoon,' she smiled.

'Good afternoon. I had a quick query about one of your customers: Chloe Burlington.'

The smile froze.

'Who are you?'

'A friend of hers. Did she come here often?'

'Give me one moment,' the receptionist said. She vanished into a side room and retrieved an older woman in a navy tunic and air hostess make-up. Her smile was harder. She scrutinised Belsey. He had entered the world that grew fat on the rich. And what it sold was discretion.

'Are you a journalist?' the woman asked.

'No.'

'Who are you?'

'An independent investigator. I was just wondering if you were aware of Chloe attending the centre in the company of Amber Knight.' She didn't let anything show at the mention of Amber's name.

'We'll deal with her family directly, if you don't mind. It would be highly inappropriate for us to speak to you.'

'I'm not press.'

She squinted at him. 'We've had words with you before, haven't we?'

'No.'

'If you don't mind, I need to ask you to leave now.'

'What if I wanted a massage?'

'We're booked up.'

'That's a shame.'

'And if it's your photographer hanging around, tell him we're willing to call the police on him too.'

Four-thirty p.m. He walked back into Marylebone, sat outside a brasserie and ordered a tenner's worth of chicken sandwich.

Next to him were four teenage girls, rich kids of West London. Girls who could be no older than fifteen, arranging themselves over coffee and talking with the unimpressed drawls of divorced forty-somethings.

He put the necklace on the table in front of him, blocked out their voices, and thought.

Two things Chloe Burlington did before dying: gave her friend her necklace, posted the Instagram photo. Three things. She called his phone.

He checked her social media again – the Instagram account and a Facebook page in her name. People were posting their condolences to the Facebook page, addressed to Chloe herself. '*Can't believe I'll never see your face again. Remembering good times.*' Some hadn't heard the news and were trying to get her to graduate fashion shows.

He tapped back to the bridge picture. Thirty-five people had liked it. He couldn't tell how many preceded the death, how many were a response to it. Comments ranged from 'Beautiful' to 'Rest in peace'. The bridge sat there, conclusive: her final post, like a destination reached.

His food arrived. Belsey ate and ordered a coffee. He turned to the teenagers.

'Can I ask you a question?' There was a flutter of curiosity. 'Are you on Instagram?'

'Yes,' two of them said in unison. The others nodded. He showed them the bridge photo on his phone.

'The people liking this, are they friends of hers? Or can anyone like it?'

'It's not private. So anyone.'

'How would they find it?'

They shrugged. 'If someone reposts. Or there's a hashtag.'

'And then there's followers, right.'

'Right.'

'Would she have to allow them to follow?'

'No. Anyone could follow her.'

'Can you see their real names anywhere? Any personal details?'

'No.'

'OK. Thanks.'

The girls exchanged glances, went back to their gossip. Belsey's coffee arrived. He drank it and rolled a cigarette. After another minute the girls left, amidst a discussion about tipping and a cloud of precociously expensive perfume.

Lives with luxurious futures, he thought. Miserable, luxurious, photographed.

Lives like Chloe's.

She went out, said something about a lawyer. The family lawyer would be an obvious one to use. Belsey had always admired families with lawyers. With infrastructure. He found the list of contacts from the concierge in Chloe's apartment block. Her father's apartment block. No lawyer listed. He called the building manager and got the same slick, nervous deference as the concierge.

'Is there a law firm that you use? That Mr Burlington uses? Sir Burlington, whatever.'

The manager provided the name and number for a person or a firm called D'Angour Strauss. According to their website, the offices were just a few minutes' drive away. Belsey called. It had gone 5 p.m. but the phone was answered promptly and, once he'd alluded to the nature of his investigations, he got put through to a man with a slight accent.

'Mr D'Angour?'

'Mr Strauss.'

'Mr Strauss, my name's Nicholas Belsey. I've been asked by Chloe's father to look into this . . . this awful tragedy.'

'Really?'

'Yes.' Belsey left it vague. That seemed to be how these people operated.

'I haven't been able to speak to him yet.'

'He said I should speak to you first. Did Chloe contact you in the last couple of days?'

'Yes. As I mentioned in the message I left him.'

'I'd like to come into the office now. I don't think we can afford to waste any time.'

* * *

The offices of D'Angour Strauss & Partners were halfway up Church Street as you ascended from Kensington to Notting Hill. They didn't reveal their opulence until you'd climbed narrow stairs and stepped through a heavy door into an oak-panelled reception area with oil paintings of men in suits. Mr Strauss met Belsey inside the door, as if Belsey needed personally escorting through the front room and the receptionist might have breached client confidentiality as she directed him. Strauss was short, tanned, greying at the temples. He led Belsey into an office the size of a rich person's living room, with similar décor.

'Please.' Strauss gestured to a deep, upholstered chair. He took a less comfortable one on the far side of a gleaming walnut desk. Pictures of sailboats decorated the walls.

'So, you are working for Sir Malcolm.'

'That's right.' Belsey got to the point. 'We don't think Chloe was killed in a random attack. We believe it connects to her contacting you.'

The lawyer joined his elegant fingers in prayer and pressed them to his lips. He gazed into the bright reflections on the desk's surface. When Belsey didn't continue he said:

'You understand I cannot say anything before I speak to the family.'

'I don't understand that.' He tried a bluff. 'The press already seem to think she was involved in something criminal, and Sir Malcolm has given me instructions to find out what was going on before they do.'

There was that flash of the concern you only get from very well-paid employees.

'A crime.'

'She visited you, Mr Strauss. Yesterday. Why?'

'She didn't visit me, she called to arrange an appointment.'

'She didn't come in?'

'No. She was due in today. Around now.'

'What did she say?'

'She was asking about confidentiality. She was crying. It was very hard to understand what she was saying. She said she had fears about her phone calls being listened to. We made an arrangement to meet in person. And then . . .' He spread his hands, cufflinks glinting.

Belsey felt himself sitting where she would have been. Not a pretty transformation.

'Why did she think her phone was under surveillance?'

'I don't know. In my experience a lot of people do. Half the time they are right.'

'Yet she was calling from her mobile?'

'No.'

'Whose phone was she using?'

'It was a landline.' He opened a desk drawer and removed a memo. Slid it across the desk's leather top. The area code looked like west London, but not the expensive part.

'Do you have access to a reverse directory?'

'I've already run it. On the back.'

On the back was an address: 5 Tonbridge Drive.

'Does it mean anything to you?' Belsey asked.

He shook his head.

'Has Chloe been in trouble before?'

'No.'

'Anything she might not have told her father?'

'Quite possibly. But I have not had direct contact with her before yesterday. I know very little about her.'

'And no indication of what she wanted to talk to you about?'

The lawyer hesitated. 'There were people with her.'

'What did you hear?'

'A voice. Someone called the name Conor.'

Conor. Belsey searched his memory. Conor – the name had come up. Was there a Conor at the club? No. Before that – Amber on the phone, pacing downstairs, Belsey on the landing in her home, wondering whether to leg it. He'd overheard her. *She said it was Conor she was worried about . . . She's just not dealing with it . . .*

'Who do you think he is?'

'My guess? A man she was seeing. Someone in trouble. The reason she was calling.'

Belsey looked at the address, stood up. The lawyer stood too.

'What is this about? What is Sir Malcolm saying?'

'He's saying hold tight. He'll be in touch in due course.'

13

TONBRIDGE DRIVE WAS A HORSESHOE of semi-detached homes tucked away on their own little development next to the sprawling White City Estate. Sedate, ragged around the edges but with pretensions to suburbia not shared by its brown-brick neighbour. None of it made any sense as a part of Chloe Burlington's life.

The front window of number 5 showed a family home, living room with a dining table at the back, rug and TV, a box of toys. The front garden was a touch neater than the neighbours'. Belsey stood on the doorstep. He heard the TV inside. A tap. A woman's voice, then a man's. He'd turned up on a lot of doorsteps needing answers, never quite as empty-handed as this.

A dog barked when he rang the bell. The tap stopped. A woman called out: 'I'll get it.'

She answered the door, wiping hands on a tea towel. Tall, dark hair with streaks of grey, hollow-cheeked. A small boy ran up and clung to her legs.

'Is Conor in?' Belsey asked. She looked puzzled, smiling uncertainly.

'Conor?'

'Yes.'

'This is Conor.' She lowered a hand to the boy's head. A man paused behind her as he crossed the hallway. He saw Belsey and came to the door. He was also tall, with messy, thinning hair, shirtsleeves rolled up above the elbows.

Conor stared up at Belsey. He held a felt-tip pen. Six or seven years old; light brown hair, brown eyes. He was pale, like his parents, but seemed in good health.

'What's this?' the man asked. Conor lost interest. He released his mother's leg and walked back into the living room.

'Do you know a woman called Chloe Burlington?'

'No,' the woman said. 'Why?'

'What's this about?' the husband asked, with well-mannered hostility. Belsey produced the lawyer's memo slip.

'Is this your home phone number?' They both peered at it.

'Yes,' said the husband. 'Where did you get that?'

'Has anyone else used your phone in the last day or so?'

'No.'

'Anyone had access to the house?'

'No.'

Belsey looked beyond the couple. Radio 4 playing, smell of a bolognese; post on a ledge by the door addressed to John and Melissa Shaw.

'There's been a mistake,' he said. 'Sorry to disturb you.'

'What's it got to do with Conor?' the man said, looking at Belsey like he was a pervert.

'I don't know.' Belsey found a pen in his jacket and wrote his number on the back of the memo slip then gave it to them. 'If anything happens, if you notice anything strange, give me a call. But – I think this is a mistake. So don't worry.' He stepped back, apologised again, turned and heard the door close behind him.

He walked to the end of the path but didn't go back to his car. He looked back, waited to see if they peered out of the window. No peering. He could see, through the bay window, the boy on the floor, drawing. No parents with him. After a shock like that, some bloke knocking at the door asking after your kid, you'd go to him. The boy sat alone on the edge of a rug, pens spread around him. Belsey took a step back towards the house: the radio had been turned off. Melissa Shaw hadn't heard of Chloe Burlington. Yet they had the radio on and it had been news all day.

None of those things necessarily meant anything.

A woman was watching him from the window of the neighbouring house. She dropped the curtain when he caught her looking.

He drove a few blocks west, stopped, checked the news on his phone. They'd released a series of photographs from the last couple of years of Chloe Burlington's life. She had a very bright, attractive smile and it was identical in every one: Chloe on a beach in a bikini; in jodhpurs with a horse; in a ball gown at an opera house.

There was a voicemail from Steve Tanner. *'You've left us with no choice, Nick; we've had to get a warrant on you. Do yourself a favour and walk into a police station, mate.'* Gabby wasn't answering his calls. He found Terri Baker's business card. She did answer.

'We met briefly at Amber's,' Belsey said. 'Yesterday. I'm the new security guy.'

'Nick. How nice of you to call.'

'I have some concerns about Amber and I wanted to see if they connected with your experiences. Do you reckon we could grab a coffee?'

'Of course. What kind of concerns?'

'Just some things I'd rather not discuss over the phone. You seem to be in the know. This might be of interest.'

'Well I'd really like to talk to *you*,' she said. 'The coffee's on me.'

14

TERRI SUGGESTED SOHO HOUSE. They could find a discreet corner, she said.

The whole place was a discreet corner. Belsey must have passed the building on Greek Street a thousand times without noticing that it existed and he wasn't allowed in. One of London's private members' clubs, as understated and forbidden as any well-preserved townhouse. The entrance hall was subtly plush. A staff member beside a desk smiled and waited for something.

'I'm here to see Terri Baker,' Belsey said.

'He's with me.' A man hauled himself out of an armchair at the side and approached fast.

'Am I?'

The man had grey hair expensively cut, a pink shirt. He looked possibly CID. Belsey checked for police kit. He saw a gold watch, gold cufflinks: no kit.

'Andy Price,' the man said. 'We spoke on the phone.' He gripped Belsey's hand. He stank of cigarette smoke. 'Just wanted to say hello. I'll take you to Terri.'

'I'm sure I can find her.'

'This place is a maze.'

Price led him into the club. They went up carpeted stairs, past a couple of nice bars, a dining room lined with bookshelves. 'So are you going it alone?' Price said.

'I'm not going it at all.'

'I've had interest.' Price scratched his nose. 'Quite healthy money. Not crazy, but tidy. Everyone wants to know who you are.'

'That's the problem.'

'Your call, Nick. Just didn't want you to miss out. What are you going to say to Terri?'

'I'm going to ask her why Amber Knight's killing people.'

Price laughed. They stopped on a landing. He took hold of Belsey's lapels and adjusted his jacket. He brushed some imaginary dirt off the arms.

'She'll take advantage,' he said.

'That's not what I'm worried about right now.'

'Everything will change when the papers get hold of your name. You might find someone on your side quite useful.'

'It's all I've ever dreamed of, Andy. Give me some space though.'

They continued into a lounge bar with olive-green walls and carefully worn leather sofas. A group of four hung by the bar, a couple occupied a table at the side. Baker sat a healthy distance away, alone in a far corner. She looked more dressed up than when he'd last seen her, in a shimmering blouse, short black skirt and mascara.

'Ah, you met Andy.' She put a wine glass down and got to her feet, beaming as she came to kiss Belsey on both cheeks. 'Andy's the best in the business,' she said, sotto voce.

'I'll leave you both to it,' Price said. He squeezed Belsey's shoulder, retreated with a wink. Belsey sat down in an armchair. A waiter appeared.

'Drinks?' Baker said. 'Have you eaten?'

Belsey ordered a whisky sour. Baker said she was fine. She smiled at Belsey again.

'So, into the limelight.'

'What's going on with Amber?' Belsey said.

'What do you mean?'

'There's some kind of situation. Her people are keeping watch over her. I was given a schedule and told to alert them if she tried to go off-piste. There was an intervention of some kind last week. You're close to the management, go through her drawers and all that. So what's the story?'

Baker sat back and studied him. She took a sip of wine then presented her own research.

'You're a police officer.'

'A suspended one.'

'Your name's Nick Belsey.'

'That's right.'

'You're not a security guard. You never have been employed by Amber.'

'That's right. I was just sneaking around her house, same as you.'

Terri didn't appear put off by this. In many ways the story had just got more interesting. Belsey decided to make her day.

'I went to the club with Amber last night. I met Chloe Burlington there. Chloe's now dead. Is there any reason Amber might be involved in that?'

This stopped the glass halfway to Baker's lips. She set it down and picked up a pen and notebook without taking her eyes off Belsey. She tried an incredulous smile.

'Why?' she said carefully. 'Is she upset? Did she know Chloe well?'

'I'm not sure. Are you aware of them knowing each other at all?'

'Not really. What do you think the murder's got to do with Amber?'

'That's what we're going to find out.'

Belsey's drink arrived, set down alongside bowls of olives and Japanese crackers.

'I don't understand what you're doing here,' Baker said.

Belsey took a cracker.

'Think of me as an angel of celebrity journalism, come to give you a story beyond your wildest dreams. But an angel that needs a bit of help in understanding where Amber's at right now, to put together the final pieces of the story.'

Baker nodded. It seemed he'd put enough on the table to start play.

'No one knows what's going on. There's money issues. Quite possibly she just overspent. A lot went on the house, the garden. Someone told me it didn't even stretch to finishing the basement. It was meant to have a recording studio and a cinema. Hence Guy Oakshott, the millionaire fiancé she's hardly met. Hence the Lancôme deal with the wedding. Everything's riding on the wedding. I don't know, this is just stuff I heard. But people are trying to keep the ship afloat.'

'I get that impression.'

'There's been other stuff, too, going on for a while. Being sued by her mum. Not speaking to her stepdad. She's been cutting off contact with her close friends.'

'When did she start ditching friends?'

'It's been getting worse over the last couple of years.'

Baker looked at Belsey like she was waiting for him to fill some gaps.

'What were you looking for in her drawers?' he said.

'Anything. There's a book usually with her, like a diary – small, black leather cover. I asked her about it once. She said she was recording the truth about things: love, fame, growing up.'

'You didn't find it?'

'No. It's your turn, give me something. What makes you think this connects to Chloe Burlington?'

'OK. How about this. I think Amber got rid of bloodstained clothing when she returned from the club last night. According to a friend, Chloe's been worried over the last few days. She called the family lawyer. She's burned paperwork. Her bags were packed, ready to skip. I think she was involved in something and it went wrong. Amber says she never knew her, which is a lie.'

Baker watched him intently, a cautious smile fixed like a legal disclaimer.

'Did Amber say anything about this last night?' she asked.

'No. But there's a man called Mark Doughty who had Amber's passport and clothes at his home. He's a stalker. I showed his ID to Chloe Burlington last night and there was a definite reaction. Maybe he connects them somehow. I've seen the guy's room. He's definitely keen on his female celebrities. I really don't know. But last night, I reckon Chloe knew something was going to happen. She gave a friend her necklace. You know, like she was saying goodbye.'

Something was dawning on Baker. 'Maybe it was her,' she said.

'Her what?'

Baker hesitated. She raised herself, hands on the arms of her chair to peer across the room at the other guests. She eased herself back down.

'Do you know about the *Sun*?'

'What about it?'

There was a final beat of reluctance. Then she said: 'A story about Amber went to the *Sun on Sunday* three days ago. I don't know what it's about. Someone said they paid seven-fifty.'

'Seven-hundred and fifty thousand?'

'It had a property attached.'

'What does that mean?'

'A recording. A picture or a video or something. We got a call from a guy called Shaun White. Do you know him?'

'No.'

'He's a publicist. I'm surprised he's not been in touch with you. He said he had a client who had a story on Amber. It was big. They wanted big money. They couldn't go into details until it was on an exclusive basis. We backed out early; it smelt wrong. And not just the money.'

'What else?'

'The hoops he was making us jump through. You don't ask newspapers to make an offer blind. That's not how it works.'

'A recording.'

'Yes.'

'Worth three-quarters of a million.'

'Supposedly.'

'A sex tape.'

'If it's a sex tape it would have to be pretty colourful. We've paid less to Shaun for bigger names. It was my first thought, of course. But seven hundred and fifty grand for a woman having sex with the man she's about to marry, that's not that exciting. Even Amber Knight. Maybe her with Jason Stanford.'

'The QPR player?'

'She used to date him,' Baker explained. 'Amber back with her semi-ex – that would possibly get a hundred and twenty. Wedding weekend. If it was filthy. Not over half a million. Has she mentioned Jason at all?'

'No.'

Baker shrugged, lifted her glass, saw it was empty.

'Who would I talk to at the *Sun*, about the story?' Belsey asked.

'Damian Drummond. He's their entertainment correspondent. But you won't get a thing out of him. People are being very fucking cagey.

From the source down. Everyone's hiding what they've got for fear of missing out on the payday.'

'What do you know about the source?'

'Just that it was a member of the public, via Shaun White.'

'Think they're still set to run it?'

'I don't know. It's gone very quiet, which is weird. But they're probably just on lockdown with it now. Waiting for Sunday.'

'Or maybe their source is dead.'

Baker paused with her hand on the stem of the empty glass. Belsey downed half his drink.

'Are you aware of Chloe Burlington ever approaching the press with stories before?'

'No,' Baker said. 'She's a millionaire. Why would she?'

'Because she's a millionaire? Because she's got nothing else to do? Even rich people try to make money sometimes; sometimes at the expense of other people.'

Baker squinted at him now, lips pursed.

'Chloe became anxious on Saturday. What do you know about Amber's movements over the weekend?' Belsey asked. 'Anything unusual? Strange behaviour? Cancelled events?'

'Nothing that I know of.'

'Chloe went out Saturday night, a last-minute thing. I think she may have been with Amber.'

'Something interesting did happen a few days ago,' Baker said, sitting up. 'That was when she fired her security.'

'Why did she do that? Because they were leaking stories to you?' Belsey said.

'I never got anything useful out of them. And no, I'm not sure that's why they were fired. I think she's just generally paranoid. She was always trying to give them the slip. The night before, Friday, she managed to lose them. Shake them off entirely before going out.'

'Any idea where?'

'Gabby overheard her on the phone before, but it didn't make much sense. Nothing useful. Apparently she mentioned a bridge a couple of times, but didn't say which one. Not Waterloo, Chelsea, or anything like that.'

Belsey paused. He put his drink down. He got his phone out, showed her Chloe's post.

'A bridge,' he said.

Baker looked unconvinced. 'Well, yes. Doesn't look like London, though, does it?'

'It's the last thing Chloe posted.'

Baker nodded: a concession.

'How did Amber go out without security knowing?' Belsey asked.

'She got in one of her cars and told the driver to drive off before the guard was in the vehicle. Pretty simple, really.'

'One of her personal account cars?' Belsey said. 'Shield Executive?'

'Yes.'

'What time?'

'Five p.m.'

'And what time did rumours about a video start?'

'Later that night.' Baker opened her notebook, touched pen to paper and seemed uncertain what to write.

'Have you tried speaking to Shield?'

'They won't speak to me,' Baker said. Belsey downed his drink and got up. 'What are you going to do?' she asked.

'I'm going to see if I can have a word. Out of curiosity.'

'Call me,' she said. 'If you find anything out. Will you?'

'Let's see.'

Belsey headed for the door. Price was waiting on the landing.

'How did it go? Is she going to run something on you?'

'I forgot to ask,' Belsey said, moving for the stairs.

'You forgot to ask?' The talent manager grinned. He thrust paperwork into Belsey's hands as he passed. 'Take a look at these,' he called after him. 'Have a think about what I said.'

15

THE MAIN OFFICE OF SHIELD Executive Cars was behind Praed Street, amongst the grey fallout of Paddington station: cheap hotels, nondescript pubs, blank-windowed sex shops. Shield tried to keep one corner respectable, with gold lettering on its window, a vertical blind, high gates beyond which eight glistening Mercedes sat like rare animals.

A woman buzzed Belsey in. Tasselled lamps cast a yellow glow over the front office, its polished wood and carpet, the photographs of vintage cars on its walls. The receptionist sat behind a pine counter, blonde, fifty-something, wiling away the night shift with a self-manicure.

'How can I help?'

'My name's Nick, from Milkshake Management,' Belsey said. She looked uncertain. 'I represent one of your clients. There's been a bit of a problem.'

'What's happened?'

'I would have called but this is very sensitive and we have issues with the press. My client thinks one of your drivers might have been a little inappropriate.'

She put the nail file down. 'Your client?'

'Amber Knight. I work with Gabby. I don't know if you know Gabby there.'

'Of course.'

'She says it's not the first time this issue's come up.'

'Really? This is the first time I've heard anything about it.'

'Well, Amber says that a couple of times your guys have asked for autographs, and this time the driver asked for it on his body.'

'On his body?'

Belsey shrugged. 'Supposedly. Amber says this happened on Friday.' He leaned in. 'I'm not saying Amber's the most rational person in the world right now. Was she even driven that night?'

The woman checked the system, typing with her nails horizontal. 'There was a job. Friday, five p.m.'

'Where to?'

'It doesn't say.'

'Is that unusual?'

'A bit odd. Paul was driving. He's here now. I can ask him.' She looked up at him again. 'She's saying Paul asked her to sign his body?'

'That's her version of events.'

'I'm sure he hasn't done anything. That doesn't sound like Paul.'

'Can I speak to him?'

'Amber's a very valued customer. We're all proud to work with her.'

'Me too. Can I speak to Paul?'

She lifted the phone on her desk, spun her chair away from Belsey and spoke quietly, then walked out of a side door into the car park.

Belsey watched a man emerge from a Portakabin in the corner, wiping his mouth with a paper napkin. He was young, with copper-coloured hair and a thin moustache. The woman met him halfway. Paul frowned as she spoke, scratched behind his ear, approached the office with a look of nervous bemusement. He was probably twenty-eight or so, but the uniform was large and made him look like a sixth-former in a school play.

'Hi,' he said. 'What's she claiming I did?'

'To be honest I'm more concerned about where she went. Is it right that you drove her on Friday evening?'

'Yes.' The driver glanced at the woman. 'It was that job I told you about. What's she saying?'

'It's important you tell me what happened, Paul.'

'She was acting strangely. Wouldn't say where she was going, directed me into the middle of nowhere. Usually, she was a bit odd, nervous. But this time it was worse. Like she was maybe being followed.'

'She said that?'

'Yeah.'

'Where did you drive her?'

'Up the North Circular.'

'To where?'

'Nowhere.'

'Nowhere's nowhere.'

'Seriously, I can show you nowhere.'

The driver took a Merc and Belsey followed in his Audi. They drove in convoy for fifteen minutes, down a descending scale of suburbia, through Swiss Cottage, Kilburn, Cricklewood, onto the North Circular. They followed the A road through Neasden – six grey lanes that seemed to expand into the landscape either side like a flooded river: vistas of business parks and warehouses behind which suburban terraces dwindled towards the horizon.

The Mercedes pulled up on the hard shoulder a minute before Staples Corner. They were deep in industrial wilderness. A hundred metres away, set back from the road, were the windowless boxes of Leatherland Sofas and an outlet for wholesale paving stone. Hedgerow was ashen, crowded with car debris: broken headlights, bumpers, hubcaps.

They got out. The driver shrugged. Traffic tore past. A low fence divided the road ensuring anyone lost amongst the channels of rubbish stayed on their fated side. To the south, the road curved left and spared you any more of the view.

'Where did she go?'

'I don't know. She told me to drive off.'

'You didn't see her go anywhere?'

'No.'

'Did she mention a bridge at all?'

'A bridge? No. I don't know anything. I said I'd take you where she went, that's all.'

'Any bridges around here that you know of?'

'No.'

'Has she been driven here before?'

'No. Never by me, at least.'

Belsey wandered a few metres amongst the faded cans and cigarette packets.

'Did she get picked up later?'

'I don't think so.'

'What was she wearing?'

Paul blew his cheeks.

'Cap. Sunglasses.'

'Dressed down.'

'Yeah, dressed down.'

'Skirt? Jeans?'

'God knows. Jeans. Trousers, anyway.'

'You said she was giving directions.'

'She was. And then she just said stop.'

Belsey looked around for anything that felt like a destination.

'Did she seem to know the route?'

'No. I thought she was making it up as we went along. It was all over the place. Maida Vale, Kensal Rise. Like I said, mate – she thought she was being followed.'

'How long did it take you to stop?'

'What do you mean?'

'She says "Stop", but you can't just slam the brakes on, right? So how long till you were able to pull over?'

'I don't know. Straight away. Ten seconds, max?'

Ten seconds' drive, at the speed of the A road. Call that about two hundred metres.

'Come with me,' Belsey said. They walked back, past the bend in the road. Belsey cut through the traffic to the central barrier. Paul stayed on the hard shoulder.

'She said stop around here?' Belsey called over a break in the traffic.

'Yeah. I suppose.'

Just visible on the far side of the road was a row of small, fume-coated shops: Vijay's News, Drinker's Paradise Off Licence, AAA Speedy Minicabs.

'OK,' Belsey said.

'What?'

'You can go.'

'I didn't touch her.'

'I know.'

Paul stared at him, then turned back towards the Mercedes shaking his head. Belsey vaulted the fence, wove through traffic to the front office of AAA Speedy Minicabs. A couple of drivers loitered at the front, smoking. Inside was a waiting area with a collapsed armchair and a broken fruit machine. It was tiny, but then they probably didn't rely on passing trade. A man slept curled up in the armchair. The controller sat behind a screen of cracked Perspex, pudgy face just visible above a handwritten notice: all jobs had to be paid in advance.

Belsey opened the office door and walked in. The controller clicked out of whatever he was looking at on his PC.

'You can't be in here.'

'I want to show you something.' Belsey sat down beside him, pulled the keyboard over and brought up paparazzi shots of Amber. He found one where she was dressed casually, baseball cap low, out shopping. 'I think that last Friday, around five-thirty p.m., this woman came here.'

'What do you want?'

'I want to know where she went. I'm a police officer,' he added, to get a bit of pace going. He sensed nervousness now, a lot of thinking about tax, work permits, all sorts of sticky things. The controller called to the men at the front. The drivers filed in uncertainly. He pointed at the picture on the screen and explained the nature of Belsey's investigation. They consulted one another in Urdu, checked the picture again. One of them went to the waiting area, put a foot on the sleeping man's knee and rocked him awake. The man stood up holding car keys. He was young, skinny, missing a front tooth. He tilted his head inquisitively when they spoke, then came and looked at the monitor. He nodded immediately.

'Friday, five-thirty p.m.,' Belsey said.

There was another exchange amongst the drivers, then the young man turned to Belsey.

'I drove her. What is wrong? She is famous?'

'That's right. Where did you drive her?'

'North.' He gestured vaguely.

'To where?'

Once again it proved difficult to explain.

'I can show you.'

Convoy again. This time following the back of a powder-blue Toyota Lexus. They drove back towards London for a mile or so. Then they swung north onto Edgware Road, and finally back onto the North Circular.

From here Amber had woven another winding route. North again, past Brent Cross, into Finchley. Wherever she was going she was determined not to be tailed. Eight p.m., not yet sunset, roads quiet. Suburb curfew. Ragged shopping arcades and more post-war houses.

The driver slowed a minute later, signalled left, turned into a sprawling car park. On either side of the tarmac, dwarfed by the car park itself, were two stretches of leisure options: chain restaurants and a plastic-looking multiplex. A sign announced the Great North Leisure Park.

The minicab stopped. Belsey got out. The driver stayed in his car.

The Great North Leisure Park, then. Closest attraction was Pizza Hut. Then Nando's, then McDonald's. At the back was a David Lloyd sports centre. Up a small gradient, past a disused Café Rouge and another fifty parking spaces, was the Comfort Hotel, like a beige and grey barracks, orange flags fluttering in the wind.

No bridge.

The driver wound his window down.

'Is this it?' Belsey said.

'Yes.'

'Where did she go?'

The driver pointed in the direction of the hotel.

'Did you see her meet anyone?'

He shook his head.

'What time was it?'

'Six. Six-thirty. What fare did he say?'

'Fare?'

'The man at the office. What did he say you pay for this?'

Belsey gave him a tenner.

He crossed the car park to the hotel, through the sliding doors into reception. The beige and orange theme continued inside. To the left, a doorway led into a darkened restaurant. No staff visible. A screen in reception showed a promotional video for the hotel in case anyone wasn't convinced yet. Beneath it were two balloons and a stack of leaflets. '*Explore Finchley from The Comfort Hotel.*' What was there to explore? 'You'll find plenty to do in the Finchley area of London. Visit the Lido, Golf Club and Brent Cross shopping centre. The Comfort Hotel offers free parking, Wi-Fi and cooked breakfasts. West Finchley Underground Station is just a 20-minute walk away.' Which meant you were twenty minutes from the middle of nowhere. Maybe that was exactly where Amber wanted to be. 'The fully air-conditioned Flames Restaurant serves breakfast, lunch and dinner every day from a Mediterranean-style menu.'

He walked into the unlit restaurant. The windows afforded an un-Mediterranean view across the car park to the cinema. A man wheeled a trolley of linen bags to a laundry van. Belsey pinched the leaf of a plastic plant and tried to piece together the holiday on offer. Sun yourself by the A1 before a walk around Finchley Memorial Hospital. Grab some Nando's, 50ml of vodka from Lidl. Finish the day watching the sun set behind the prefabricated office units of the North London Business Park.

What was Amber Knight doing here?

He walked past reception to the lifts. There was a screen set into the wall between the two lift doors showing BBC News. He caught a helicopter shot of the Mayfair crime scene. Chloe's face again. It made for a chilly form of decoration. He was watching it, thinking about ash on an oven tray, when the lift doors opened and a pair of hotel staff appeared. Two girls, neither much older than twenty, one with a name badge that said Shannen, one Habiba. They smiled, and when he followed them over to the reception desk Shannen said, 'Sorry to keep you waiting, sir. Are you checking in?' Shannen was plump, freckled; Habiba pretty in a blue headscarf.

'No. I've actually got a bit of a crazy situation. You know Amber Knight? The singer?'

The girls gave a confused smile. 'Yes.'

'Well, I'm Amber's manager. I think she might have been around here on Friday evening.'

'Here?' They looked doubtful.

'Between you and me, we're worried about her. Please don't tell anyone, OK?'

'You're joking.'

'No. Were you working on Friday evening?'

'I was,' Habiba said.

'Did you see her? Maybe dressed down, wearing a baseball cap and sunglasses?'

'I don't think so. Are you serious?'

'You'd remember, right?'

'Yes.'

'Can you check the bookings for that night?'

The girls huddled around the reception monitor.

'No rooms booked under her name.'

'Can I see?' Belsey walked around the desk. He scrolled through the list of bookings for that day. Fourteen of the sixty rooms had been occupied, none in any name he recognised.

'I need to see any CCTV you have for that time.'

'I can get the manager,' Shannen said.

'Thank you.'

She returned three minutes later with a broad, ginger man in his early thirties. He walked with a bounce, hands clasped in front of him. Graham, according to his badge. He was smiling in a way that suggested he was prepared for a nutter.

'You think Amber Knight was here?' he said.

'Yes.'

'And what is the problem?'

'A lot of potential problems, Graham. Would it be possible to see the CCTV?'

Graham now looked appropriately tickled by all this. He opened a door behind the reception and led Belsey into a windowless office crowded with left luggage. A desk at the back had a widescreen monitor divided into nine squares of surveillance. He sat down, clicked into the main menu.

'When exactly?'

'Last Friday, around six p.m.'

The first channel he selected was a high shot from above the reception desk itself. He typed in 'Friday, 17.30'. The screen showed a couple of businessmen wheeling luggage past. The camera filmed three frames per second which made the footage juddery. He skipped ahead. Then, at 17.37, a woman came into view at the bottom of the screen. She wore a black Emporio Armani baseball cap, shades, jeans. No luggage. She walked in, past the desk to the lifts.

The hotel staff looked from the screen to Belsey.

'That's not really her, is it?' Habiba said.

Graham played it again. The woman entered alone, looked around much as Belsey had done. Except there was someone on reception; you saw a corner of headscarf to the far right.

'That *is* her,' Shannen said, wide-eyed. 'And that's you.'

'Oh my god,' Habiba said.

'Where did she go?'

'She must have gone up to a room. Someone else must have already checked in.'

They scrolled backwards. 17.30: the two businessmen passed through.

'Go back further.'

17.21, a man alone checked in. He also wore shades, two days' stubble, hair tied in a short ponytail.

'Let's get a better angle.' Graham clicked back to the menu screen. Nine options. He brought up a camera covering the car park.

17:19, a silver hatchback parked: a Renault Clio with the passenger door dented. The man got out, glanced around. He took a hat and glasses from the passenger seat and put them on. But before he did that it was obvious enough he was Mark Doughty.

Graham switched to a camera above the entrance. They all watched Doughty walk in. Up close, he looked nervous. A little more groomed than the ID photo: still gaunt, but the stubble was shaped.

He checked in, took the lift up.

Amber appeared sixteen minutes later. She went straight to the lifts.

'Could you check the bookings again?' Belsey said. 'Double-check there's nothing under the name Mark Doughty?'

Shannen went to the PC at the front desk.

'No,' she called through. 'Nothing. Who is he?'

'Not someone you would have heard of.'

Belsey studied the footage again. 'Who checked in at seventeen twenty-one then?'

'Seventeen twenty-one. Someone checked into the Finchley Suite. No name.'

'No name? How was it booked?'

It took Shannen a moment.

'The room was reserved by a Mr A. Majorana. But it was paid in cash.'

'But you would have needed a card as deposit.'

'Yes.'

'When was it booked?'

'Hang on.' He heard typing. 'A couple of hours earlier.'

'By a Mr A. Majorana.'

'That was the name on the card.'

'Who took the booking?'

Habiba spoke up, a little sheepish, with a glance at her manager as if she might have done something wrong: 'I think it was me. I remember the name.'

'Did you ever see the card?'

'No, it was over the phone.'

'Did you run the card number past an authorisation department?'

'No.'

That was well-studied discretion on the part of the guest. Almost professional.

'What did he sound like on the phone, Habiba? Foreign?'

'Maybe. A bit. I don't know.'

'Which room did you say?'

'The Finchley Suite,' Shannen said.

'When does it say they checked out?'

She looked down at the screen.

'Two and a half hours later.'

He found the moment on the security footage. Amber walked out at 20.05. Again, straight through reception, alone. She looked no different than when she'd arrived.

Mark gave it two minutes. Two other guests walked out before he appeared at 20.07. He checked out, counted out cash from a wallet, took the printed receipt.

Back to the Renault, head turning as he scanned the car park.

Belsey left the back office and walked outside, stood where Mark Doughty had emerged from the Renault and stared back at the hotel. The world around it was growing dark. Dark, yet rich with possibilities. A world more extensive than it had seemed five minutes ago.

Mark Doughty. You player.

That online personality test in Mark's room – the same one he'd seen on Amber's laptop: *What's stopping you living the life you want to lead?* Not as much as one might suppose. Maybe Chloe Burlington had been stopping her. He returned to the reception.

'Are there any bridges near here?'

'No. Why?'

'Just a thought. Do you have cameras up on the floors themselves?'

'No.'

'Can I see the room?'

Shannen took a key card and went up in the lift with Belsey. 'I literally cannot believe this,' she muttered. The fourth-floor corridor was beige. Shannen knocked tentatively on the door of the Finchley Suite, inserted the key card, walked in.

The suite consisted of two rooms with dividing doors that folded open to create a continuous space. It was clean, empty. To the right was a large bedroom with double bed and en-suite bathroom. The rest of the suite was a living area with a sofa, dining table and kitchenette.

'Know what state it was in, afterwards?'

'No idea.' Shannen shrugged. They took the lift back downstairs. In the back office, he wrote down the registration number of the Renault Mark Doughty was driving, then emailed himself a copy of the footage. He stood up, said he'd be in touch.

'Is this a secret?' Habiba asked.

'A secret?'

'Can I tell people?'

'That's up to you.'

He sat in the Audi. Did Mark film something in that room? Try to sell it to the papers? That seemed ungrateful to say the least. Film something and then someone else got their hands on it?

He drove back through north London, stopped at the Gate Lodge in Golders Green. It was a shop-conversion pub, plastic Paddy, with its windows painted over and no sober clientele. He ordered a toastie and a coffee and took a table at the back in time to watch the news on a screen above the bar.

Chloe Burlington was third on the schedule, below terrorism and a hurricane. They showed CCTV of her leaving Loulou's. Alone. Phone in hand. Rope unclipped, doormen watching her back a little uncertainly as she steps between two parked cars and heads directly for the darkness. They showed her parents crying. That was all.

He watched a report on a factory closing. Then the news ended with Amber. '*Back in top shape for her wedding.*' Her public life continued, shining, unruffled: Amber beside a poster for the perfume, her face airbrushed out of reality. Amber in a short dress with gold sequins, taking selfies with prizewinners at an awards ceremony. Glossy. Unmurderous. Mobbed by people fighting for their piece of magic.

A lot of questions condensed to a simple one: how did Mark meet Amber? The Retreat Boutique & Wellness Spa seemed unlikely, though not impossible. Selling drugs? Not implausible. How long had they been . . . what? Lovers? Surely not. And if, somehow, they had been, how long could they have kept that secret? You'd run out of suburban leisure parks eventually. Someone would see past the baseball caps and shades.

Was this the secret Chloe Burlington had stumbled across? Was it worth seven hundred and fifty grand?

16

TEN-THIRTY P.M. QUEEN'S CRESCENT AT night was edgy. Men walked fast, alone, hoods up. Most of the local population kept to the high-rises. TV screens flickered in the blocks like pilot lights. Two teenagers assessed Belsey's mugging potential and cycled on. Someone stumbled out of the Sir Robert Peel, held onto a bus stop, then lowered themselves carefully to the ground.

The lights were on in Maureen Doughty's home. No Renault Clio parked up. Belsey walked the length of the street and back, but it wasn't there. He listened at Maureen's door: no male voice, no suggestion that Mark was at home. Knocked.

Maureen Doughty answered, sleep-dazed, wrapping a cardigan over a nightie.

'It's you,' she said.

'Can I come in?'

'Have you found Mark?'

'Not exactly.'

'Where is he? What's happened?'

'Does Mark own a car?'

'I don't think so.'

'Anywhere he might keep one?'

'No.'

Maureen felt for the sofa and sat down stiffly. Belsey went upstairs. Mark's room still stank. But, in light of the Comfort footage, there was something fascinating about its compulsive hoard. As if the very force of Mark's obsession had burst the membrane between fantasy and reality. Belsey was dealing with the aftermath.

He returned to the living room. Maureen looked frailer, more disorientated than yesterday.

'Have you eaten?' Belsey asked.

'A bit.'

He couldn't see any new washing-up in the kitchen. He found a tin of soup in the cupboard, cleaned a pan and put it on. He opened the bread he'd bought her yesterday and buttered a slice. Mark and Amber. Two outsiders. Two lonely people. But people on different tracks. He leaned against the rusted sink as the soup heated and savoured the improbable. Had Amber Knight been here?

He brought the food through on a tray and sat down to watch Maureen Doughty eat.

'Did Mark ever say that he knew Amber Knight?'

'Knew? Mark has an imagination. His teachers always said . . .'

'I think he did know her.'

'No, I don't think so.'

'I'm sure of it, Maureen. Did Mark go anywhere special ever? Anywhere he might have met her?'

'I don't know.'

She ate hungrily, dipping her head to the spoon. Dabbing her mouth with a tissue between sips.

'Tell me about his life since uni. What jobs did he do?'

'He was a lab technician. At a school. He lost his job.'

'How did he lose it?'

'He quit. Then he didn't leave his room for weeks. Months.'

'When was that?'

'A few years ago. Then he started going to the centre.'

'Which centre?'

'The one in Islington. It was a way of getting him out of the house. That helped. He got some more work – at a shop, a newsagent's. On weekends.'

'When did he start getting interested in celebrities?'

'Maybe at the shop. Reading the magazines.'

'And maybe he started going to events with celebrities. Red-carpet things, signings.'

'Sometimes, if there was a first night of a film. Or a concert. He's friendly when you get to know him. People think he's a loner, but he isn't.'

'Apparently not.'

Belsey left her to eat, went and sat on Mark's bed. Had Amber been in it? That was quite a thought. Were the soiled sheets what turned her on?

Mark hadn't bridged fantasy and reality by accident. Nor by magic. He was clever, that's what Lee Chester said. How did you do it, Mark?

A police siren opened up a few blocks south. Belsey tweaked the curtains. A black Ford Mondeo was sitting in the middle of the road outside, gleaming like oil under the orange street light. No one got out. A minute later it crawled to the end of the street and turned. Belsey watched the brake lights disappear towards Gospel Oak.

He was being paranoid.

He went downstairs, checked the front door was locked. There was a pile of unopened letters on a ledge by the door. Two were addressed to Mark Doughty. He glanced back at the living room. Maureen was resting, her head back, eyes closed. He slowly tore the post open. *'Essex Police is committed to making the roads of Essex a safer place for all who use them.'*

It was a speeding notice: 9 May 2015. Saturday, 11.43 p.m. Mark Doughty had been camera-flashed going 30mph over the limit. They'd skipped the fine and points and gone straight for a court order. The offence took place on Woodford High Road.

The next letter had been sent on the Monday, courtesy of Epping Forest Council: 'To the owners(s) of: Renault Clio (blue), vehicle registration: A053 JVU.' Sunday 10 May, Mark's car had been found abandoned at the Fatboy Steak House car park, High Road, Epping. 'Under the terms of the Refuse Disposal Act 1978 it is a criminal offence to abandon a vehicle on public and private land . . .' They threatened him with a fine of up to £2,500 or three months' imprisonment. 'The Council can also claim back the cost of removing and disposing of the vehicle.'

Belsey stepped back into the living room. Nudged Maureen.

'Any idea what Mark was doing in Epping on the weekend?'

She blinked up at him. 'No.'

Belsey showed her the letter.

'Do you think he's OK?'

Belsey sat down. 'I hope so.' He looked at the grease stains up the wall behind Mark's armchair. Maureen was staring at the letters in his hand. He read them again, then got to his feet.

'I'll take a look.'

'Would you?'

'Sure. Why not?'

17

LONDON BECAME ESSEX AROUND CHIGWELL. Clusters of habitation
with quieter roads between them. The landscape became scattered
things looming out of darkness: lorry parks, burger vans, desolate
picnic spots. After twenty minutes Belsey was on Woodford High Road,
where Mark Doughty had been caught speeding – long and straight,
past golf courses and reservoirs. He continued past Chingford onto
Epping New Road. The forest began.

He stopped by the turning for an air museum, checked the map,
kept going. Trees clustered tightly on either side. Belsey kept an eye
out for a steakhouse. Past the Wake Arms Roundabout, signs for
Woodridden Hill, one for an equestrian centre. When he started getting
signs for the M25, he knew he'd gone too far. He stopped at a petrol
station, showed the letter to a cashier. The man pointed him back to
the roundabout.

'The restaurant's just the other side, back towards Loughton, but
it's shut down.'

The second time round Belsey saw it. He also saw why he'd missed
the place originally. It was the only facility on a barren stretch of
road; once, no doubt, a beacon of shelter and meat, now a ruin.

Lights were off, windows boarded, boards graffitied. Someone had smashed the neon bulbs on the roadside sign, a depiction of Fatboy himself, a red-cheeked man in a chef's apron. A kids' play area had accumulated a carpet of empty cider cans. Beyond it was the car park, stretching to the forest itself, a single car in the far corner: Mark Doughty's Renault. Belsey stopped close to the entrance and walked over.

The back right door was dented; the front left tyre was flat. Nothing to suggest it had been stolen or hotwired, though. The doors were locked. It looked like someone had turned up for a steak one night and the restaurant closed before they could leave.

There was rustling amongst the tightly packed trees. Doggers? That was the local sport, wasn't it. Liven up the Essex nights.

He approached the trees. A section of branches was broken. Snapped quite recently. The ferns on the ground lay trampled into the mud. Not enough for a regular route. Someone had forged a new path.

Belsey went back to his car and found a small penlight in the glove compartment. He took it into the woods, shone it around. The trail continued.

Twigs scratched his face as he followed it deeper. Brambles scraped his legs. He lifted an arm. Branches flexed and swung back behind him as he forced his way through. After a moment he looked back and couldn't see the car park. The trees had closed ranks. He listened. There was a low hum a few metres deeper into the darkness, like an electricity pylon, but modulating in pitch. He walked towards the sound. Thirty seconds later a fox bolted past, retinas bright in the torchlight, mouth smeared with blood.

That was the rustling.

Then he smelled the decomposing flesh.

Belsey covered his nose and mouth. A second fox stopped mid-sprint, fronted up like a cornered offender before diving sideways into the undergrowth. He continued into a thickening mist of blowflies. Another twenty seconds and he'd found the epicentre.

A body lay amidst the trees. Its skin rippled. The face and arms were made of skipper flies, which seemed to pour upwards out of the earth. Belsey stepped back. He found his lighter, took a fallen branch with a lot of dead leaves and lit it. He stamped the flames out and smoked some of the insects away. Under the coating of flies was a man, Caucasian, some dark hair, remains of a T-shirt, blue jeans. White jawbone and teeth flashed out. The eye sockets crawled with larvae. Beetles made forays from his nostrils and ears.

No stab wounds that Belsey could see: they would have their own entomological party going on. Belsey felt along the neck, through the insects. It was unbroken. The windpipe was also intact, skull in one piece. He bit the torch so both hands were free then rolled the body. It forced liquid out of the lungs and over his arms. He gagged, then went back to work.

No socks or underwear. Suggesting he'd been killed naked, dressed after death.

The less edible surfaces were more informative. Enough skin remained on his back to see he'd been dragged – brambles wedged into the flesh. Belsey searched the pockets, brought out a handful of bluebottles, no wallet. At the bottom of the left-hand pocket he found a pack of breath-freshening mints and a small piece of paper. A receipt. Flames Mediterranean Restaurant, Comfort Hotel, Finchley. A double of 'Mediterranean whisky' had set him back £6.40 – cash payment. 8 May. Last Friday.

It seemed he'd found Mark Doughty.

Belsey allowed himself a moment's pause – some sympathy for Maureen Doughty, at least. Pity for one more dropout who'd found himself on a bad journey, as glamorous and unexpected as it may have been. Then he traced the path of trampled leaves back to the car park.

He picked up a chunk of broken concrete from the side of the restaurant, smashed a side window of the Renault, reached in, opened the door. The driver's seat was pulled forward so that his knees hit the wheel when he climbed in. As if someone significantly shorter than Mark Doughty had been driving. The glove compartment was empty. He climbed through to the back seat, lifted the cover of the boot and separated two tangled bedsheets: Egyptian cotton, according to the labels. They were still damp from whatever they'd last enfolded.

Belsey walked out of the car park to the road. Cars sped past every thirty seconds or so. The roadside lamps cast a syrupy yellow light. He flicked two maggots off his jacket. The stink of corpse lingered in his nostrils. He looked down the road. He could see the tall silhouette of a camera a couple of hundred metres away. The court summons sent to Mark Doughty had him snapped by a speed trap at quarter to midnight on Saturday. Woodford High Road, half a mile further south. But it would be the same model: Truvelo D-Cams, digital with wireless comms. They took face-on pictures. They would have a shot of the driver.

He was staring at the camera's silhouette, wondering what the shot might reveal, when a police car turned the bend.

Belsey stepped back. But there was nowhere to hide. Just him and a corpse and a couple of foxes: the only action for miles around. The car slowed, two men already undoing their seatbelts. It pulled up by the Fatboy sign.

'Evening, sir,' the older of the two said as he climbed out, adjusting his radio. His colleague slammed the driver's door and joined him. Two uniformed male officers; duty sergeant and constable, both in stab vests. They looked wary, heavy with kit.

'Evening,' Belsey said. 'I've just found a corpse.' He didn't have the energy for convincing dramatics.

'What did you say?' The sergeant was moustached, the constable thinly bearded, gangly. Both stared at him.

'I've found a corpse.' He waved towards the trees. 'A dead body, in the woods.'

The two men studied his face, then glanced towards the two cars in the car park, and finally the woods themselves.

'Where, exactly?'

'About fifty metres into the trees, a straight line from the Renault.'

'What were you doing there?'

'I was taking a look at the abandoned car, the Renault. Then I found the corpse. I can show you.'

'What's your name?'

'Robert. Robert Peel.'

'Live around here?'

'No. Central London.'

The older officer turned away to radio an update. Belsey could feel the younger one scan him up and down for weapons. The sergeant came back, nodded at his colleague, adjusted his protection kit.

'After you, sir.'

Their police torches were more effective. The beams picked out the corpse just as the smell reached them. The officers took a few steps closer, glanced at each other again, then at Belsey, eyes now sharp with adrenalin.

'Know what this is about?'

'No.'

The younger one began sweeping his beam in all directions, as if an assailant might be lurking. Belsey watched the older one make an assessment of the scene's forensic fragility.

'We're going to mess this up if we go any further,' he said.

They marched back to the car park. The sergeant radioed through for full Homicide response. Belsey could hear two sets of sirens starting up a mile or so away. The constable went back to the squad car, took a roll of tape and began sealing off the area.

The sergeant turned to Belsey. His moustache twitched.

'Tell me again what you were doing here.'

'I was actually looking for a friend. It's his car.'

Belsey unfolded the council notices addressed to Mark Doughty. The sergeant took them and read them through.

'You think it's this Mark Doughty?'

'Maybe.'

'Do you know what happened?'

'No.'

'Is that your car, Robert? The Audi?'

'Yes.'

The first back-up pulled in. A woman in a grey suit climbed out of a silver Vauxhall Insignia, clearly senior, maybe an inspector. An area-response car containing two more CID suits arrived a few seconds behind.

'The car was caught speeding,' Belsey carried on to the sergeant. 'The cameras along this stretch of road look like new ones. Forward-facing. So it will have taken a shot of the driver.' The sergeant nodded once, squinted.

'Who are you exactly?'

'I was thinking – if Essex Police sent the court order, you'd have the shots. The original photographs.'

The sergeant walked over and consulted the senior officer. A Scene of Crime van rolled up. An exploratory party headed into the woods.

The senior officer took Mark Doughty's penalty notices and studied them. Then the woods ignited. The white light of a halogen lamp back-lit the trees, throwing their shadows across the gravel. A few minutes later Belsey saw officers huddled around the initial squad car, leaning in to study the dashboard-mounted data screen. He walked over, alone. They'd got the speed-trap shot. Mark's Renault, going 90mph at 23.43 on Saturday night.

It looked like at least three people in the car. A man driving: glasses, dark hair, jacket zipped up to the neck; hard to see much else. Beside him – Amber. Belsey wouldn't have recognised her if he hadn't been looking specifically: dark jacket, black baseball cap. A third person sat in the back, a meaty forearm resting along the edge of the window.

'Recognise them?' someone asked, turning to Belsey.

'Can't see much, can you,' Belsey said.

Behind the Renault, driving close for an empty road, was a second vehicle: a grey Peugeot 5008 people carrier. Both front seats were occupied. It looked like a man and a woman, and the woman could just possibly have been Chloe Burlington.

He peered closer. Chloe Burlington? The woman's face was very faint. She wore a pale cardigan or coat, hair tied back. But he thought he recognised Chloe's long neck and round face. He didn't recognise anything about the man beside her: white, clean shaven, possibly a receding hairline.

A second vehicle might explain how Amber got out of there.

What else might it explain?

The first two officers he'd encountered were talking to the Vauxhall Insignia woman now, thumbing in Belsey's direction. She gave an instruction and the sergeant glanced towards Belsey's Audi, lifted his radio and read the licence plate.

It would come back registered to Nick Belsey.

Nick Belsey would come up as wanted by the police.

That would be thought-provoking.

Response vehicles kept piling in, Metropolitan Police as well as Essex. It was a Tuesday, late turn; no one was going to miss out on a corpse. More tape wrapped the scene as the SOCOs ordered an outer cordon. Soon the road would be blocked entirely: two more forensics vans were already struggling to park, another squad car and a traffic-police motorbike queuing behind.

Belsey walked back to the Audi.

'I'll move this out of your way,' he said, climbing in. The classic crime-scene mistake: not man-marking their witness. Bigger the scene, messier the operation. He started the engine, swung out fast, tearing past the DCI and the sergeant. The fresh roll of tape snapped out of someone's hand as he caught it.

Belsey stepped on the accelerator and headed to Primrose Hill.

18

HE SPED BACK INTO LONDON, once again wondering at the limits of Amber Knight's abilities. Amber in the passenger seat. Mark Doughty in the boot. Mark Doughty, who she'd been with twenty-four hours earlier in the Comfort Hotel, wrapped in a pair of sheets.

There'd be an alert on his vehicle now. Belsey kept to back roads, away from cameras and patrol cars. He arrived in Primrose Hill shortly before one a.m. The streets were quiet. He left his car a block away from Amber's house and walked. He could see lights on in her home. Three fans in blankets waited by her gate, two paps with Thermos flasks encamped across the road.

Belsey went around the back, into the neighbour's abandoned garden. He shifted the ladder into place, crossed to the roof of the shed and dropped down to the garden. All was still, dark, no security lights. He took a breath then moved slowly towards the back window. Amber was curled up on the sofa in the living room, oblivious behind her wall of glass. She looked like something trapped in a vast block of ice. She looked normal.

He spent a voyeuristic moment wondering at her calm. Pink shorts, white vest. No make-up. Hair in a messy bun, face pale in the light of her MacBook. He tried to imagine her dragging a corpse through a wood. It wasn't easy. Beside her, splayed face-down on the sofa, was a small black book. Leather cover. The diary Terri Baker had mentioned. The one she'd been looking for. *Amber said she was recording the truth about things: love, fame, growing up.* She'd been doing plenty of growing up in the last week or so. Belsey wondered what observations the book might contain.

No movement in the other windows of the house. No sign of the new security. Belsey took another step and the security lights came on. Amber looked up, couldn't see him in the glare. He knocked on the glass and she got to her feet, startled. She peered out, then saw him. She approached the glass cautiously, opened the sliding door.

'Are you gave me a heart attack.'

'Are you alone?'

'Yes. Why?'

'I need to speak to you.'

Belsey slid the door closed behind him. Amber moved the MacBook and diary. He sat on the sofa, beside her.

'What are you up to?' he asked. 'Just chilling?'

'I guess.' She looked at him, then down at the floor. 'I'm sorry you got caught up in the fuss about us going to Loulou's. These things blow over fast.'

'It's been pretty insane, to be honest.'

'Welcome to my world. Enjoy it while it lasts, that's what I say. I heard you're going to do some stuff on TV.'

'Am I?'

'I don't mind. Good luck to you.'

'What's going on, Amber?'

'What do you mean?'

'What do you think I mean?'

Her expression faltered.

'Do you want a drink?'

'That's not what I'm here for.'

'I'm going to get some water.'

She went to the kitchen, taking the diary with her. Belsey opened the MacBook. Online, five tabs of news sites, UK and international. He shut it as she returned. She sipped water from a crystal wine glass, sat beside him, put the glass down. No sign of the diary.

'Who sent you here?' she asked.

'No one sent me. I'm very much self-motivated right now. In fact, I was just in Epping. Why do you reckon I was there?'

She nodded, which was an odd response. She looked down at the floor again. Finally she made eye contact.

'Trust me,' she said.

'Trust you.' He stared at her. Gave her a moment. 'So who killed Chloe Burlington?' Amber flinched. Again, it struck him as an odd response, not so much guilty, but as if he was being crass, transgressing propriety.

'There's something you're not going to understand,' she said.

'Give it a go.'

'I can't.'

'Somebody's making you do this.'

Amber put a finger to his lips. She shook her head, eyes brimming. She was scared, but it didn't feel like it was entirely for herself.

'I can help,' Belsey said. 'If you tell me what's going on.'

She shook her head again, slowly. 'Please, just stay away.'

'What's it got to do with a kid called Conor Shaw, Amber?'

The tears stopped. 'How do you know about him?'

'That's not the urgent question here.'

'This is nothing to do with you. Don't come stumbling in.'

'Don't come stumbling in?'

Something was driving her. He had no doubt about that. When someone's in a situation like hers and doesn't crumble, it's because they have a greater fear than their own imprisonment. She was drawing a desperate strength from something.

'Seriously—' She paused, breathed '—this is nothing to do with you.' Another breath. 'You'll get more people killed if you keep going around asking questions.'

'Why? What's going on?'

The front door opened. A woman called out: 'Amber?' The manager, Karen. Belsey turned towards the sound. Amber smashed her wine glass into the side of his head.

He felt the blow like a punch, got instinctively to his feet, staggered out of reach. His fingers came away bloody when he felt his left temple. He saw the glass broken in Amber's hand. It had cut deep. Fat drops of blood appeared on the carpet around him. Amber came at him again. He grabbed her wrist and the glass fell. He pulled her to the ground and got a knee in her chest.

Karen entered the living room with a security guard. She screamed. The guard picked up the piano stool. He was built, shirt straining.

'Help me,' Amber called from the floor. Belsey clambered back to his feet.

The guard approached, stool in his right hand, arms spread as if dealing with a wild animal. 'Call the police,' he said to Karen. She was already fumbling for her phone.

Belsey, bleeding, moved for the sliding doors.

19

HE HEADED FOR THE AUDI, trying to staunch the bleeding with a wad of used Kleenex from the depths of his coat pocket. A guy on a Vespa appeared from out of nowhere, lifted his camera and fired off a round of shots. A second man pulled up in a Mini, blocking Belsey's car, climbing out with camera raised.

Belsey turned away, stumbled back to the high street. He crossed the bridge into Chalk Farm. An area-response car passed, heading towards Amber's, braked hard, pulled a U-turn. Belsey cut across Chalk Farm Road. There was a drunk crowd spilling out of Marathon Kebab House in the wake of a brawl.

He dived in.

Marathon was one of the few local places where you could buy alcohol after hours. A live band played in the back room, oblivious to the fight at the front. Kebab meat was strewn across the floor. Belsey pushed his way through. People stared at the blood, but it all seemed part of the fun. He moved between guitarists, over an amplifier, found the 'Staff Only' door. It opened onto an outside rubbish area. Up onto a beer crate, to the wall, to the back of a budget hotel with a gate to the Belmont Street Estate.

Breathe.

No one following. He reckoned he knew the estates better than the paps. Probably better than whichever area sergeant he'd almost encountered on the high street. Another siren called: faint, back towards Primrose Hill. Belsey headed deeper into the maze of public housing, sat for a moment behind someone's wheelie bin as he tried to clean the head wound with a hose tap.

He needed to fix up properly, lie low, rehydrate. Only one place came to mind.

The power had cut again at Maureen Doughty's. It allowed him to get to the bathroom before she could see his injuries. He undressed and rinsed himself, fashioned a makeshift bandage, dressed the wound. He swallowed some of Maureen's painkillers. He took a shirt from the cupboard in Mark's bedroom.

He came back downstairs, checked the window, drew the curtains.

'Don't answer the door to anyone. Especially other police.'

'Why? What's going on?'

'Nothing. We just need some peace for tonight, Maureen. OK?'

'OK.'

He took an armchair, sat in the dark with her and let the meds kick in. Listened to squad cars crawl the estate outside, searching for him. He could see her eyes in the darkness, wet points of concern, studying the strange man who kept turning up where her son should be.

'How long's the electricity been gone?' Belsey asked.

'Not too long.'

'Do you know how to charge the key?'

'I think so. I can never find it.'

'Is there anyone else who can come and help for a bit?'

'Mark will come back soon.'

'Maybe.' He couldn't bring himself to make a death announcement. Not wearing the dead man's shirt. 'What if he doesn't?' Belsey said.

'He will.'

'Do you have any other relatives in London?'

'No.'

'You go to church, don't you? Know people through that?'

'I can't get there any more. Hip.'

When the sirens faded, it was peaceful. Belsey took his phone out and searched for news on the Epping body. Nothing yet. He pictured Amber, that scene.

Maureen Doughty dozed off. He thought of his own mother, and the belated gesture of his sitting vigil in Lewisham Hospital. An individual spent by those around her. Broken by his father in more ways than one. And by him, no doubt. That a life can be that, fuel used up in other people's fire. Propping up and excusing cuntish men.

He eased himself out of the armchair, up the creaky stairs to Mark's room. Lit a candle.

If you seek his monument, look around you.

Notes, print-outs, magazines, books. Belsey sifted the clippings again. At the bottom of a pile he found one that wasn't about the world of celebrity. Not directly anyway.

It was three sheets of advice on counter-surveillance.

The sheets had been printed recently by the look of the paper. The first few tips were obvious enough: 'Avoid SMS text messages. Leave mobiles at home, or remove the battery to defend against tracking. Face-to-face conversations are the safest bet.'

It got more paranoid as it proceeded. 'Detach external microphones and cameras from your laptop or cover the lens of attached cameras with a small piece of tape when they aren't in use. This ensures that remote activation of those mics and cameras is one less thing to worry about.'

There were instructions on how to securely delete data, how to encrypt iPhones and Windows devices. How to use encryption tools 'to "tunnel" communications securely over the Internet'. Finally it listed commercially available bug detectors and signal jammers.

Who did Mark think was bugging him? Press? Because of Amber, maybe. Maybe she gave him the documents. How exciting. Transgressive. Had it all been worth dying for, some hours snatched in the Comfort Hotel? A blinding flash as all your dreams ignite at once; a fuck in return for your life. Would Mark consent to that deal?

Then the line of thought broke – and he heard the smooth voice of Chloe Burlington's lawyer: *She said she had fears about her phone calls being listened to.* Mark wasn't the only one with worries, was he.

Belsey cleared enough papers off the bed to find a seat. The mattress retained the hollow imprint of a living Mark Doughty. Encrypted now and for ever. The moon shone through the curtains, a cold, unflinching light. He looked around and wondered when Mark's obsessions would realise their master was gone, and the lonely clippings would start to curl.

He put a finger to his bandage. It came away warm, tacky. What was possessing Amber? Something terrifying, for sure. *There's something you're not going to understand.* Turns out there was plenty.

The landline rang.

Belsey got to his feet. He checked the time: 2.50 a.m. His first thought was police, but police didn't ring. Not when something needed doing at 2.50 a.m.

'Hello?' Maureen answered. Belsey stepped slowly down the stairs. There was a long silence, then she spoke again: 'Yes. Yes . . . No. But sweetheart, I'm so worried about you.' She saw Belsey, covered the receiver. 'It's him.'

'Mark?'

'Yes.'

'Are you sure?'

She nodded. Her whole being had lit up.

Belsey leaned close, heard a man's voice on the other end of the line: '. . . won't be long, Mum. I promise. It's just not safe right now.'

'And you can't say more, darling?'

'No. I wish . . . I wish I could explain.' It was the voice of someone trying hard not to sound scared. 'If you don't see or hear from me, it means I'm safe.'

'OK, love.'

'Has anyone visited you?' There was a pause. Then Mark said: 'Mum – is someone with you now?' Maureen's eyes flicked to Belsey. He let her decide how to play it.

'Yes, darling,' she said. 'A police officer. He's been looking after me.'

Belsey took the phone before it was too late.

'Mark,' he said. 'I can help.'

'Who is this?'

'My name's Nick Belsey. I understand you're in a difficult situation, with Amber.'

Mark hung up. Belsey winced, gave the phone back.

'He's gone.' Maureen kept her ear to the receiver. Belsey saw the body lying in Epping Forest and wondered who he'd found. 'Do you know where he was calling from?' She shook her head, put the receiver down gently in its cradle.

'He couldn't say. He's hiding.'

'Did he say why?'

'No.'

'Is he in London?'

'I don't know.'

'Did he say anything about Amber Knight?'

She shook her head.

'If he phones back tell him I'd like to speak to him. I can help.'
Belsey wrote down his number again. 'Tell him I understand that
something's going on and it's not his fault.'

'OK.'

She returned to her armchair. Belsey went back upstairs.

He picked the counter-surveillance instructions up from the bed,
lay back with them held to his chest. Passed out. Woke to the sound
of prayers.

Someone was holding his hand. He turned. Maureen Doughty knelt
beside the bed. Four a.m. light through the curtains.

'You're alive,' she said.

The pillow was wet. Belsey sat up. His bandage had slipped. The
pillow and sheets were blotted a rich scarlet. Maureen Doughty watched
him, wide-eyed.

'It's not as bad as it looks,' Belsey said. He went to the bathroom.
He'd rolled in the blood during his sleep. His face and hands were
sticky with the stuff.

'You wouldn't wake up,' Maureen said.

'I'm awake.'

He was fixing a new bandage when he heard the sirens – approaching,
then cutting out.

'That's not for me, is it?'

'I thought you were dying.'

'You called an ambulance?'

'Yes.'

Belsey shut his eyes. The sirens weren't just ambulance sirens.
There would be an alert out for male IC1s with head injuries in the
Camden area.

He went to the window and watched them pull up. The ambulance,
and right behind it the police convoy. They'd killed their lights and
sirens before entering the estate, but it wasn't a discreet arrival. Ambo

and two squad cars, at this time of night. Curtains twitched in the ground-floor flat opposite. Then torchlight shone through Maureen Doughty's front window. There was a heavy knock at the door.

'Have I done something wrong?' Maureen Doughty asked.

'No,' Belsey said. 'It's fine. Thank you. And thank you for praying.' He answered the door before they broke it down.

20

'DID SOMEONE CALL AN AMBULANCE?' an officer asked. Tall, with stubble shadow, eye-balling Belsey. Behind him was a stocky colleague.

'It was for me.' Belsey gestured at his bandaged head.

'Is this your home?'

'No.'

'Whose home is it?'

Belsey pointed into the darkness behind him, towards Maureen Doughty.

'Can we take a look inside?'

'Ask her.'

The tall constable walked in, the stocky one guarded Belsey.

'Nasty knock you've picked up. What happened?'

'I slipped and fell. It looks worse than it is.'

'Want to take a seat?' Belsey was encouraged out of the front door as the officer's radio confirmed the description of a man wanted in relation to an aggravated burglary in Primrose Hill earlier that evening. He was given a seat on the wall of the front garden.

'Been out tonight, sir?' the officer asked.

* * *

They were courteous enough not to cuff him until he'd been checked by the paramedics. He got butterfly stitches and a new bandage. Once the paramedics gave him the all-clear, he was put in the back of a squad car and driven to Kentish Town police station. No familiar faces working the night shift. He sat in a holding suite for twenty minutes while a drunk was processed, then his arresting officer took him through to custody.

He was searched, possessions bagged. He'd accumulated a confusing array of notes, contracts, all folded into one papery mass. The custody sergeant wasn't interested in them, a man in his sixties with a Scottish accent and tufts of hair coming out of his ears. Belsey handed over his belt and shoes as instructed, declined the offer of a phone call.

They assigned him to the furthest cell. Last time he'd been in the station he'd spoken to a kid being held in this very cell – third time in a month he'd been picked up transporting weapons in his school bag, nunchucks and a kung fu sword, convinced he was under threat. An underdeveloped comic-book fantasist who collided with one of the sporadic crackdowns on gangs and was looking at time in a young offenders institution. Belsey knew he wouldn't survive Feltham and put in some effort arguing for a caution instead. That failed. He wondered where the kid was now.

The cell's orange and white tiles reminded Belsey of public swimming baths from his childhood. A line of thick glass bricks in the centre of the back wall gave the approximation of a window – but he knew the other side was just a corridor. Belsey got as comfortable as he could on the blue, plastic mattress. They had twenty-four hours before they needed to charge him or let him go. He put his hands behind his head, smelt vomit and thought of Amber Knight.

No great investigation had ever been conducted from a cell. Apart from those by the prisoner into their own soul, and even then not as often as commonly believed. Who had he found in Epping Forest? The dead man, whoever he was, had been at the Comfort Hotel at the same time as Amber and Mark. Belsey knew that much. Mark Doughty was in danger and on the run. Good luck, Mark. But what are you running from? The thought faded to black.

At 6 a.m. he woke to the sound of the cell being unlocked. Detective Inspector Geoff McGovern walked in.

McGovern held a preliminary pathology report and a rolled-up tabloid newspaper. Behind him, on the bench in the corridor, Belsey saw his own shoes and the bag of his possessions, freshly rifled.

'You attacked Amber Knight.'

'Self-defence,' Belsey said.

'What were you doing there?'

'I was asking her some questions.'

'You were in Epping before that.'

'That's right.'

'Why?'

'I thought I'd found Mark Doughty, the guy I told you about.'

'You thought?'

'It's his car. It's not his body. Have you ID'd it?' Belsey glanced at the file in McGovern's hand. 'Is that a pathology report?'

But the Inspector hadn't finished.

'You've got a necklace amongst your possessions that belonged to Chloe Burlington.'

Belsey lifted himself onto his elbows then swung his feet to the ground.

'She gave it to her friend. Her friend gave it to me.'

'The friend you tried to stop giving a statement.'

'I didn't stop her. I just spoke to her first.'

'You're a fucking tool.'

'Amber was with Mark Doughty at the Comfort Hotel in Finchley on Friday night.'

'Of course she was.'

'Seriously. It's on CCTV.'

'I thought Mark Doughty was some crazed stalker.'

'I think he was.'

'So why the fuck would she be at a hotel with him?'

'That's a good question, Geoff. I don't know. The joy of degradation, perhaps. Maybe she likes the smell of public transport on his clothes. You know what I mean?'

'I've no idea what you mean.'

'Maybe they're in love, against the odds, one of those miracles that makes life worth living.'

'Right. And where's Mark Doughty now?'

'Hiding.'

McGovern took a breath. 'Apparently you're coining in on all of this.'

'Am I?'

'I hear a guy called Andy Price is managing the income from your new-found celebrity.'

Belsey laughed. 'How much has he managed so far?'

'Fuck knows.'

'Show me the forensics report, Geoff.'

'Explain to me why you think Amber Knight would be caught up in all this.'

'Someone went to the papers with a recording.'

'Of what?'

'I've no idea. It may have been from Chloe. Maybe it was Mark. Maybe both. Who knows?'

McGovern stared at him. His phone rang and he answered.

'I'm with him now. Kentish Town. I'll bring him to you.'

Belsey held his palm out for the report. McGovern threw the file over, still talking on the phone. 'We'll be there in twenty . . .' Belsey turned the pages. The line for victim name was blank. No ID. No fingerprint connection on the database.

Cause of death: asphyxia due to aspiration of fluid into air passages.

The pathologist had found white froth in the lungs, water in the stomach and intestines.

Salt water.

Another wave of confusion, crashing in. He read on. There were traces of salt in the victim's hair and on his skin. The report noted the lack of socks and underwear. It was all commensurate with someone who'd drowned in salt water. Been drowned.

The image that came into Belsey's mind was of those freak occurrences, storms that pick up water and drop it along with whatever else it contains: frogs, stones, bodies. He imagined the victim storm-tossed, lifted by a tsunami.

Belsey flicked through the rest. The skin had badly decomposed where clothes had ripped as the body was dragged along. But the arms were relatively well preserved. One flap of skin in particular had been carefully salvaged from the corpse's upper right arm, cleaned and dried, like a fragment of parchment, before being photographed. It bore a tattoo. Insects had eaten away the edges, but you could make out what looked like 'Angel' in gothic black script, and, below this: 'Jack'.

Angel Jack.

McGovern was still on the phone, eyes not moving from Belsey.

'He's said he was there. It's not clear. No, he hasn't expanded on that.'

Belsey leaned back against the cool tiles. McGovern had left his pen clipped inside the report. Gold, monogrammed. When had Geoff McGovern started using monogrammed pens, for Christ's sake? It was heavy. In their old CID office it would have been nicked in minutes. Mocked, then stolen. Belsey took the pen and set it down on the floor, behind his left foot.

'He was admitted into custody at two a.m. It's OK, I've got the car. Get Steve there.'

Belsey took a final look at the photographs of the tattoo, angling them to get full light on the image. The ink on Jack looked fresher. He flipped back through the print-outs, to a photograph of the victim's left hand. No wedding band.

'Come with me,' McGovern said, hanging up, snatching back the report.

Belsey stood and stretched, followed McGovern into the corridor and collected his bag of possessions.

'Your pen.'

McGovern turned, saw his pen on the floor. He stepped back into the cell and Belsey shut the door.

21

YOU GET A LOT OF people banging and shouting in their cells. No
one rushes to respond. But they get there eventually. Belsey took his
possessions and walked fast, from the station to the residential
backstreets, cutting through to Camden Road.

Out in the free world, it had gone 7 a.m. Camden Road was bleak
and busy enough to lie low for a while. He sat in Cantelowes Gardens,
transferred his possessions to his pockets, threaded his belt. Realised
what was missing.

His passport.

The bastard.

Belsey closed his eyes, took a breath, continued down Camden
Road.

The bandage was conspicuous and identifiable. He dropped into
the Parma Café. He knew the chef there, Miguel. A little while back
Miguel had given him some Spanish lessons in return for help with
his cousin's visa.

'Your head,' he said, seeing Belsey.

'I walked into a door.'

Belsey went down to the bathroom, removed the bandage. The wound had scabbed under the hair. His ear was amply dressed with the adhesive stitches. Dried blood rinsed off, he binned the bandage. Got a tea to take away.

'No time for a lesson?'

'*Hoy no. Gracias*, Miguel.'

Belsey cut south towards King's Cross. By the time he was at the back of St Pancras he felt safe. He found the number for Detective Sergeant Gary Livermore, the least principled officer he'd ever had the pleasure of working with, which was saying something. Livermore answered over the sound of traffic. 'Who's this?'

'It's Nick. Got a business opportunity for you.'

'Fuck's sake.' Livermore hung up. He called back a minute later from another mobile.

'What do you want?'

'You at work?'

'What do you want?'

'A favour, Gary. I'm looking for a family where the wife's called Angela and there's a son called Jack. I need the name of the father.'

'You're all over the Internet.'

'That's right.'

'You know there's a warrant on you? What you playing at?'

'It's been a busy few days. I need you to run a check.'

'You've got to be joking. Shit's properly hit the fan, Nick.'

'Who says?'

'Geoff.'

If McGovern had a true disciple it was Gary Livermore.

'What did he say?'

'Nothing to me. People say he thinks you've fucked it – everything's going to come out about Borough when they get this inquiry going.

Only you're so fucked yourself he thinks he can shut you down before you get the chance. You're a suspect in a murder. Soon you're going to be out of action. Out of credibility once and for all. So no worries.'

In a way it was a relief having McGovern's strategy spelt out so clearly. It told him unambiguously what he was up against.

'Your last chance to fleece me then,' Belsey said. 'Name your price.'

'What's the surname?'

'I don't have it, that's the point. But let's give this a go. I'd put money on them being somewhere in the system. Search divorce records, Domestic Violence Prevention Notices, social-work case files. Angela and her son Jack.' Belsey checked his watch. 'It's quarter past seven. The office will be quiet. You can make a couple of hundred quid before morning prayers.'

'Five hundred.'

'It's an hour's job.'

'It's hot.'

'Not too hot for you, Gary. It will be in the last three or four years, I reckon – plaintiff called Angela. Won't be too many. One will have a son called Jack.'

'Five hundred.'

'Sure. Start with the London area: Camden, Middlesex.'

'I'm going to need some time, yeah.'

'I don't have time.'

'Whatever. I'll call you. Don't call me on that phone again.'

He hung up. Belsey walked into St Pancras station, slipped into the crowd. The only police here carried automatic weapons and had bigger things to worry about. He bought newspapers from WHSmith's, took them to the Pret to read over coffee.

His altercation at Amber's had been too late to make the print run. The entertainment pages had a lot on her wedding plans:

150 guests are expected at the reception on Saturday at the Dorchester Hotel in London. The celebrations are rumoured to have cost in excess of £1 million. Some of the costs include £200,000 for flowers; £350,000 for food, including caviar, Kobe beefburgers, truffles, and cupcakes; £300,000 in Perrier-Jouët champagne; £5,000 for hand-painted Lehr & Black wedding invitations.

But that was it – nothing more spectacular in the world of celebrity. The *Sun on Sunday*'s £750k exclusive hadn't caused any advance ripples; they were sitting tight. He checked online, scrolled past a photo of himself, head bloodied 'after violent altercation days before wedding'. Nothing from Damian Drummond, the *Sun*'s entertainment correspondent. Keeping it all for himself, no doubt. Something huge. Keeping it for Sunday when it would explode.

All the papers had a few inches on the ongoing Chloe Burlington murder investigation. Which seemed stuck. Still on appeals from friends and relatives. It wasn't clear who they were appealing to. He checked his phone. A couple of messages from Terri Baker: *Call me.* Against the stark landscape of his current predicament she almost looked like a friend. He called her.

'Is it true?' she asked. 'You were at Amber's last night?'

'I was there. The body found in Epping last night, it connects to her. I think Amber was involved in dumping it.'

'What?'

'Seriously.'

'Why were you at her house?'

'I was asking her what's going on. Didn't get an answer.'

'Listen. Have you come across someone called Katja?'

'No.'

'I've been going through the last few months of Chloe Burlington's social media. I've spoken to everyone. There's one girl who shows up in three or four photos, tagged as Katja D. I can't figure out who she is exactly. Her Facebook page says she was born in Krakow, twenty-two years old. Now lives in London, studying business at Westminster Uni. Everyone I've spoken to has said Chloe became distant over the last year or so. But not from this girl, it seems.'

'What are the pictures? Partying?'

'Not exactly. There's only a handful. But look, none of Chloe's friends know who she is. None of them. One of Chloe's old schoolfriends, she thought she might have got in with a bad crowd. Says she hadn't seen her in ages. She was acting strangely – Chloe had asked her once if she wanted an adventure. The friend thought maybe sex parties. She said it would involve being taken somewhere blindfolded.'

'To what? An orgy?'

'That's what the friend thinks. I've got to start writing this up. Will you call me if you get more? Anything.'

Belsey went back online, found Chloe's Facebook page, looked for 'Katja D'. Katja D turned up in inoffensive restaurant shots. '*Out with friends*'. A pale girl with dyed red hair who favoured T-shirts and jeans, didn't use much make-up. No hints of orgies. There was one picture of her holding shopping bags on an expensive-looking high street: Knightsbridge or Chelsea. Then '*Day trip*': Katja standing beside a grey Peugeot people carrier. He knew that people carrier. It had been caught on speed camera, a few yards behind Mark Doughty's Renault as it sped to Epping.

There was more. One recent photograph, posted three weeks ago, had been taken in the mirror of a dressing table: Katja and Chloe, both bare-shouldered, hair up, glowing. '*Feeling much better*'. There was a large, white bedroom reflected behind them. Chloe Burlington's place. Belsey examined it closely. Some kind of kit on the bed. Maybe a hair dryer, and something plastic-looking, with two loops at the end, like an oversized key. More grooming kit? Sex toys? Something that made her 'feel much better' in the bedroom of a girl who was killed on Monday night.

Belsey searched through Katja's profile. Not A-list. Not much anything, as far as he could tell. But real enough that her own friends were concerned. In June 2013 there was a flurry of messages congratulating her on getting a grant to study business. There was a photo of her celebrating with ruddy-faced parents in a poor-looking home. Then she came to London and posted a few photos of Big Ben – then, a year or so later, a few with Chloe Burlington. A succession of messages had been posted to her wall over the past week or so, mostly in Polish, none garnering a reply.

He pasted them into Google Translate: 'Where are you?', 'Call me.' One friend, Irena, gave a mobile number.

After a couple of experiments with international dialling codes, he got a ring tone.

A girl answered: '*Tak, stucham.*'

'Is that Irena?'

'Yes. Who is this?'

'My name's Nick. I'm a friend of Katja's, in London. I'm worried about where she's gone. I saw your message on Facebook.'

'What's happened?'

'I don't know. I'm trying to find out. When did you last hear from her?'

'Last week.'

'Do you know where she was staying?'

'I have an address. From a year ago.'

'Can I have it?'

'Please wait.'

She got the address. He wrote it down. 236a Turnpike Lane.

'How long's she been in London?'

'A couple of years.'

'Doing what?'

'You are a friend of hers?'

'Yes, but I don't know her well.'

'She is studying.'

'At Westminster University?'

'Yes, I think so. She won a grant, from a foundation. You will speak to her parents?'

Belsey rang off with promises to phone Katja's family and keep Irena in the loop. He flicked through the rest of Katja's pictures. There was nothing to do with any university. No uni friends. No parties, no campus, no happy hour in the union bar.

He downed his coffee and headed to the Piccadilly Line.

22

TURNPIKE LANE: A BUSY THOROUGHFARE several miles long, with flats above an endless parade of all-night grocers', kebab shops, cheap Indian and Chinese restaurants. It wasn't Primrose Hill.

Katja's address was above a pub, the Admiral, currently clad in scaffolding. A banner announcing YES, WE'RE OPEN sagged from the first floor. A delivery lorry was parked outside, boxes of crisps being trolleyed in.

Belsey found a worn white doorway down the side of the pub: one bell, no name. Junk mail for 'Katja Dabrowska' was jammed in the letter box. He pulled it out. Through the letter box he could see narrow beige-carpeted stairs and a spread of letters that looked a few days old. There was a bicycle pump beside a radiator, space for a bike but no bike.

He checked the street, swung himself up onto the scaffolding, followed it round to the back of the building. He climbed up to the second floor, found a window looking into a small bedroom with a single bed. The window was locked. Beyond the room he could see a corridor, then a kitchen with what looked like a one-hob portable electric stove. Not much else. No books anywhere. No photos or ornaments.

He climbed back down to the pub and walked in. It was mostly carpet, with fluorescent stars stuck to the laminate walls advertising house spirits. There was a double act behind the bar, both in their sixties. The landlord was pulling taps, red-faced, stained suit jacket over his vest. A woman with the same years of pub management worn into her complexion moved stiffly around him, hair backcombed so that it stood up and framed her face.

'Not open yet, love,' she said.

'I'm looking for Katja – the girl who lives upstairs.'

'Not seen her. Not for a while.'

'Know her?'

'Not well. She's not been around, the last few days. We'd been wondering where she's got to. Hadn't we?'

The man nodded.

'I'm from her university. We're concerned about her. Did she rent the room off you?'

'No. It's the same landlord owns the whole building. Not us.'

'She's not been at lectures. Have you seen her with anyone recently? Any signs of trouble?'

'No.'

'I heard she was a bit of a party animal. Had a bit of a lifestyle.'

'Living up there? No. She'd be in by seven most nights.'

Belsey considered this.

'You never saw her dressed up – anything like that?'

'No.'

'With a man?'

'No.'

'Do you have a number for the landlord?'

She hobbled into a back room, returned with a name and number in shaky blue biro on a piece of notepaper: Mashru & Co Property Investments. Belsey stepped out of the pub and called.

'Viraj Mashru.'

'Are you the landlord for Katja Dabrowska? 236a Turnpike Lane.'

'That's right.'

'This is Detective Constable Nick Belsey. We're concerned about Katja's whereabouts. It seems she's gone missing.'

'Katja Dabrowska?'

'That's right. How much does she pay for the flat, Mr Mashru?'

'One hundred and twenty a week.'

'And how did she pay that?'

'Cash.'

'No standing order set up?'

'No.

'What about the deposit?'

'Same.'

'Was she working, Mr Mashru?' Belsey asked.

'She was a student.'

'Where?'

'University of Westminster, I think.'

'Did she say why she was paying in cash?'

'No.'

'Any idea where she was getting the money?'

'Her dad or something. I spoke to him once, on the phone. He gave me his name and number in case there were any problems. I can find it.'

'What kind of problems?'

'I don't know. That's just dads, isn't it. Worried about their little princess.'

'And you think the money came from him?'

'He *said* the money came from him.'

'Can I have those details, please?'

'Hold on.' The landlord changed rooms. A moment later he said: 'Andreas Majorana.' He read out a mobile number. Belsey thanked him and hung up.

A. Majorana: he'd heard that name, but in another voice – Shannen at the hotel. The name on the card used to book Mark and Amber's three hours of Comfort.

A man shuffled past, checked his watch, headed into the off-licence next door. Belsey dialled the number for Majorana. Dead. A pay-as-you-go SIM with no address connected to it, he suspected. Probably long-destroyed.

He called Westminster Uni. He was eventually passed to a woman in the registrar's office. She ran a check.

'No. A Katja Dabrowska has never been a student here. Are you sure it was Westminster?'

Belsey went back into the pub.

'Did you get through to him?' the landlady asked.

'Yes. It looks like Katja had money coming from somewhere.'

'Money? She didn't have a TV, for god's sake. Did she?' she asked her husband. He shook his head.

'You've been in her flat?' Belsey asked.

'No.'

'How do you know she didn't have a TV?'

'Because she came down here. To watch the news.'

'I thought she wasn't down here that much.'

'It was just the once. Wednesday. We had the match on and she asked to change channels. There was no one watching anyway.'

'Wednesday last week.'

'That's the one.'

'Was there something in particular she wanted to see?'

'I don't know. Just the news. She tore a page out of the paper as well.' The woman shuffled into the back again. He saw her riffling through a pile of old newspapers. 'Will you look at that,' she said, returning with a copy of the *Mail*, a torn strip where page 7 had been. 'Not affording a TV I can understand, but she could have bought her own paper, no?'

23

BELSEY CUT THROUGH RESIDENTIAL STREETS to Wood Green, north along the busy High Road to the tarmacked square crowned by Wood Green Central Library. He went in, asked to see the last week's papers and was directed to a large grey filing cabinet in the reference section.

He leafed through the stack of dog-eared *Mails* from last week until he had Wednesday's edition. Page 7, a half-page advert for conservatories and one story: 'DUTCH POLICE PLEA FOR MYSTERY WOMAN. Dutch police have appealed for help in identifying a 40–50 year old woman found in a disorientated state near the town of Spier on Monday. The woman, who has not spoken, is believed to have travelled to the Netherlands from the UK . . .' The 'mystery woman' had been picked up by Dutch police wandering outside Spier, in the north of the country, just above Hoogeveen. She didn't have any money or ID on her, hadn't eaten for several days as far as they could tell. She had curly greying hair, was wearing a blue North Face jacket, blue jeans, black Adidas trainers with grey stripes. She didn't appear to speak Dutch and hadn't responded to any of the interpreters they tried, but the labels on her clothes suggested she'd recently been living in the UK. It was possible she was suffering from trauma-induced amnesia. Possible she wasn't.

The woman had been treated for mild hypothermia at Bethesda Hospital in Hoogeveen before being transferred to the University Medical Center Utrecht.

UK police were heading over to help identify her, along with officials from the British embassy.

The *Mail* mentioned injuries to her hands. And there were inset pictures the police had released of both hands, front and back. The palms had been lacerated. There were scratches up the wrists and forearms.

To Belsey's eyes they looked like someone gripping on to things not meant to be gripped. Barbed wire. Fence-climbing injuries. There were red markings around her wrists – they hadn't mentioned this in the article. They looked like old restraint marks.

He was staring at the article when his phone rang. A fellow library-user tutted as he answered.

'Meet me in an hour,' Gary Livermore said.

Belsey walked out to the corridor.

'You've got a result?'

'If you've got five hundred quid.'

'What's the name?'

'Back of the Elm Grove Trading Estate, half-ten. Off the Old Kent Road. It's the turn-off after Chicken Cottage. And don't fuck me about.'

Belsey returned the paper to the cabinet. He found the number for Andy Price at AP Total Media Management and dialled as he left the library. If Price was going to appoint himself manager he could sort some cashflow.

'Nick, my man.' Price sounded delighted. 'I was worried you'd gone reclusive.'

'I hear my career's going well.' There was a nervous laugh. 'I need some money.'

'Of course. Did you look at the contract?'

'I've got it in front of me. I'm looking forward to working together. But I need five hundred pounds in the next hour.'

'Where are you?'

'Wood Green library.'

'I'm in Barnet, heading into town. I can swing by.'

Price drove by fifteen minutes later in a worn-looking maroon Bentley. There was an iced coffee in the drinks holder. The back seat was covered in signed prints of a woman Belsey didn't recognise.

Price wound the window down, eyed the butterfly stitches, a little disappointed.

'So is this your neighbourhood?' he said.

'No.'

'Jump in. I'm on my way to the office. We can finalise things there.'

'Do you have some cash at the office?'

'Of course.'

Belsey climbed in. They began to drive. Price checked an incoming call – 'The intern' – killed it. 'I saw that photo of you bleeding,' he said.

'What did you think?'

'I think we need a strategy. First thing, have a look at this, give me your thoughts.' He passed Belsey a brochure from a company offering celebrities for openings, club nights, promotions. Discreetly tucked in was a flyer about teeth-whitening services. 'It's no one's dream come true, but it gives us something to build on. Gets your face out there.' Belsey read about teeth whitening. Price's phone rang again. 'She struggles to open the post,' he said, answering the call. Then his face fell. 'Don't do anything. We're ten minutes away.'

* * *

186

The office was a small room above a tanning salon behind Tottenham Court Road. It had one desk, one leather sofa, the contents of its drawers and cupboards across the floor. The place had been turned over. Copies of *Entertainment Weekly* lay scattered amongst old invoices. The intern was a shaken eighteen-year-old in thick-framed glasses.

Price went straight to the desk. He dropped his laptop and car keys, opened a cash box, checked it.

'What happened?' Belsey asked the girl.

'It was the police.'

'What did they want?'

'Anything about you. They said they'd be back.'

'Were they in uniform?'

'One was.'

'Show a warrant?'

'I think so.'

'How many officers?'

'Four. Three men and a woman.'

'Did you get any of their names?'

'No. They asked me if I'd spoken to you. When you started working with us. If we had bank details. If we had a record of where you've been.'

'How long were they here?'

'I don't know. Ages. Twenty minutes.'

Belsey thought of Livermore's words: *Only you're so fucked yourself he thinks he can shut you down before you get the chance. Soon you're going to be out of action. Out of credibility once and for all.* Bullseye. A man who always had his minions. Who knew how to shut someone down.

'It's bullshit,' Belsey said to no one in particular.

He went to the window. Someone was opening up the tanning salon. A couple of months before Hampstead station closed they found needles on a fifteen-year-old girl, brought her in. There was a minor panic over drugs, before someone pointed out the orange hue of her skin. She and her friends had been injecting melatonin. It seemed a long time ago now.

Across the road was a young man with a goatee, wearing shades, a black jacket, fingerless driving gloves, ear-piece in. He looked up at the window, met Belsey's eyes, looked away. Then he turned his back and browsed the menu of an Italian restaurant.

Belsey checked his watch. 10.05 a.m. Livermore would be on his way to the Old Kent Road. He went to the cash box, counted out five hundred in twenties, then another eighty for expenses. Took Price's car keys.

'I need to borrow your car for a couple of hours.'

'My car?' Price smiled, disbelievingly.

'I'll bring it straight back.'

24

THE BENTLEY DROVE LIKE NEW. He crossed London in half an hour. Old Kent Road was flashback territory, south of the river, a high street that had been a ragged, bustling handful when he was patrolling it, but had become sullen, emptier by the year. Belsey passed the turnings for Rotherhithe and Surrey Quays, saw the Chicken Cottage, cut left.

Industrial estates and builders' warehouses filled the no-man's-land north of the main road. Livermore's chosen rendezvous was a gutter behind the windowless backs of kitchens and launderettes, blocked at one end by an avalanche of abandoned mattresses. Belsey parked, alone amongst the waste. He realised he'd been here before – a furtive moment with a young lady. With a woman he'd loved, in fact. Every corner of London seemed to hold associations these days, streets overlaid with scar tissue. He spent a moment thinking about that woman and the possibility that drug-fuelled back-seat sex might not have been what she needed. Then a red Mazda pulled up beside him and cut the nostalgia.

Livermore kept the engine running. Belsey climbed out, got into the Mazda, kept the passenger door open.

Livermore was lanky, cramped in his sports car, eyes cynical and alert. He wore a navy suit, hair slicked and side-parted. It had been a couple of years since Belsey had seen him and he'd kept in shape. There was a retractable truncheon in the door pocket, police radio on the back seat.

'What did you get?' Belsey said.

'Money first.' Livermore checked the mirrors. Nothing had changed. Belsey envied him that. While others had fled the toxic mess of Borough CID into various forms of cover, Livermore had blithely maintained his corruption. Whatever native wit kept him employed it didn't extend to ethical self-reflection. Belsey gave him the cash. He counted it and dropped it into his jacket.

'So you're famous now.'

'What did you get?'

Livermore checked the mirrors again. He reached between his legs, retrieved an envelope from under the seat and handed it over. It contained two folded sheaths, five photocopied pages each. First was a police report dated 12 March 2010, from Notting Hill CID. Officers attended what they termed a 'domestic disturbance' at Westbourne Park Road. Called in by an Angela Harper – wife, at that time, of Ian Harper. Paper-clipped to this, a file courtesy of Kensington and Chelsea social services concerning their son, Jack Harper, born 30 May 2003: medical stats, psychological surveys, educational assessments.

The second sheath consisted of five sheets from the Child Support Agency: correspondence from last August detailing Child Maintenance Enforcement Charges. This dossier included Ian Harper's supporting evidence of financial hardship. Now there were two addresses listed: Angela and Jack in Ladbroke Grove, Ian in Ravenscourt Park.

'Ian Harper on any of our lists?' Belsey asked.

'No.' Livermore revved his engine. Belsey got out. Livermore leaned across.

'Is this something to do with Amber Knight?'

'This is someone Amber killed.'

Livermore laughed. 'Have you shagged her?'

'I appreciate your help, Gary,' Belsey said. 'If you speak to Geoff again, tell him to give me my passport back or I will tear his life apart.'

Livermore grinned, gunned the engine and splashed muddy water, reversing at 30mph back into the past.

25

BELSEY CLIMBED INTO THE BENTLEY and looked through the paperwork again. The most recent document, the CSA file, described Ian Harper as having been director of two companies, Digital Ad Solutions and Regent's Property. Both had gone into administration last year. He'd moved out of the family home and appeared to have drifted around the less salubrious parts of west London before turning up with the foxes and skipper flies of Epping Forest. His most recent address was 9 Waterside Heights, Ravenscourt Park.

Belsey cut back across London through late-morning traffic. This felt like the strongest lead he had. Someone worth killing. Someone police were yet to ID. Caught up in a very odd circle of individuals.

Waterside Heights was a new tower block, part of Thames Village, a development that involved six high-rise residential towers constructed out of yellow, machine-hewn bricks. The development was barely out of the box, ground-floor commercial units obscured with builders' sheets and the promise of a Tesco coming soon. There was a startled air to the place, as if it had gone up too fast and was trying to catch up with its own existence. Flats on the upper floors still had manufacturers' stickers on their windows. Grey sacking showed around the bases of trees. An arrow attached to one of those trees pointed to the show flat: 'Waterside Living Starts Here.' Belsey couldn't see much water or living. Eventually a group of Chinese students walked towards Harper's block carrying shopping. Belsey followed them in.

Inside it smelt of fresh plastering. Belsey climbed dusty concrete stairs three floors to number 9. The door was open a crack. Undamaged. No scratches around the lock suggesting a more sophisticated break-in. His guess was that whoever last entered the flat had the key – but they weren't Ian Harper, and weren't too worried about Harper returning.

Belsey knocked, walked in.

The flat was clean, compact, with all the curtains drawn. Appliances were new; some still sat amidst polystyrene and instruction booklets. But the place had been searched: drawers were out, papers and files on the floor and table. Ring-binders lay open. A Slazenger bag had been upturned on the sofa. In each room, receipts and crumpled paperwork sat at the top of the bin, as if someone had fished sheets out before returning them. A framed photograph of a man, woman and small boy lay on its back on the coffee table. No sign of struggle. Furniture remained aligned. The bedroom was tidy to the point of impersonality.

The bulk of Harper's paperwork was fanned across the kitchen table: copies of polite letters about financial ruin: from NatWest to Harper, Harper to NatWest; to utilities companies and Ealing Borough Council. Then an HMRC Statutory Notice of Bankruptcy. Belsey was familiar with that one. It was dutifully hole-punched like all the rest.

The bathroom was more like a generous-sized shower cabinet, used but tidy: shaving kit, one toothbrush in a drinking glass. One discordant note: tangled knots of Sellotape filled the bin. Off the removal boxes?

Belsey sat down on the living-room sofa and, staring around the room, considered all this. According to the paperwork, Harper had been paying just over three hundred a week for this shoebox. As if to make up for lack of space, whoever designed the flats had installed a lot of plug sockets. Two were in use, side by side in the corner. They contained identical black charger plugs, leads trailing on the faux-wood floorboards. Not a type of charger he'd seen before. He went over to them. No phone insignia on the plug.

Belsey returned to the bathroom, took the Sellotape from the bin and untangled it. It was opaque. Not Sellotape at all, in fact. Surgical tape: breathable, rough in texture, made for use on skin. Maybe two metres of the stuff. He stuck it to the mirror, turned the shaving light on. There were hairs on it. Body hairs. He took a length of tape and wrapped it around his chest.

It had a property attached. A recording. A picture or a video or something.

Belsey went back to the chargers and wondered what kind of device they charged. The only time he'd used a concealed recorder was on an undercover drugs score. He had sworn never again; the police devices were huge and heavy. Most undercover officers forked out for their own equipment – preferable to being shot when it fell down a trouser leg. There was much better stuff on the market.

You wouldn't wear two, though.

He looked around, saw the Slazenger bag. It was in good condition. The style didn't seem to fit with the rest of the flat. He lifted it to the light and peered through a small hole bored into one end. Just big enough for a peephole camera.

Now Belsey sifted the bankruptcy paperwork more attentively. Ten days ago a significant chunk of Harper's arrears became the responsibility of a professional debt-collection agency. Not friendly people in Belsey's experience. But good at prompting money-making schemes.

£750k for exclusive world rights.

He thought of the receipt he'd pulled from Harper's trouser pocket in Epping. A whisky at the Comfort Hotel, Friday – the night Mark and Amber turn up. Harper's ready to get his £750k scoop. But he's going to have to film something without taking his clothes off. Maybe just the pair of them entering and departing. You could build a story out of that. You could also just rip it off the security cameras. And it wasn't worth £750k. Not to anybody.

Belsey tweaked the living-room blind. The narrow balcony outside granted you a view of the next wave of construction. It also gave a view of two cars parked close to his borrowed Bentley. One was a black Ford Mondeo. Belsey felt sure it was the car that had swung by Mark's last night. Sitting in the driver's seat was the young man he'd seen across the road from Price's office. Same goatee, same Oakley sunglasses. He had a sightline on the entrance to Waterside Heights.

Paparazzi would get out of the car to take a photo. They wouldn't have binoculars on the dashboard. They wouldn't have been tailing him for twenty-four hours.

Belsey let the blind fall and turned on the TV. News of foreign wars, then more local matters: Harper's demise arrived right on schedule. *'Police are appealing for assistance today as they struggle to identify the body of a man found in Epping Forest last night. The body is described as that of a white male between thirty and fifty years old . . .'* They'd reconstructed the outfit Harper was wearing. They'd tried a reconstruction of his face. Belsey picked up the family photo and compared them. Not bad. Not great. £750k. Someone with £750k of footage who goes missing – that's going to be noticed. Certainly by the people trying to profit out of him. The story went to the *Sun on Sunday*, Baker had said. Via a broker: Shaun White.

Belsey took his phone out and searched online for the Shaun White Agency. White, it turned out, was quite a character, dominating the market in sleaze: self-styled 'Mr Showbiz', a clearing house for every titbit with market value, a companion for those who'd fallen into fame and needed a guide. He got his clients deals, fed the papers scandal, and found himself fabulously rich. The wealth was part of the sales pitch, it seemed. His fat, shaven head sweated in photo ops with disgraced soap stars, teenage singers, kidnap victims. All looked delighted; most were one or two feet taller than him. It was hard to find White's name without the words 'six-figure deal' hovering nearby. But then publicity was his job.

I'm surprised he's not been in touch with you, Baker had said. Belsey was a little surprised too.

No answer from the Shaun White Agency when he called. He left a message saying he was fucking Amber Knight and needed representation. He sent an email and got an auto-reply: 'Due to an exceptionally high workload the Shaun White Agency will not be taking on any more clients until further notice.' All enquiries were directed to a mobile number. Belsey called the number and it went to voicemail.

Not what you'd expect from the market leaders.

The agency listed an address in east London. Belsey found a number for the building's main reception and called. A woman said the agency was temporarily closed for holidays.

Unfortunate time to close, given the current workload. He'd tried that tactic in his own career and it proved a temporary solution at best. He checked the window. The Ford was still there. He left

Harper's flat, got in the Bentley and began the drive towards Old Street. The Mondeo stuck close to him. Belsey stopped a couple of times and checked his mirrors. There they were. He drove in a couple of circles, around a few blocks, one direction then another, and wondered if they felt as foolish as they looked.

26

SHAUN WHITE OPERATED FROM A warehouse conversion close to
the Old Street roundabout. Bare bricks, unpainted concrete and some
of the most expensive office space outside of the Square Mile. A young
woman sat at the building's front desk, disgruntled simultaneously by
two couriers and a maintenance man.

Belsey walked through to the stairs, past offices for music labels
and online clothes stores to a door on the fourth floor with a sign for
the Shaun White Agency. A notice had been stuck to a frosted-glass
panel above it: 'Closed due to bereavement.'

The door was locked. Through the frosted panel you could see lights
were on. Belsey felt the glass. It was cold. He felt the handle. Freezing.
The air con was audible through the door.

He went back down to the front desk. The little crowd remained.
The receptionist was trying to convince one of the motorbike couriers
they were in the wrong building.

'Shaun White—'

'I'm dealing with someone,' the woman said.

'I'm waiting too, mate,' the maintenance man pointed out.

The receptionist got up, led the biker to the front of the building and flapped her hand towards the end of the road. Belsey walked behind her desk, opened all the drawers and found a bunch of master keys. He went back up to the office, waited for a group to clear the landing, tried a couple of keys and opened the door.

Shaun was in after all. He sat at his desk, looking at Belsey. His head was tilted, purple and swollen. Air con had forestalled most of the decomposition, but there was nothing to stop the bloating and the livid blotches. His wrists were duct-taped to the arms of his swivel chair. His feet didn't reach the floor.

It was a nice office. New Macs, translucent furniture. Around the walls were framed pictures of Shaun himself, smiling triumphantly at his corpse. There were two desks close to the door and one for Shaun in the centre, plus a small meeting room behind a clear glass wall. The ice-cold air con rippled the leaves of plants and the pages of open magazines. On his desk, the little finger of White's left hand sat detached in a small pool of congealed blood.

Belsey turned the desk light on. The finger was pinkish-blue, childlike. The mutilated hand remained taped to the arm of the chair, the floor beneath it black with blood. But not enough to have killed him. Belsey considered the victim's age and BMI and read the cause of death as a heart attack brought on minutes after the enhanced interrogation began. He pressed the skin on White's forearm and it stayed discoloured. Over twelve hours dead. Rigor mortis worn off. Clouded lenses, but the eyes weren't bulging with gases yet. Maximum two days dead.

He angled the light and checked the skin around the mouth. There were no signs it had been taped. Suggesting Shaun hadn't had much time to scream. Also suggesting his attacker had wanted him to speak.

The door of the meeting room was open. A long glass table, more framed pictures on the wall, one of them on the ground. Set into the wall where the picture had hung was a black cabinet safe with combination lock. It was open.

Belsey approached the safe. Inside was a mess of incriminating material in every medium: Polaroids, paperwork, flash drives and a couple of video cassettes. Some items had been thrown to the floor. Belsey took an armful, dropped them onto the table. A minor royal in lingerie, blurred people with rolled twenties up their noses, a burnt spoon on a hotel bureau, a man and a woman holding hands on a secluded beach. Decades of shame. Envelopes of grainy black-and-white prints, rolls of Kodak, three floppy disks and a VHS labelled 'Christmas oral 1988'.

He searched the rest of the safe. Whatever Shaun had on Amber Knight had flown.

Belsey returned to Shaun White at his desk, switched the computer on, tried a few passwords. Then he nudged the corpse aside and searched for an address book. He opened the top desk drawer and removed a bulging Filofax. Shaun was old school. He checked D for the journalist who made the offer for Harper's property – Damian Drummond. Not there. Belsey tried S and found Drummond amongst a whole page of *Sun* contacts. Belsey took his mobile out, then put it back and picked up the desk phone instead. Drummond answered on the first ring.

'Shaun, where've you been?'

'It's Hugo,' Belsey said. 'Shaun's assistant.' There was a pause.

'Is Shaun there?'

'Yes. He says he's sorry he's been busy. He wants you to come in. He's got what you need.'

'He's got it?'

'Oh yes.'

'It's OK? There's no problem?'

'Plenty of problems. That's how we make our money, isn't it?'

Drummond laughed uncertainly. 'I'll bring my chequebook.' It sounded like he was moving already.

'Bring the big one. Shaun can't wait to see you.'

Belsey hung up. He set up a third chair by the desk. He took a sheet of paper from the printer and wrote the chronology as he had it while he waited. A story had gone to the *Sun on Sunday* four days ago, Saturday, according to Terri Baker, from a member of the public via Shaun White. The receipt in the Epping corpse's pocket suggested Ian Harper had been at the Comfort Hotel early Friday evening, same time Amber and Mark paid a visit. Say Harper approaches Shaun White on Saturday morning with whatever he's recorded. By Saturday night, Mark Doughty's on the run, Shaun's taped to his chair and Harper's an ecosystem.

Belsey looked at the corpse beside him. While his estimation of Amber was rising by the hour, he couldn't see this as her handiwork. What about Mark Doughty, torturing Shaun for Amber's sake? To close the story down.

But what story?

The door to the office opened at twenty past three. Drummond walked in, stopped, stepped back again. He froze on the threshold, professional curiosity counterbalancing disgust. The journalist was tall, stubble greying, tie loose. He stared at the corpse, then at Belsey.

'Come in. Shut the door.' Belsey gestured to the empty seat. 'We've been waiting. I mean, I have. Shaun's dead.' He kicked the sliding chair towards the door, where it hit Drummond's legs.

'What is this?'

'A corpse, an open safe, evidence of torture. Choose your headline.'

Drummond came over with his chair, staring at the space where Shaun White's little finger should have been.

'You killed him?'

'No. Have another try.'

'What's going on?'

'Someone taped Shaun's hands to the arms of his chair and cut his finger off. Shaun told them the code for the safe. Then he had a heart attack. They stole what they wanted. Everyone lived happily ever after. Apart from me and Shaun White and quite a few other people. I think they took a recording of Amber Knight that was being sold to you. So tell me about that.'

Drummond considered all this, aspects of the situation coming into focus.

'We never got it. I don't know what it was.'

'You offered seven hundred and fifty k. I don't believe you were taking a total punt.'

The journalist glanced around the office, the open safe, having another go at comprehension; then back to Belsey.

'You're Nick Belsey.'

'No points for that.'

'What are you doing here?'

'Trying to establish why people are dying and how I can avoid being held responsible.'

'I'm going to call the police now,' Drummond said, taking his phone out.

'I'm going to call Terri Baker, so fuck off out of here. I thought you were a journalist.'

Drummond relented, took a seat on his sliding chair. Belsey admired him for that. He was still wielding his phone though.

'Are they about you?' Drummond said. 'The films.'

'No. Shaun must have said something when he spoke to you.'

'A man had come to him with a set of recordings. That's all. We never found out what exactly he had.'

'A set?'

'Yes.'

'When was that?'

'Early last week. He said he could get us something special but needed operating money.'

'Meaning?'

'Five grand – to cover his expenses and recording equipment. The source said he was going to give us something special but would need to get away afterwards. That his life would be in danger. We promised up to eight hundred depending on what he brought us. Shaun was doing his usual, playing the papers off each other. But I don't think it was entirely bluff. There was something special about this one.'

'Maybe the life-endangering aspect was a giveaway.'

'Yes.'

'Who did the source think would be putting his life in danger?'

'I don't know.'

'Did you meet them?'

'No.'

'What made you invest?'

'Shaun had pictures from him already – of Amber at home, no make-up, with a man. No one knew who the man was.'

'How did he get these?'

'I don't know. This was just the start. He said he could get video that would blow our minds. He had access. Shaun said his client had detailed knowledge about her: her routine, her life. A secret life.'

'Involving what?'

'I'm telling you everything I know.'

'Any idea how he had that knowledge?'

'No. He wasn't staff. We know all the staff through Karen. Do *you* know?'

'I have no idea.'

'I got a call on Saturday morning saying they'd got the footage. Shaun had seen it and said it was crazy.'

'Crazy like what?'

'Different from anything I'd have ever seen before – that's what he said. I had to come in to his office to see it. He wouldn't talk on the phone. Couldn't say what it related to exactly. But it was definitely Amber, so you knew it was going to be huge. Then he stopped returning my calls.'

'That's one way of putting it.'

Drummond's eyes cut to Shaun. He looked away again.

'I thought we'd been outbid. It's happened before with Shaun. I was waiting for Sunday. I expected to see it in the *Mail*.'

'When exactly did you last speak to him?'

'Saturday lunchtime.'

'What did he say?'

'He said his client had delivered one tape and we should hold tight.'

'Well, someone found out about what his client was doing. In between whatever he got on Friday night and being dumped in Epping Forest twenty-four hours later. How many people on the paper knew about this?'

'Just me, the deputy editor and the editor.'

'Someone leaked.'

Drummond shook his head, more in wonder than denial.

'I don't see how.'

'You know about the body found in Epping Forest last night, right?' Belsey asked.

'Yes.'

'He was your source, a man called Ian Harper. He was killed on Saturday night – I don't know where – and dumped in the woods. He was a bankrupt divorcee, former online advertising salesman. I believe Chloe Burlington was involved somehow and started panicking about all this. She's dead two days later. And there's a guy called Mark Doughty. He's on the run now.'

Drummond slipped a notebook from his jacket pocket and wrote this down.

'How do you fit in?' he asked.

'I don't.'

Drummond turned back to the main office. 'I'd like you to put all this on record. There would be a fee, for a full interview.'

'Not right now, Damian.' Belsey stood up.

'Are you represented by Andy Price?'

'Not really. We're in talks.'

'There are people trying to sell stories about you.'

'Good luck to them.'

'We spoke to a DI Geoff McGovern. He knows the editor.'

Belsey sighed. 'Yeah, Geoff McGovern. He's talking to you, but where is he? You know what I mean? Here we are at a crime scene trying to stop a killer and where's super DI Geoff McGovern?'

'I don't understand.'

'Me neither, Damian. Maybe he's not all he's cracked up to be. Maybe he's talking about me because I'm one of the few people off statins who knows what a dark bastard he is. Maybe he's not investigating at all. But someone needs to sort this out, don't you think? Before more people get killed.'

Drummond nodded warily.

'What did he say?' Belsey asked.

'You might have the money.'

'What money?'

'Amber's money.'

'I get the impression she's been disposing of it quite well herself. Why would I have it?'

'I don't know. But it's gone. To the extent that they can't pay people meant to be doing the wedding.'

'Hold on. How much is gone?'

'About forty-five million in the last few weeks.'

Belsey tried to accommodate this new information. Drummond's eyes flicked to the corpse, then the meeting room. Both men sensed the presence of this fact in the room. A missing £45 million is rarely an irrelevance.

'I don't have Amber's money,' Belsey said. He walked to the window, called Drummond over. 'Know this guy?' He pointed to the Ford Mondeo parked across the street, the goatee.

'No. Who is it?'

'He's been tailing me for the last twenty-four hours. I might try to find out.'

Drummond nodded, walked into the meeting room. 'Holy fuck.' He picked up the royal lingerie shot, then put it down and picked up the Polaroids. 'Are the police on their way?'

'I haven't called them. I thought you could do the honours.'

'Sure.' Drummond turned to the safe. 'I might hang here for a minute.'

'Knock yourself out.'

27

BELSEY RETURNED TO THE BENTLEY. He waited for his watcher to climb back into the Mondeo, then he drove west, up City Road, turned fast into a cul-de-sac behind a council block and hit the brakes. The Mondeo followed him in. Belsey reversed back past the Ford, swinging his car so that it blocked the exit. He got out, opened the Ford's passenger door and got in.

'Why are you following me?'

The driver gripped the wheel. He didn't turn. He still had shades on, but Belsey could see he was in his late twenties, beard thin, sleeves rolled up to show well-honed forearms. There was a click of miscalculation and he reached for the door handle, about to get out. Belsey opened the glove compartment and sifted through paperwork. The man leaned across and tried to snatch it out of his hand.

'Get out of my car.'

Belsey kept a grip on the papers and eventually the man gave up.

'Take a walk.'

'Fuck off.' The man got his mobile out. Belsey took it from his hand and threw it out the window.

'Go on – take a walk.'

The driver tore his shades off, held Belsey's glare for a second, then opened the door, heading to retrieve his phone. According to the car papers, the Mondeo belonged to Sisco Private Intelligence. Belsey knew Sisco: big company, but not the one he'd hire. They were greedy, took on jobs they couldn't support. Overstretch led to sloppy recruitment: graduates and fantasists. The young PI had rigged himself with an excessive amount of kit: night-vision binoculars, a Nikon with zoom lenses on the dashboard. On the back seat were headphones connected to a sound-amplifying mic. Amongst the papers were briefing notes on Belsey: his name, age, vehicle details; ID photos ripped from his police file. The notes were addressed to a Stefan Keydel.

Keydel got back in with his phone. He tried to grab the papers again. Belsey chucked them out the window.

'Stefan.'

'Get out.' Keydel clutched the steering wheel again as if that might go next.

'Your car, Stefan, or Sisco's? Maybe it's Neil Ferguson's car. He still runs Sisco, doesn't he?'

'For fuck's sake.' The private investigator stared straight ahead. 'What do you want?'

'Me and Neil go way back.' That was a half-truth. He'd had three pints in the bar of a Travelodge with Neil Ferguson after a race-awareness training session. 'We used to work in the same unit.'

'I don't care.'

'Who's the client?'

'I don't know.'

'I'll ask Neil directly. We can have a chat.'

'Queens Park Rangers,' Keydel said. Belsey checked his face. He wasn't joking.

'I'm being scouted?'

'No.'

'Why are QPR interested in me?'

'It's their player – Jason Stanford.'

'He used to date Amber Knight.'

'That's right.'

'Jason Stanford's hired you to follow me?'

'It's his people. They want to know what's gone wrong.'

'What has gone wrong?'

'Everything.' Keydel exhaled, released the wheel.

'Come on, Stefan, give me some insight. It will make both our lives easier. Save me making that phone call.'

'He's had some kind of breakdown. No one knows.' Keydel didn't sound sympathetic. 'Money's missing.'

'How much?'

'A lot.' Keydel climbed back out, started trying to gather up his papers. 'You can get out now,' he said through the open passenger window.

'You haven't said why you're following me.'

'We're following everyone connected with him.'

'I'm not connected to him.'

'Sure.'

'Have you tried following Jason himself?'

'Other people are on him.'

'What have they found?'

'Nothing.'

'So your colleagues are about as good as you. When did Sisco get hired?'

'Last Thursday.'

That was something approaching good news.

'So you know Jason's movements over the weekend?'

'Not off the top of my head.'

Keydel walked back round with the papers. Slid back in.

'Has he been with Amber in that time?'

'I think so.'

'When? Where?'

'I don't know, mate. It's another lot on him. I just told you.'

'What kind of team's Neil running?'

'About fifteen on rotation: three tail teams, two photographers, data analysis back in the office.'

'And you're assigned to me?'

'I was asked to investigate you. To see how you connect.'

'Do you know whose flat I was in at Thames Village?'

'No.'

'He was called Ian Harper. I think he filmed something involving Amber Knight. Have you heard anything about a recording made over the weekend?'

'No.'

'Nothing about any tapes?'

'We have a tape – of Jason, not Amber. From Saturday.'

'Doing what?'

'Acting fucking weird. Near Great Portland Street.'

'Like what?'

'It's hard to explain.'

'You got a copy?'

'In the office.'

'I need to see it.'

The PI turned to Belsey.

'I've just had a kid, a son. I've bought a home.'

'Congratulations, Stefan. What are you saying? You're tired?'

'I can't afford to lose my job.'

'Few can. But mutual desperation's a wonderful thing. Is Sisco still based on Grosvenor Street?'

Keydel shut his eyes. Belsey got out.

'I'd like to see what you've got. The awkward way to achieve that is I walk into the office myself; much easier is if you get the tape and I wait around the corner.'

Keydel nodded.

'That's where I'm going, anyway,' Belsey said. 'If I were you I'd tail me.'

28

KEYDEL KEPT A FEW METRES behind, through rush-hour traffic, all
the way to his office. It was an impressive address just off Berkeley
Square, a Georgian block with a Porsche showroom on the ground
floor. A suited security guard watched the lobby. Belsey stopped on the
next corner. Keydel drew level, wound his window down.

'Do people at your office like Indian food?' Belsey asked.

'What?'

'Do they ever go for curries after work?'

'No.'

'There's a restaurant called Knights of the Raj, a couple of blocks
north of here, on South Molton Lane. Should be pretty empty. I'll meet
you there.'

'Give me twenty.'

'Take as long as you need.'

Belsey drove to the curry house and asked for a table at the back.
He was the only diner. The place was low-lit, white tablecloths, a
recording of a woman and a sitar. He ordered two beers, some
poppadums and a jalfrezi. He ignored the incessant calls from Andy
Price, possibly wanting his Bentley back. Keydel arrived fifteen minutes

later, carrying a bulging Waitrose bag. He sat down, glanced around, bemused.

The bag contained a laptop and the file on Jason Stanford. Its first few pages put the whole thing in context: Stanford had been bought from Newcastle on 3 August 2013. QPR had paid £4.2 million to Newcastle, £900,000 to Stanford's agent. Stanford was on £42,000 a week, rising to £60,000 the following season. The club had bought him a Bugatti and his parents a £2 million house in central London. Additional clauses included a £1.4 million bonus for European qualification. This was all followed by ten pages about image rights and commercial endorsements totalling another £2 million.

There was a copy of a report from the medical he had passed with flying colours. There were copies of the drink-driving conviction he picked up in October 2013, and the official statement from his agent released subsequently, which included references to anger management. He'd stayed clean enough from then on. He'd promised to put his troubles behind him. But he seemed to have put everything behind him.

A log of curiosities followed, prepared by the club's lawyers: Stanford not turning up for training, or turning up in body only. Extended periods out of contact. Not just out of contact with the club but with friends and family as well. Visits to addresses that didn't make sense – residential properties in poorer areas of London. Then Sisco Private Intelligence were hired, Thursday May 7. Neil Ferguson must have been eager to impress: he rustled up a fifteen-strong team to service this one lucrative client. Maybe he thought he'd found a potential niche in the market.

Concern over the possibility that Amber Knight was involved led to closer scrutiny of her life, which led to Belsey: 'Monday 11 May: Amber seen out with former police detective, Nick Belsey.' He could see how that might get people thinking. But this was the problem of such comprehensive surveillance: they'd got everything, except what was going on.

A fresh stack of poppadums arrived.

Belsey slid the food over. 'Help yourself.' He slid a beer over too. Then he flicked through photos of Jason Stanford's home life, his friends, his nights out. A lot of the material was taken off social media. Lazy. In photos Stanford looked content; he looked like a lad out on the town: fresh haircut, designer stubble, tattoos. Only difference was he carried with him a few million pounds' worth of accuracy in front of a goal. Or had done until this March.

'What's Neil's interpretation?' Belsey asked.

'He says Jason's probably got caught up in something. Big boys.'

'Like what?'

'Gangs. Betting. Like he was told to do something and fucked up. Now he's having to pay out money, either for some kind of protection or blackmail.' Keydel cracked a poppadum and scooped fragments into his mouth.

'You said you had a video of him.'

Keydel opened the laptop, loaded up a file, pressed play. It was grainy black-and-white footage from an off-licence's external security camera: 23.14, 9 May, junction of Great Portland Street and Cavendish Street. Stanford stood at the bottom of the shot. He wore a bathrobe of some kind: thin material, dark. He was barefoot.

He seemed to walk in slow motion. Up to the kerb.

'He's walking strangely.'

'It's like he's seeing things that aren't there.'

At 23.21 Stanford entered a convenience store. Someone approached him and he backed out. He spent a minute looking east across Cavendish Street. Watching for someone, or something.

'How did he get there in the first place?'

'We can't figure it out.'

After another five minutes he managed to cross, disappearing from shot towards north Euston.

'We found him two hours later, in a school playground near Euston station, totally naked.' Keydel took a swig of beer.

'And you managed to keep that out of the press?'

'Just. We found the robe half a mile away. It was wet. With salt water.'

Belsey put his drink down.

'Salt water?'

'You could smell it. And see where it had dried – there was white sediment.' Keydel saw Belsey's expression. 'What is it?'

'What did Jason say? About the water.'

'He said it was tears.'

The investigator's mouth twitched with the beginnings of a smile. 'Tears.'

'That's right. Go on. What do you know?'

'I just found a body in Epping Forest. A bloke called Ian Harper. He'd been drowned in salt water. So I'm curious about where all this salt water is coming from. Did you recognise the robe?'

'No.' Keydel shrugged, dipped poppadum into Belsey's jalfrezi. 'He'd been acting increasingly weird the last few days. We picked up a phone conversation with a friend where he says he wishes something wasn't a secret. Wishes he never knew it. That his life's not going to be the same again. That kind of stuff. Basically, he's losing it. Since then, he's just spending all his time playing games on his computer. Shut indoors, not really speaking to anyone. Like he's trying to shut stuff out.'

Belsey turned through the reports. The back of the file contained a somewhat dull and uninformative log of the gaming sites Stanford had been visiting. Belsey ripped them out. He turned back to the log of Stanford's movements, skimming for any mention of Mark Doughty,

Chloe Burlington, Ian Harper. Any Andreas Majorana. None of their names came up. He trawled the log again, slower this time. Four days ago, Saturday night, Stanford had turned up on Great Portland Street, half-dressed, covered in 'tears'. Friday night he was tailed to Finchley.

At 17.45 Stanford parked by Majestic Wine in Finchley. Then ran. Lost the operative tailing him on Ballards Lane.

A few hundred metres from the Comfort Hotel.

Belsey read it twice, to be sure, then drew Keydel's attention to the incident.

'Do you know about this?'

'Yeah.'

'What was he doing there?'

'We don't know.'

'Connected him to a place called the Comfort Hotel?'

'No.'

'You said Jason has lost a lot of money.'

'That's right. It's not clear where it's going. He's been withdrawing huge sums of cash every week over the last eighteen months or so. That's why Neil's got it pegged as gambling.'

Belsey turned back to the log of Stanford's movements.

'Amber was also at this hotel on Friday night. She's also haemorrhaging big money. I'd chase that angle. What's causing the cash outflow?'

Keydel nodded.

'Are you confident you weren't followed here?'

'Yes.'

'Would you check the street?'

Keydel shrugged, went outside. Belsey tore a selection of pages from the file. He folded them into his jacket.

'Nothing,' Keydel said, returning. Belsey put a twenty on the table, got to his feet.

'Give me your number. I'm going back to the hotel to see if I can find out what it was hosting on Friday. You concentrate on figuring out where the money's going. I'll give you two hours.'

He headed for the Bentley.

29

COMFORT. QUARTER TO NINE IN the evening. The leisure park had assumed an unexpected floodlit beauty. Darkness framed it like something precious. Beneath the lights, first dates ensued, peer groups laughed, nuclear families moved unhurriedly between the cinema and the dining options.

The hotel itself remained quiet. Habiba was on the front desk, accompanied by a boy with a shaving rash. Her smile faltered as Belsey approached.

'We spoke about Amber Knight,' Belsey said.

'Yes.'

'I think she was with other people that evening. A larger group. I wondered if you remembered them.'

Habiba frowned. 'Like a band?'

'Maybe. Or not quite like that. There was the man we saw the first time, checking in. But maybe another two men – a footballer, Jason Stanford, and a fourth man, possibly with a Slazenger tennis bag.'

'Jason Stanford?' the boy said.

Habiba shook her head. 'I didn't see that.'

'I need to recheck the security footage.'

'My manager's not here at the moment.'

Belsey walked behind the reception and opened the door to the back office. 'I spoke to him on the phone. He said it would be OK.'

He sat down in front of the security monitor, typed in the time and date for Friday evening, figured out how to split the screen between the reception's camera and the one above the entrance, facing the car park.

Harper's receipt – a whisky in the restaurant at 17.08. That was earlier than Amber or Mark's arrival. Belsey found the moment Harper entered, 17.01. He was recognisable from the family portrait, but a little heavier maybe. Head down, waxed jacket, jeans. Straight into the restaurant.

Carrying his sports bag.

Belsey wondered about the logic of the timing. Get there early to set up his kit, maybe; in time for a double whisky, calm the nerves.

Twenty minutes later, Mark Doughty, 17.21.

Belsey fast-forwarded through the pair of middle-aged men in suits who appeared between Mark and Amber's arrivals. Then he stopped. He wound back to them.

They didn't check in. Just walked straight to the lifts.

'Habiba.'

She stepped into the office.

'Recognise these guys?'

'No.'

He paused the footage. One tall, tieless, receding hair and a long, thin face. The other built like a rugby player, with ruddy features and small eyes.

Amber walked in less than two minutes after the suits, followed the same course to the lifts.

Now Belsey watched each new arrival.

A black Hyundai drove into shot, parked close to the hotel entrance. A man climbed out. He had light brown hair neatly combed, a raincoat over a grey suit. No luggage. He flicked a cigarette to the ground as he crossed to the entrance.

Straight to the lifts.

A yellow Aston Martin V8 drove in fast, parked askew. Chloe Burlington climbed out. She wore a trench coat, skinny white jeans, black ballet pumps. Expressionless. Hands in the pockets of her trench.

A couple emerged from a grey Peugeot 5008 people carrier. Belsey took a second to recognise them: the Shaws – Conor's parents. The back-up vehicle that had tracked Mark Doughty's Renault through the Essex night, on a mission to dump Harper's corpse and bring back the troops.

Over the next twelve minutes another sixteen individuals entered the Comfort Hotel. A significant number emerged from hi-spec cars: Mercedes, BMWs, SUVs. None carried luggage. Seven men, nine women. All arrived alone. Some entered via a side door into the restaurant before cutting through to the lifts and stairs. Jason Stanford used this route, pulling down the hood of a grey tracksuit top as he stepped into the lobby.

The one other thing they had in common: the arrivals didn't look comfortable being there. They walked fast. They ducked into the hotel as if escaping rain.

'Know what this is?' Belsey said. The hotel staff shook their heads. 'An event? A function of some kind?'

'We don't do anything like that.'

Belsey switched to footage of the reception area. Men and women gathered by the lifts, waiting to go up but not talking. No contact between them.

He tracked through on high speed. One hour, two hours.

At 20.02 they began to leave.

First out was a bespectacled young man, followed thirty seconds later by a very thin young woman with straight black hair, wearing a denim jacket and black leggings.

They left one by one, at intervals of thirty seconds. Belsey checked the women's hair. Not dishevelled. He checked the men's shirts and suit jackets. Two hours in a twenty-four-strong orgy should leave its marks. All looked fairly neat.

'Let me see the suite again,' he said.

They went back up. The room was unchanged. In total there was just enough space for twenty-four people to gather. If this was really where they wanted to be.

Two hours in here, Belsey thought. Something had occurred worth filming. Worth £750k. Amongst the complimentary bottles of Highland Spring and the dog-eared edition of *South East Tourism* magazine.

He opened the curtains, pushed the netting aside and peered through the double glazing down to the car park.

'Are there any cleaners still about?' he asked.

'I think they've just finished.'

'Could you see?'

Habiba disappeared. She returned with two women in jeans and coats. One clutched a purse; the older of the two held a pack of cigarettes and a lighter.

'I'm interested in the people here last Friday,' Belsey said. 'Do you remember? Quite a lot of people. They left around eight-thirty p.m. Did you clean it?'

'Yes.' The older one spoke.

'When? That night?'

'The morning.' Her English was limited but she understood him well enough.

'How was it? Was the room dirty?'

'No problem.'

'Clean?'

'Very clean. Very good.'

'Had the bed been used?'

The cleaner shrugged. She consulted her partner, who looked puzzled. 'Very clean,' she said, eventually.

'Rubbish in the bin?'

She shrugged again. Both cleaners glanced around the room, wondering what they'd missed.

'Do you think they cleaned the room themselves?'

'Maybe.'

'And the bed was made? Like this?'

'Yes.'

Belsey told them to talk amongst themselves. He stepped into the corridor, shut the door, listened to their voices. He wandered the landing, couldn't hear much. It wasn't soundproof though. He knocked and they let him back in.

'Was there anyone else staying up here?'

'I can check,' Habiba said and led him back down to reception. He went into the back office while she typed something at the main desk.

'No,' she said, walking into the office. 'Just them.' Belsey was connecting the CCTV monitor to the printer.

'Did the manager say that's OK?' Habiba asked.

'Graham said I'd be doing him a favour.'

What he had: twenty-four people but in varying degrees of anonymity. Of the thirteen cars that came into shot, eleven had licence plates that he could read. Fourteen of the faces hurrying past were in clear view of the camera. Seven he already knew: Amber, Mark, Harper, Chloe, Stanford, Conor's parents. The rest he wanted to know.

'Do cars using the car park need to register?'

'No.'

Which meant he was limited to the licence plates he could see on camera.

'What is this?' Habiba said.

'I have no idea. Tell Graham to call me if he's got any suggestions.'

Belsey stepped outside. He looked up towards the inscrutable orange curtains of the Finchley Suite. He crossed the car park to the 24-hour McDonald's.

Five minutes to ten p.m. It was quiet. Blank, immutable light, a homeless sleeper, a family with suitcases. He got a black coffee, took a seat in the corner and called Stefan Keydel.

'Can you talk?'

'Just about.' Keydel changed rooms. A door shut.

'Have you got anything yet?'

'I went through bank statements. I couldn't see anything. There's more I can look at in the morning.'

'How's Sisco's access to the DVLA database?'

'What do you want?'

'I'm going to give you eleven registration plates. They all connect to people who were with Jason Stanford at the Comfort Hotel on Friday evening. I need you to get me their details.'

'Eleven people?'

'Out of a total of twenty-four. These are just the ones I can get registrations for right now.'

'Doing what?'

'I'd really like to know. I'm thinking that if we establish who they are it might help us find out.'

Belsey gave him the information.

'Get everything you can, from dates of birth to points on the licence. Cross-check with the PNC and any other databases you can access.'

'The DVLA won't be open until eight.'

'The details will all be on the Police National Computer. I'm sure you can get access to that. And it's open all night.'

Keydel muffled a groan.

'Just call me as soon as you've got anything.'

Belsey finished his coffee facing the window, but couldn't see much beyond the reflected glare of the fast-food restaurant: a black smudge of car park, occasional headlights. What did he have? A group. A little crowded for a book club. A little heavy on the counter-surveillance. A group engaged in planning a crime of some kind, maybe. Is that what was filmed – a plot? Or a renegade meeting of AA, NA, some anonymous pain which only fellow sufferers could get you through. Was that a £750k revelation? He had never known an AA group meet in a hotel suite. But he'd never attended any with pop stars or premiership footballers.

A group takes co-ordination. Someone sent the invites out.

Someone organised the silence.

Someone called up and booked the Finchley Suite in advance.

Andreas Majorana. His card used for booking. He was the 'dad' coming up with Katja Dabrowska's rent money, whoever she was.

Belsey saw them all filing into the lifts one by one. Silent amongst themselves. It seemed an unnecessarily deep discretion.

The spread of arrival times, most in the ten minutes before six o'clock, suggested a group convening for a scheduled meeting. If it started at six then it lasted two hours exactly. Harper gets a recording worth £750k. Next day he takes it to Shaun White. Both killed within twenty-four hours.

Chloe's at the hotel. And that weekend Chloe panics.

Stanford's walking through Fitzrovia wet with 'tears'.

Mark Doughty's gone AWOL.

And at Loulou's, maybe Amber Knight's trying to stab her way out of a predicament.

Belsey looked again at the CCTV images he had. None carried luggage, but two individuals – a blonde woman in a long, padded jacket, and a man with glasses and a checked shirt – were carrying equipment of some kind. It was hard to see, as their bodies obscured it – a stick with two loops on the end, about the size of a ping-pong bat.

It looked familiar. Belsey stared at the shots for a minute before he realised where he'd seen it before. Katja Dabrowska's Facebook. *Feeling much better*. That picture, in the towel, in Chloe's bedroom: the same contraption was behind her on the bed.

He searched for the picture online. He found her Facebook page. The picture had been taken down.

Belsey sat back. The travelling family were getting up to leave, one child crying, gripping a portable games console. Belsey thought of Stanford. Shutting out the world, just playing his computer games. He looked through his pages from the Sisco file until he got to Stanford's Internet history – webpage details, wads of screen grabs. It wasn't the kind of gaming he'd expected. Not shoot-em-ups: brain teasers, puzzles, memory tests. Belsey took his phone out, tried one of the memory tests. It showed you twenty symbols, each above a number, then changed the order and asked you which number they'd originally been above. You had thirty seconds to do it.

Belsey got six.

'Do not expect to remember them all,' the test warned.

But Stanford did.

According to the screen grabs, out of ten exercises he got seven fully correct – twenty out of twenty – two more with just a single mistake, and on his final attempt he dropped three to get a score of seventeen.

There were similar exercises in perception, finding duplicates in a series. Stanford was getting incredible scores.

Most of the puzzles seemed to come from the same website. The URL came up repeatedly in Sisco's notes: www.advancelogin.com. It struck Belsey as an odd URL. He typed it into his phone's browser. The home page didn't mention puzzles. It showed a map of Europe. The continent appeared in luminous green against a black background, cross-hatched with lines of longitude and latitude, national borders marked. Orange dots illuminated select locations, several in Germany, a single dot in the Netherlands, three in France, a couple in Scandinavia. He searched the screen for tabs. No 'About'. No 'News' or 'Contact'. In the top right corner: 'Members Login'. He clicked and a box appeared asking for username and password.

It was tantalising and opaque. Belsey looked across the locations and paused on the Dutch dot. Northern Holland. Not Amsterdam.

He knew where, though.

He brought up the *Mail* story: 'Dutch Police Plea for Mystery Woman'. Found in Spier, north of Hoogeveen. That was his dot. Belsey found a map of Spier online. It was nothing special: a small village on the east side of a major motorway. There were two hotels marked, a restaurant and a campsite. Nothing else; few streets even. Only, half a kilometre away was a network of grey blocks, a facility marked 'Onderzoeksinstelling'. Belsey posted it into Translate. It came back as 'research institute'.

He pushed away the dregs of his coffee. The homeless man slept on. A few new customers ate steadily, leaning into their burger boxes.

He walked back to Price's Bentley and drove to Hampstead.

30

AS SOON AS HE WAS close to the station, Belsey saw that someone had been in. An upstairs window was open. He climbed the fence into the car park. The back door was ajar, his padlock lying on the ground.

Belsey listened at the threshold. No sounds or movements. He took a step inside, stepped cautiously through the darkness. The canteen was empty. His clothes hung down in the courtroom like bedraggled bunting. He continued silently up the stairs.

Things had been moved: the gas stove, bottles, his sleeping bag. He returned downstairs, checked the door they'd breached. The wood of the latch was splintered. There was nothing else he could fasten the padlock to, no alternative way of locking the door. And even if there had been he couldn't see himself getting another good night's sleep in the place.

He pulled a set of spare clothes down from the courtroom, packed his sleeping bag, the *Teach Yourself Spanish* book, took the half-bottle of rum that remained.

He drove north, checking the mirrors. There was no one following; roads empty. Past the East Heath car park, up to Whitestone Pond. He slowed as he reached Sandy Heath: marshy woods, birch and beech standing ghostly amidst the hollows. One access road for a private estate led away from the street lamps into seclusion. Belsey took it, pulled into the trees, killed his lights.

Looked at the map of Spier again. *Onderzoeksinstelling.* 'Research institute'. Nature of research unspecified. He looked at the CCTV screen grab, the contraption being carried into the hotel.

Only one person came to mind who might have an idea. Gordon Douglas was twenty-five years old with his own technology start-up doing something involving transport and artificial intelligence. At the age of nineteen he invented a fold-up satellite dish and made a lot of money off the military, some of which went on Amazonian psychedelics. That brought him to the attention of Hampstead constabulary, which brought him to the attention of Belsey. Douglas's studio flat was crowded with everything from old transistor radios to DIY virtual-reality headsets. Belsey had spent good times there. He made a call.

'Gordon, did I wake you?'

'No.'

'I've got a weird bit of kit you might be interested in. I'm going to send through a picture.'

'Sure.'

'If you've got any idea what it is I'd appreciate the insight.'

Belsey emailed the shot and waited. Tried Keydel. No answer. Left a message. Warm in bed with his wife, no doubt. Belsey stepped out of the car and breathed the night. A bird flapped, cawing into the branches above. He spent another few moments feeling the darkness, listening to nature, then returned to his car.

His phone rang twenty minutes later. Startled him.

'I wasn't sure,' Douglas said, 'so I woke up a doctor friend. She says it's a Transcranial Magnetic Stimulator.'

'What does that do?'

'What it says on the tin: stimulates the cranium, using magnetism.'

'Why would you want to do that?'

'A number of reasons. Maybe it helps with mental illnesses, depression. There's always research going on for that kind of thing.'

Transcranial Magnetic Stimulators. Belsey thanked him, put his seat back and watched the trees starting to appear from the gloom like a developing Polaroid.

At 5 a.m. he opened his eyes. More trees, still no call-back from Keydel. There was enough light to make him feel conspicuous. He drove back to Hampstead Lane and into town, not sure where he was going until he got to the Edgware Road, where he descended the ramp into the underground car park of the Grosvenor Hotel and walked up three flights to its 24-hour casino. Nowhere felt more secure than a casino. And it was low-key: free entry, coffee shop, smoking terrace, some big old poker tables and a room of fruit machines. Not a place you're ever going to feel underdressed or conspicuous.

It was quiet, fruities jingling softly. Belsey drank two large whisky sodas, played some slots. He had a conversation at the bar with a sweaty man who told him solemnly never to fall in love or invest in currency. A bit after seven he went and slept in a toilet cubicle.

His phone rang at 10.30. Belsey sat up, answered.

'I've got DVLA records for the vehicles,' Keydel said. Belsey took the pen from his jacket, found a receipt for this morning's drinks and turned it over.

'Go for it.'

'Are you saying these people were with Jason Stanford?'

'Yes.'

'Can I get that footage?'

'It's all at the hotel. Who are they?'

'One's Peter Blayney. He's a financier, has ties with the Confederation of British Industry, lives in Holland Park. That's the Aston Martin Rapide. The Ford Galaxy belongs to Addison Lee. We've got someone there getting us the account holder. The Toyota Corolla is hired from Europcar.'

'Europcar do airport hire.'

'Yeah, mostly. I'm checking on it. There's a couple of strange ones.'

'What do you mean?'

'Two vehicles connect to names of people reported missing.'

'Recently?'

'No, a few years ago.'

Belsey saw that strange, silent parade into the hotel again – it was becoming rapidly more sinister.

'Who?'

'The white Kia Sportswagon is owned by a Sajit Rajikumara. Twenty-three years old. If I'm right, then he's the Sajit Rajikumara reported missing in 2011. But the DVLA issued him a licence two years ago – same name and date of birth as the missing man.'

'Who else?'

'Juliet Turner, forty-six years old, from Bournemouth. She owns the L-reg Citroën Aura. Again, the name and date of birth match that of a woman reported missing five months after Sajit. Missing from Bournemouth.'

'Have you looked into their stories at all?'

'There are a couple of pieces online. Nothing recent. Juliet Turner walked out on her family. Sajit was at Merrill Lynch. There's no ongoing investigation into either of them.'

'What else?'

'I can send it all through. Nothing that stands out.'

Belsey gave his email address. 'Keep going,' he said. 'We need whoever's in charge. That's the jackpot. Cross-check with police lists, the electoral roll, HMRC. If you get any sniff of anything that might tell us what's going on call me. And try this name: Andreas Majorana.'

He dropped into King's Cross, to the tattered sanctuary of the Junction Hotel. There were few traces of its nocturnal misdemeanours in the late-morning dust. The manager gave Belsey a wink when he entered. Belsey went up to the first floor, showered in the gym, cleaned his head wound and changed into his spare set of clothes. Then he continued along the corridor to the business suite.

In reality, the suite was a former breakfast room with photographs of London buses on the walls, now hosting a glass-topped table, two PCs, an old printer and a set of phone directories.

That was enough.

He opened his emails. Keydel had sent through the list of vehicle owners. It was a strange collection. Two with particular edge.

Sajit Rajikumara, reported missing aged twenty-three. He'd made the news four years ago, though not extensively, which was telling. 'Concern mounts over gifted maths graduate last seen on way to work.' Described as polite, shy, obsessed with chess and cricket, Sajit had just started working at Merrill Lynch and, while he'd expressed some worry about settling into the environment, colleagues believed he would excel. He'd been living in Wapping at the time of his disappearance. His family were in Hounslow. They appealed to him directly in the press: 'Let us know you're safe.'

Reading between the lines, it suggested this hadn't come out of nowhere. There'd been some kind of disagreement, warning signs.

Juliet Turner, missing three and a half years, left a husband and two children. Only the *Bournemouth Reporter* saw this as newsworthy. Maybe because Juliet had had previous issues with drugs and mental health. There was 'concern' from her friends and family, but not enough to secure any more press coverage.

The disappearances had been logged, investigating officers assigned. Keydel had gathered information about the police involvement but it didn't amount to much. Going missing wasn't a crime. Files would have been opened as a matter of course. No one would have sweated over them. Belsey knew the sharp divergence in how missing people were dealt with. One call from the possible victim, a postcard or the suggestion of a ticket bought, and the distraught relatives were pointed towards life's small print: *Sometimes adults who go missing may wish for their location to remain anonymous, and they do have that right which we must respect.* As such, you can stop being missing without reappearing. Police couldn't do much for the estranged.

Belsey worked through the CCTV screen grabs. He managed to match seven faces to names, using a combination of Keydel's research and social media. The only thing they had in common was their randomness. Helen Woods, entering the hotel at 17.47. A Facebook page confirmed the identity, with a picture of Helen in a small, well-kept back garden with two dogs. She lived in Stroud Green, trained as a social worker, liked animals, good books and cake. There were forty photos of her life, none involving Amber Knight, Jason Stanford or the Comfort Hotel. Just behind her, parking a blue Volvo close to the hotel entrance, was Leon Brooks. A Dr Leon Brooks came up on the website for a dental surgery in Fulham. His photo matched the CCTV. Time of entry: 17.49. Neat brown beard, balding. Belsey printed out the screen shots and began putting pictures and personal details side by side. He got a computer programmer, a beautician and a tax accountant. He got an employee of the Retreat Boutique & Wellness Spa.

The connection gave him a moment's pause. The Marylebone spa Amber and Chloe had frequented, the ones who went tight-lipped when he'd turned up asking questions. It felt like the beginning of a thread that might lead to something that finally made sense.

Christopher Duval was on camera entering the Comfort Hotel at a brisk pace, 17.57: tall, closely cropped hair. Belsey looked up Duval and got his own page on the Retreat website with a list of services: personal trainer, massage therapy, nutrition.

Belsey called the Retreat. He recognised the manager's voice at once, the stern air hostess, sounding initially welcoming.

'Good morning, the Retreat. How can I help?'

'Is Christopher Duval there?'

'I'm afraid he's not in at the moment.'

'I wanted to book an appointment with him today.'

'He's had to call in sick.'

'Really?'

'Yes.'

'OK. I haven't trained with him before – can I just check: he's experienced, isn't he? How long has he been with you?'

'Christopher's been here since we opened.'

'Is it true he treated Amber Knight?'

There was a long pause. He could hear the water feature trickling in the background.

'You're the man who came in yesterday,' she said, finally.

'No – when exactly did Christopher Duval call in sick?'

She hung up.

He went back to his research. Vehicles and faces. He sensed two tiers of guests: the randoms, then those with weight, the ones who pulled up in the BMWs and SUVs, the hire cars. The Addison Lee vehicle was a lead that should generate a name without too much digging. Ditto the Europcar hire vehicle. He called Keydel and chased both.

'No luck yet,' Keydel said.

'Listen. Addison Lee will know who ordered that job. To open an Addison account you need to give bank details. They see a bank statement, proof of ID. You can do a lot of things with cash and PO boxes, but you can't open an Addison Lee account. So lean on them.'

'OK.'

'What about Europcar? Any more on that?'

'No. But the licence plates definitely have it belonging to Europcar. It's just we haven't got an in with them.'

'An in?'

'I'm thinking we might have to hack into their system or something. It will take a few hours.'

If you need a job doing . . .

Belsey found a number for Europcar and called.

'This is Detective Constable Nick Belsey. Got a Toyota Corolla here, registration GUV 47W, coming up as belonging to you.'

He heard typing. 'Yes, that's one of ours.'

'Bit of a situation here. The car's on Edgware Road. There's a child locked in the back.'

'Right?'

'Yeah, little chap been here a while, starting to look a bit hot and bothered. We can't find the driver anywhere. Have you got contact details?'

'We've got the car rented by a Ms Lindy Voskuil.'

Belsey asked her to spell out the name.

'Nationality?'

'Dutch.'

'Good. Great. Know where she's staying?'

'At the Park Grand in Kensington.'

'I'll take her mobile if you've got it.'

The girl gave it to him. 'Who *does* that?'

Belsey promised he'd have a word.

The number had a foreign prefix. No answer when he called. One prominent Lindy Voskuil came up online. Giving a talk in 2009 on 'The Future of Security Technology in Europe' for the Global Research Council. Its programme listed her as 'an employee of the Government of the Netherlands'. No department specified. He googled her name again, combining it with 'Government of the Netherlands'. Nothing else came up. But here she was, staying in expensive hotels well off the tourist track.

'Morning.'

One of the Junction's guests came in and sat at the other PC. He cast a curious eye over Belsey's research. Outside the window, the day was bright. Thursday. The computer screen said 13.15. Belsey gathered up his sheets and left the hotel.

He checked the street. No sign of anyone tailing him. He got a coffee and breakfast at a greasy spoon behind the old town hall, took a copy of the *Sun* from the adjacent table. News, courtesy of Damian Drummond's sister paper: 'Death of Star Publicist'. Shaun White had never gained himself so much free publicity: four pages of photos, eulogies and expressions of horror. The suggestion by an unnamed police source that his death could be linked to the Chloe Burlington murder was buried cautiously in the middle.

It had been a good couple of hours' work. Eleven of the twenty-four Comfort attendees identified. Belsey was curious as to what kind of explanation they'd come up with. Where to start? He looked through his notes again until he got to the Shaws and their people carrier. Definitely the tail vehicle going to Epping the night Harper's corpse was dumped in the woods. He thought about the trail that had led him to the Shaws in the first place – Amber's phone conversation: *She said it was Conor she was worried about.* Chloe's lawyer, the debonair Mr Strauss, thought he heard the boy's name in the background when Chloe called.

He'd start his enquiries with the Shaw household.

31

THE LIGHTS WERE ON AT 5 Tonbridge Drive. No radio playing. No movement visible.

No answer when he rang the bell.

He gave a knock on the front door and it creaked open. The Shaws' dog lay in the hallway with a Sainsbury's carrier bag over its head, rubber bands sealing the bag around its neck, flies circling above the corpse.

Belsey stepped over the dog.

'Hello?'

Toys sat neatly in the corner of the living room, brightly coloured books had their own shelf. A wooden chest sat open, empty, in the centre of the floor. Three bin bags had been stacked in the kitchen, next to the bin. Crockery gleamed in the drying rack. On the kitchen table were three sealed envelopes, two bunches of keys, a child's inhaler, packaging for three disposable barbeques. The envelopes were addressed: to 'Mum and Dad', 'Fiona', 'Mr Philip Shaw'.

Belsey checked the bin. No food packaging. Vegetarian cookbooks lined the kitchen shelves. The barbeques didn't make sense.

He took a set of keys from the table. There was a remote beeper for a garage.

When he went back outside a middle-aged woman was standing beside the garden gate, staring into the Shaws' hallway where the dog lay.

'Know John and Melissa?' Belsey asked.

'Yes. I – I live next door. Who are you?'

'When did you last see them?'

'Yesterday.'

'Where's their garage?'

She led him down a path between the two houses, to a row of lock-ups at the back.

He smelt the charcoal from outside.

'Go back to the front of the house,' he told the woman. When he was sure she'd fully retreated, Belsey covered his nose and mouth and raised the garage door.

Most of the smoke had dispersed. The people carrier sat in the tight, concrete space, two people leaning together on the back seats, as if they'd fallen asleep on a long journey and the driver had thought it best to get out and leave them there. He didn't risk opening the doors. The barbeques were on the front seats. Upholstery singed and the roof blackened.

No Conor.

Belsey returned to the house. Walked past the neighbour sitting on the garden wall. Gave her a grim smile.

'Just stay put, OK?'

He searched through the rooms until he heard whimpering in the bathroom.

Conor sat on the floor beside the bath, his breathing laboured. Belsey checked his pulse and air passages. He was dehydrated. Nothing more serious. Belsey took the boy downstairs, grabbed the inhaler from the kitchen table. Got out of the house.

He handed Conor into the care of the neighbour, gave her a look which she seemed to understand.

'No—' she said, managing to stop herself.

'Stay out here. Wait a minute, then call the police.'

'Where are you going?'

He returned to the living room, checked the empty chest: key in its lock, empty cardboard folders and plastic ring-binders around it, an unlabelled CD snapped in half.

He dashed back to the kitchen, tore open the bin liners and emptied a pile of ash onto the floor. A lot of paper had been burnt, along with what looked like an oxygen mask and heat-resistant silver clothing. This hadn't burnt so well. He found a couple of singed scraps of text caught up in the material, still legible. One contained a graph, headed 'Performance over Time'. The other seemed to be part of a cover sheet: 'For group-selected trainees embarked on Stage Three training only'. Belsey took the scraps, headed out past the neighbour.

'Have you called them? Call the police. And get an ambulance for the kid.'

He jumped into the Bentley, drove fast, east again, towards the centre of town. He stopped by Paddington station and tried to figure out what he'd got.

The graph. It plotted 'Signal Noise' against 'Threshold of Awareness'. That didn't tell him much. There were only a few words legible beneath the title of the cover sheet: '. . . the level of resolution with which we are able to view our surroundings. Knowledge is contingent on data . . .' Both items had been printed from a website. Across the top of the scraps was a familiar URL: www.advancelogin.com.

He brought up the website again. The map of Europe, the box asking for username and password. Behind that, he felt sure, was what he needed: names, places, a suggestion of who was in charge of whatever this was, and what Belsey could do to halt a run of premature deaths.

He thought through hackers he'd arrested. There weren't many. One now toured with a sound system, one had resettled in Berlin. Then there was Maya.

He called a mutual acquaintance, Dimitri Passadakis, an anarchist chef in Deptford.

'Is Maya in London?'

'Yeah. The Language Centre.'

'Still at Theobalds Road?'

'That's the one.'

Belsey kept an eye on the mirrors; the Hampstead break-in had him paranoid. That and the lack of sleep, the small matter of West End Central having a warrant on him – and Geoff McGovern on his case again.

He parked on Great Ormond Street, walked swiftly through the residential streets to the south, then turned off Theobalds Road into an alleyway filled with metal bins. It was closed at the far end by the back of the former language centre, a tall, narrow building that was boarded up now, boards covered with eviction notices, upper windows covered with tin foil, flags and a painted bedsheet: 'Gentrification is Class War'.

Belsey checked he was alone, then banged on the steel door. The bedsheet twitched. A first-floor window opened and a bearded man stuck his head out.

'I need to speak to Maya,' Belsey said.

A minute later the steel door opened and the same man admitted Belsey into a hallway filled with bicycles. The place smelt of hash and garlic and bike oil.

'Top floor,' he said.

Belsey continued past the old reception counter. A lot of people were sitting around a table of candles in a kitchen at the back. He went up to the third floor, stepping over drying laundry and camping equipment, knocked on the door of what used to be the administrative office and entered.

A reptile tank in the far corner gave the room its only light. Mandala wall hangings obscured the windows. Books on physics and computer programming were piled beside the wall. A desk supported two monitors. Belsey crouched beside the figure in the corner wrapped in a sleeping bag.

'Maya, it's Nick.'

She half opened her eyes. 'Am I under arrest?'

'I need a hand.'

'Want to climb in?'

He passed her one of the burnt sheets of paper, pointed at the URL.

'I need to get into this website. It's password protected.'

She glanced at the sheet, put it aside. 'What time is it?'

'Daytime. I'll make some coffee.'

Belsey gave her the second sheet and went downstairs. He fixed two instant coffees in the kitchen, declined the spliff, declined involvement in a debate over consensus democracy, put a fiver in the communal box and took the coffees upstairs.

Maya was sitting up when he returned, studying the scraps of paper more attentively. She'd found a hoodie and her glasses, put her hair up in a bun.

'What is this?' she said.

'That's what I want to find out. If you can get me into the site, we may be a step closer. Do you think you can do anything?'

'Yeah – I'll have a go.' Maya went over to her desk and turned her computer on. Belsey took a beanbag in the corner.

After ten minutes of playing around she said, 'OK. So this isn't particularly secure.'

'No?'

'No. Do you care if they know someone's attempted access?'

'I don't think so.'

'This will show up in traffic and log entries, though.'

'My priority is seeing what's there, who they are, what they're doing. It doesn't need to be subtle. Just work your magic.'

She spent another few minutes typing; ran a program that filled her screen with rapidly moving text. Belsey stared at the scraps again. 'For group-selected trainees embarked on Stage Three training only'; 'Performance over Time'. Performance of what?

After five minutes Maya said: 'I think we're in.' She sat back. The screen showed what looked like any desktop: rows of folders against a white background. Belsey took a seat beside her.

'You're a genius,' he said. But Maya looked unsettled.

'It really wasn't very well protected. Are these people big?'

'Why?'

'Because when something's that easy to hack, it sometimes means they're monitoring you. If it's a government site, or a bank.'

'I don't think it's either of those. What's there?'

Maya angled the screen towards him. There were tabs across the top of the screen, opening three separate pages with further files. The pages were titled 'Home', 'Research', 'Training'.

'It's a shared drive. There's a network of other groups and individuals who can access it remotely. We're in Group 9, apparently.'

'Of what?'

'The Bridge Foundation.' She pointed at the screen. Belsey saw the name in the directory heading. He thought of Chloe Burlington's final posting, a bridge over blue water. 'Heard of them?' he asked.

'No. You?'

'Not directly.' Belsey clicked a folder marked 'Introduction to Methodology'. A message appeared: 'Do not save on unencrypted software.' He closed the message and read on.

If you are reading this, you have been chosen to participate in ground-breaking research. Our work concerns the comparatively new area of bio-magnetic fields. Please familiarise yourself with the central tenets of our methodology.

Bio-magnetic fields are generated by the atoms of which we are made. These atoms date to the origin of the universe. All hydrogen atoms were produced in the big bang, while heavier atoms such as carbon and oxygen were forged in stars between 7bn and 12bn years ago. These atoms never touch. The closer they get to each other, the more repulsion there is between their electrical charges, causing them to vibrate. It is these vibrations that generate the magnetic fields with which we work.

He clicked on the 'Training' page. Eight audio files, twelve PDFs, titles ranging from 'Neuroplasticity and Genetics' to 'Precognition: Accessing the Future'. He opened a few at random. They seemed to be a mix of articles lifted from academic journals, some authored by the research committee of the Bridge Foundation, some papers by Professor A. Majorana himself. He was feeling the heat of it now; getting closer.

One caught his eye. It came from a US military base: Fort Meade, Maryland. 'Controlled Remote Viewing'.

'It's CIA research,' Maya said.

'Do you think it's authentic?'

'I don't see why not. They were doing a lot of pretty cranky stuff in the sixties and seventies, weren't they?' She read aloud: '"A channel exists whereby information about a remote image or location can be obtained by means of a developed perceptual modality. Current research identifies electromagnetic bio-fields as the likely conduit." Brilliant. They thought you could train people to go and spy on Soviet bases just using the power of the mind.'

'Did they manage?'

'What do you reckon. Listen to this: "As with all biological systems, the information channel will be initially imperfect, containing noise along with the signal. It may be that remote perceptual ability is widely distributed in the general population, but because the perception is generally below an individual level of awareness, it is repressed or not noticed." Right.' She clicked a sound file. Belsey crashed back on the beanbag and listened. Nothing happened. Maya turned her speakers up. The room filled with a droning sound. She tried another track and it appeared to be identical.

'Nothing livelier?' Belsey said.

'It's binaural beats. You're meant to listen to them on headphones so you get a slightly different tone in each ear. It produces a third frequency inside your mind which influences brainwaves, takes you down to low-delta brain frequencies.'

'Sounds fun.'

'According to this, if we hit the right frequency we can start increasing our cognitive ability.'

'To the extent that we can see things remotely.'

'Exactly. Want to try?'

'I want some proper information: names, places, money. Something slightly more bound to reality.'

Maya went quiet for a while, kept clicking. Until she hit something.

'There's a protected area.'

Belsey got up and came over. The folder was entitled 'Level Three Only'.

'It asks for another authorisation code,' Maya said. 'I can give it a try. But it will take a bit.'

Belsey printed a selection of documents to read while she worked. These came from a folder called 'Timeline' and lent the group a more political edge. They involved report after report on deforestation, climate change, disease. He was on his third article about the global population crisis when Maya gave a whoop.

'Here's your proper information,' she said. The screen was filled with files carrying individuals' names and dates of birth. She opened a couple. Each contained what looked like results from a full medical: BMI, cardio, eyesight, speed-of-response tests.

'Who exactly are these people?'

Belsey took the mouse and scrolled down to the end of the members' personal files, to a folder entitled 'Guide Materials for Advanced Trainees'. This contained an eye-catching selection of papers: 'Mission Preparation and Pre-Launch Operations', 'Sleep-Wake Cycles and Light Exposure During Spaceflight', 'Neurocognitive Performance in Microgravity'. Maya gave a low whistle.

Belsey opened a document on Space Motion Sickness. 'Space Motion Sickness is an event that can occur within minutes of being in changing gravity environments. These range from 1g on Earth to more than 3g during launch, and then from microgravity in space to hypergravity during re-entry.'

'Space cadets,' Maya said.

'So it seems.'

A final folder contained wave-form graphs. They looked like more cardio readings, EVG graphs, but no subjects named this time.

'What is that?' Belsey asked. Maya squinted at the screen.

She took the mouse and started clicking through. Page after page of what looked like heat maps, abstract shapes with red cores, pixellating out through yellow and green to blue and then black. 'This is astronomical research. Spectroscopic data,' she said. 'Measurements of, like, stars and galaxies.' She clicked back to the homepage, the map of Europe, tapped the screen. 'I bet you these orange dots are all locations of radio telescopes.'

'Really?'

'Just wait. I'm a geek for this.'

She went online, brought up another webpage.

'This is all LOFAR data,' Maya said. 'The Low-Frequency Array for radio astronomy. It's a network of radio telescopes, thousands of antennae all linked.'

'Go back to the map.'

Maya clicked back.

'See this. It's a research centre near Spier, in Holland.' Belsey pointed to the location. 'Is that on the network?'

Maya brought the LOFAR window back up. Spent a minute searching.

'Got it. That's ASTRON. The Netherlands Institute for Radio Astronomy. But these telescopes, they're a completely different thing to your Bridge Foundation. It's not about physically getting people into space. It's stargazing.'

Now Belsey clicked back, through the Level Three materials on space travel to the 'Timeline' page, with its reading list for a sick planet. It was starting to make sense.

'They're not really training astronauts, are they?' Maya asked.

'No. I don't think so.'

'Is it a joke?'

'I don't think it's a joke, exactly. What's eclosis?'

'What?'

'There's a folder there named "Eclosis".'

'No idea.'

'Useless.'

He opened a new window, ran a search. Eclosis was the process by which a butterfly emerged from a chrysalis.

'Great,' Maya said. 'Now we know.'

Belsey closed the window and opened the file. It contained a countdown timer, currently at 29 hours, 55 minutes. It clicked down to 54 minutes as they watched.

'That's weird,' Maya said. She took the mouse and returned to the main page. Her face fell. 'Someone knows we're in.'

She lifted her hands off the keyboard. Files were disappearing, being deleted before their eyes.

'Save what you can,' Belsey said.

She put a USB in the hard drive and copied the last few files as the Bridge Foundation sunk back into secrecy.

32

THEY MANAGED TO SAVE TWELVE documents. Belsey took the flash drive, promised Maya a place on the first shuttle out of here and returned to his car. The afternoon was greying into evening. He waited for sirens to pass, then drove north to Eversholt Street, spent twenty quid printing sheets off the USB at an internet café in Mornington Crescent and took them to a pool hall at the junction with Hampstead Road. It was owned by the same Kurdish gang as the rest of the bars nearby, all part of one money-laundering operation. Which suited Belsey fine right now. They knew him; they weren't going to be answering the door to any other police too quickly.

He climbed the stairs, got a steroid-enhanced hug from Afran, the manager, asked for a table at the back. The light came on over the furthest table. Belsey kept the cover on, spread the notes. He separated the sheets into piles and tried to figure out what he was up against.

He started with a directory: 'For group contact only'. It listed fifteen groups in ten countries: seven in Europe, then India, Australia and Russia. Individual membership lists within the groups were anonymised, only initials given. There were fifty or so per group. Phone numbers were listed, as were professions; they included lawyers, journalists, government officials.

Each group had a director, sitting on top of a hierarchy of management. Budgets were listed, along with holdings running into the millions, mostly involving land and property. It all looked worldly enough. But then he looked at Majorana's papers again. They hit a different note entirely.

What we commonly call depression is the felt pressure and weight of our own unactualised life potentials. As trainees, we do not deny the experience but let it press us down into ourselves and help us reach our own deeper fields.

To reduce essential pain to evident pain is to deny the essential nature of this planet: that it is a world of essential pain, a world that has constantly to disguise itself as a realm of opportunities for the purchase of temporary pleasure.

As pain in an individual signifies new understanding, so there is pain that accompanies a new epoch. We live amongst it.

Be in this world but not of it.

His other lectures to devotees included: 'On Tertiary Evolution', 'Beyond Psychological Time', 'How the Vanguard Prepare'. The vanguard prepared by developing their control of 'the bio-magnetic fields'. This was a knowledge passed between several ancient civilisations, encrypted in their writings but lost in modern times. 'Bio-magnetic fields' allowed an individual to reconnect with the universe, transcending limitations of time and space to explore other dimensions. These fields could also be used to assess the health of one's personal energy store. Bridge recruits were expected to purify themselves of Earth's negativity so that, wherever they settled next, it would be uncontaminated. Which was a nice idea.

So far, the Foundation had discovered five consecutive 'fields'. There was the physical one; then the 'Emotional Body' – the layer dealing with emotional responses such as love, hatred, envy, loneliness. The third field was the 'Mental Body', where all our memories and belief patterns could be found. These were stored as small crystalline energy forms, observable psychically. They revealed the hidden personality traits of an individual. 'It is through regaining control of the third layer that we can learn to broadcast a powerful magnetic energy signature to others.'

'Magnetic energy' rang a bell. Belsey took his phone out, opened the browser, typed: 'Positively Happy Survey. What's stopping you living the life you want to lead?' It appeared right away: the test Amber and Mark had both been so interested in: 'Find out how to become the most attractive version of yourself and be magnetic in personal and business relationships. Are you amongst the 3 per cent of the population with a High-Receptive Personality?'

Belsey thought it was time he found out. The site informed him that the test took 'no more than twelve minutes' to complete. 'Answer honestly.' It gave him a list of statements and told him to mark them on a scale of 1 to 5 according to how much he agreed:

You don't usually initiate conversations.
You feel a constant need for something new.
Your dreams tend to be vivid.
In groups and parties you place yourself nearer to the side than in the centre of a room.

It got deeper:

You sometimes stand close to a person and begin to feel anxious for no reason.

You see images, faces or objects in your mind's eye and don't know
   what it means.
You have put your hands on someone to help ease pain.

Belsey graded all thirty statements. It asked for his email address
to receive results. He gave the anonymous address he used for porn
sites, clicked send. A minute later he checked his inbox. An email had
come through from amajorana@thebridgefoundation.org.uk:
'Congratulations! You are in the top 3 per cent of respondents to this
survey. As data is sensitive we must ask you to conduct the subsequent
process in confidence. If you are interested in undergoing the next
steps towards self-transformation please reply "Yes" to this email
address.'

Belsey replied 'Yes.'

An auto-response pinged back: 'Thank you for your interest in
this ground-breaking experiment.' Attached was a non-disclosure
and confidentiality agreement asking for his electronic signature.
'This agreement is made on the date of the last signature below,
between i) The Bridge Foundation, 8 Avenue du Mervelet, Geneva;
ii) Nick Belsey (please confirm if details are correct).' The Bridge
Foundation address didn't exist: there was no 8 Avenue du Mervelet
in Geneva. Belsey confirmed his details were correct and sent it back.
It was only when he'd clicked send that he realised he'd never given
them his name.

He took a beer, watched the islands of baize across the pool hall.
Read on, learnt about the final two 'fields'.

What we term the Spiritual Body is the fourth layer of our
bio-magnetic field, which is like a giant storehouse of information
regarding our past, present and future deeds.

The fifth layer is our Astral Body, the form in which we overcome the last terrestrial boundaries. As we progress beyond self we dispose of emotions such as guilt and self-doubt in order to discover new sources of power. Centuries of religion and politics have encouraged us to retreat into the smallest forms of ourselves. We shelter inside a familiar shell of identity. This is easy, even if it causes us pain. Energy rebounds, causing mental and physical illness, inhibiting our power to transform.

If you want success, harness the energy of the future. Become a chrysalis, as Earth itself is a chrysalis in which the future is being born.

A chrysalis.

Belsey took Chloe Burlington's necklace from his pocket, held the glass pendant up to the light. That was what it was: a chrysalis. Like an elongated acorn, but not quite symmetrical. He saw the very faint lip a third of the way down where it began to gently taper. He admired the craftsmanship, wondered who was producing them. Did this Majorana get a job lot? Someone in China knocking them out on demand? Did you receive it when you signed up, a free gift – or were you given it at a graduation ceremony? He put it back in his pocket, stepped out to the fire escape.

The evening was mild. He lit a cigarette and looked at the street below. Three teenagers hung out beside the bus stop, hoods up, bikes aslant. Two homeless men sat on the shelter's bench, pooling their small change, peering into each other's hands like they were comparing collections of something exquisite. Then the windows of the three tower blocks by Hampstead Road, gaining visibility against the evening sky. Boxes, stacked. A neat, modular storage system for oddly shaped lives.

Lonely lives. As police you see inside the homes no one else sees. You see what isolation means. You start to understand the power of company. Nocturnal London was a city of hidden congregations, refusing to feel ashamed. Of pubs like the Crown in which Borough CID crammed itself, men sinking their guilt into a communal pool. Other groups praying together or trying to stay sober; gambling or trying not to gamble. Turning their backs to the world. Warming themselves off shared secrets.

In the third layer of the bio-magnetic field we store our experiences, memories and belief patterns, crystalline energy forms which can be observed psychically . . .

Belsey saw the Crown. Hard to leave a group. Hard to step away, as the distance between identities stretches. Your old life on one side, the truth on the other. Every group's a trap. It happened with police. Old friends grew distant, you found yourself cutting ties, seeking out the company of those who'd understand. You sunk yourself in – into the most faithless cult around – curious about where it led. Then part of you was owned. That was the problem. The Bridge Foundation didn't quite get it. Your truth wasn't written in the cosmos, it was in the memories of the bastards you were drinking with when you thought you could get away with anything.

Everything's going to come out about Borough . . . Only you're so fucked yourself he thinks he can shut you down.

Sometimes it's not the obvious moments that get caught in memory. The incident that came to mind most often wasn't the messy end of Borough CID or one of the interminable benders with tabloid hacks and various exotic hangers-on, but a more routine night somewhere in between. He and McGovern, first at the scene of a road traffic accident on their way back from interviewing the owner of a string of brothels. Saturday night, all other police elsewhere, the two of them kneeling in the centre of the Old Kent Road, scooping teeth out of a woman's mouth so they could perform CPR. He remembered spitting her blood onto the tarmac as they took turns. It was twenty minutes before an ambulance arrived. She died. They went home. McGovern had just separated from his wife and was trying hard, for once, to stay dry. Belsey got home and thought of McGovern returning with the same taste in his mouth. He hadn't answered his phone when it rang. He thought: that's Geoff, and he didn't answer. He couldn't imagine what conversation they'd have.

There were other moments that challenged the story he usually told himself. Heart-to-hearts, lock-ins; their first drink together, when he retained some awe, and it took six pints for McGovern to try explaining something, and Belsey realised he was saying: Get out of Borough – don't stick around, it's rotten and it will suck you in. And he'd been offended by that, as if his tenacity was being questioned.

He finished his cigarette, went inside and looked at his CCTV print-outs of the individuals who'd attended the Comfort Hotel, the information he had on their inconspicuous, terrestrial lives. He stared at Mark Doughty – his ponytail and shades. *He's hiding.* That was how Maureen Doughty had put it, her last conversation with her son. He remembered Mark's voice on the phone. Someone trying hard not to sound scared. Somebody stuck in something; some kind of situation where they wanted out?

Belsey thought of the injuries on the Spier woman's hands. The *Mail* article. Trying to scale a fence? Maybe succeeding. Getting out. Lost, disorientated. Hard to leave a group; hard for it to end in a civilised fashion. Chloe – Chloe didn't get the opportunity to walk away. Did Katja? Belsey was trying to see in; but there were others, surely, trying to see a way out.

He went to the counter with a fiver in his hand.

'I need to use your computer for ten minutes.'

Afran took his money, said: 'No porn, no jihad.' Told him to keep an eye on the place and went out for a smoke. Belsey sat behind the desk and typed in 'free website'. He clicked the first result that came up, 'Your own website. Live online in minutes', and keyed his details in.

It asked him to choose his domain name. He typed in 'bridge9survivors'. It was available.

By 8.45 he was the proud owner of bridge9survivors.webspot. com. He chose a white background. Found a picture of a chrysalis. Across the top of the page he wrote: 'Others have escaped. Talk in confidence.'

He opened another window and set up a new email address, made it prominent across the top and bottom of each page, along with his mobile number. He typed: 'Any information, please call or email.' Then he added: 'We can help.' He didn't feel entirely confident about that. He added some references to magnetic fields, Group 9, radio telescopes, clicked 'publish' and went live. Then he sent a link to every Comfort attendee for whom he could find an email address or social-media page.

No sign of Afran. Belsey helped himself to a beer, switched the big screens on and watched highlights of a rugby match between England and Italy. He kept an eye on his phone. Afran returned and he paid for the beer, got one more. He ordered a pizza from the delivery place next door and, when it arrived, ate in front of the TV screen. He watched France vs Ireland. A couple of teenagers in caps came in and shot a few frames. At 10.45 an unknown number called, hung up as soon as he answered.

At 11.30 he got an anonymous text that said: 'Sleep tight.' Belsey tried calling the number; his call was rejected. When it got to midnight he put a tenner into Afran's oversized fist and went down to his car.

33

BELSEY DROVE INTO THE CITY. He parked around the side of Waterloo station and fell asleep on the back seat. He achieved several hours' blissful unconsciousness, woke at 9.20 a.m., shivering, phone ringing.

'Hello?' a man said, uncertainly.

'Hello.'

'Who is this?'

'My name's Nick Belsey.'

'The website . . .' He was hushed but well spoken.

'Yes.'

'Do you know where Thomas is?'

'Who's Thomas?'

'My son.'

Belsey paused. No Thomas on the list of Comfort attendees.

'I don't know where he is. But I may have information related to his whereabouts. I can't guarantee that. Tell me his story.'

'Are you part of it?'

'The organisation? No. I want to help people who've been part of it. I have concerns about the organisation. I work for the police. What happened to your son?'

'He broke off all contact.'

'When?'

'Two years ago.'

'And what made you call exactly?'

'Can you come round?' the man said. 'I'd rather not speak over the phone.'

He gave Belsey an address in Highbury, close to the Emirates Stadium. The door was answered by a tall man with thinning white hair. He wore a jumper with a hole in the shoulder.

'Come in.'

He let Belsey into a hallway filled with books, introduced himself as Jim Arnett, didn't offer a handshake.

'Have you also lost someone?' he asked.

'Not exactly. How did you see the website?' Belsey asked.

'Because of this.'

He led Belsey through to a study. A silver MacBook on the roll-top desk gleamed amongst old furniture, sagging bookcases and a Persian rug.

'This is where you showed up.'

The screen showed three windows: in-boxes filled with alerts on keywords: 'bridge', 'Group 9', 'Majorana', 'evolution'.

'These were all terms we found in papers in his room. In emails and websites he'd been looking at.'

'Was he living here at the time?'

'Yes. We thought he should. For his first year. He was at university. Imperial.'

'Can I see his room?'

There was a second of what appeared to be hesitation, then he led Belsey upstairs, opened the door to his son's room and stepped back. The room was tidy, with a music stand set up, a violin case on the floor, maths books, school prizes. It felt like a museum reconstruction. A can of shaving gel had rusted beside the sink. The duvet cover had a Ferrari on it. But the detail that drew the eye, lending something quietly horrific to the scene, was a figure drawn onto the wallpaper above the bed. It was the crude figure of a man. The figure had large eyes with no pupils. One of its arms was raised. Around the head was what looked like a halo or helmet.

The father cleared his throat. 'It appeared a week or so before Thomas disappeared. I've done some research. The image is taken from rock carvings in Peru. Three thousand years old or thereabouts. I don't know what it's doing there.'

Belsey walked into the room. The image had been outlined in pencil first: you could still make out some of the preparatory drawing. The ink looked like biro.

'Do you know if Thomas drew it himself?'

'He must have done. No one had visited him. He was in here alone often enough. We didn't like to disturb him.'

A book sat on top of a pile of papers on the floor. A black, leather-bound diary – identical to the one he'd seen splayed face down on Amber's couch the night she attacked him. The one in which Amber was recording the truth about things. Belsey picked it up. Inside, the title page announced 'The Lost Light: Two Lectures by Prof A. Majorana'. The paper was thin, text printed in narrow lines.

Chemically all life processes are a burning. Oxidation is a slower burning, as in rust. Decomposition is a burning. Hence all energic activity amongst the elements of life is thought of as the work of fire. Man's whole life is cast in the midst of fire. And so Egypt described the world as the lake of fire, or again, 'the crucible of the great house of flame'.

'It was amongst his university notes,' the father said. 'There are loose papers as well. Written by the same man.' He indicated the pile the diary had been sitting on. 'Odd lectures. That kind of thing.'

'When exactly did Thomas go missing?' Belsey asked.

'Twenty-fifth of February that year. 2013.'

'Any word from him since then?'

'He called a month later. He said he was well. He wouldn't tell us where he was. The number was blocked so we don't even know where he was calling from.'

'How did he sound?'

'He sounded OK. But not entirely himself. His voice seemed *older*. Then, on Monday, we got a call. That was the first time in two years. We were out. We missed it.'

The man didn't visibly express his anguish.

'Did he leave a message?'

'Yes. He said not to worry.'

'Not to worry about what?'

'That was all he said. "It's me. Don't worry. Everything is OK." Seven words.'

'And no idea where the call came from.'

'No.'

Belsey went over to a photo display frame by the bed, a glass box with prints jumbled together.

'This is him,' he said.

'Yes.'

Thomas looked awkward in all the photos: amongst friends, amongst family. Angular, in glasses, with the same long, thin face as his father.

'How old was he when he went missing?'

'Nineteen.'

Nineteen in February 2013. Belsey thought through the faces on CCTV, allowed for the time that had passed. He wasn't one of the attendees for whom Belsey had a clear shot. Possibly one of the others.

'Can I take the notes and book?' Belsey asked.

'If they help you find him. Will we be able to have them back when you're finished?'

'Of course.'

They went downstairs to the living room.

'Do you have any idea how he became involved with the group?' Belsey asked.

'No. We've tried to find out. The university hasn't been able to discover anything. He had become slightly uncommunicative. We thought it was a good thing, maybe. He was doing brilliantly on his course, no problems there. As we expected. He'd never been in any kind of trouble. We'd thought he might take a while settling into university life, making friends . . .'

'How long was he at Imperial before he disappeared?'

'Five months.'

'And he seemed OK.'

'He seemed better than ever. Top grades, fencing team, orchestra. Even seeing a girl. Everything was tip-top. Then he vanishes, middle of the night. Doesn't even take his wallet.'

'Any suggestion he might have been forced in any way?'

'None at all.'

'What did the police say?'

'Not much. There wasn't a great deal they could do, apparently.'

'Not easy for you.'

'No.'

'You said you didn't want to talk over the phone.'

He nodded.

'Why was that?'

'Just . . . caution, I suppose.'

'What's made you think you need to be cautious?'

'Nothing really. Well, just one thing.' He hesitated again; glanced at Belsey to make one final assessment. 'In the first week or so I thought there might be people watching us.'

'In what way?'

'There were two cars in particular, that I saw parked across the street four or five times. With someone in them. Sometimes two people. As if they were taking turns to watch the house. This could be a total overreaction on my part.'

'I'm not sure it is. Were Imperial aware of other students who may have been involved?'

'No.'

'Did the girl he was seeing notice he'd changed?'

'To some extent. She said he'd been seeing her less. She had concerns, but she didn't know what was happening.'

'Do you have a number for her?'

He went to a chest of drawers at the side of the living room. 'This was in his desk.' He produced a square piece of card with 'Josie' written on the back in a young woman's handwriting, a heart, then the number for a landline in south-east London. On the front was a picture of a chrysalis.

34

BELSEY PROMISED JIM ARNETT HE'D be in touch as soon as he found anything out. He took the notes, sat in his car at the side of the Holloway Road. Studied the card. It was an extraordinary photograph, close up. You could see the black stalk at the top of the chrysalis, by which it hung from the stem of a plant, the veins of a wing within the translucent green wrap, pressing against the outer skin. He turned it over, called Josie's number. The line was disconnected.

Belsey looked at the notes. No contact from Thomas in two years. Then a call on Monday. *He said not to worry.* Which meant there was something to worry about.

He skimmed the notes for any suggestion as to what it might be. He hit this:

To advanced recruits:
   Trainees who have successfully completed the initial stages must prepare themselves for the psychological demands ahead. Those granted access to the past and future will inevitably undergo exile from the present. Be patient and guard your new knowledge. Do not expect the uninitiated to accompany you on

this journey. Man's collective reality is an expression of fear, and no fear is greater than that of advancing beyond the terrestrial.

Life does not necessitate acceptance of the human condition. Humanity is a stepping stone. Our vow, as vanguard, is to conquer new potentialities before they can be exploited by the forces of greed. The time is coming when Earth may lose, once and for all, the possibility of fulfilling its role in the universe. Civilisations have risen and disappeared, each advancing man's knowledge of the journey ahead. Yet none have displayed a level of self-destruction such as ours.

Belsey looked at the chrysalis picture again. Josie Christie. Not a unique name, but unusual enough. He googled it and found three Josie Christies currently in the London area, one a retired headmistress, one a twelve-year-old. The third worked for a PR firm called Kingsley Mackintosh Promotions. It was accompanied by a brief biog, which had her graduating from Imperial in 2011.

There was a picture of her on the firm's website: quite glamorous, long, wavy brown hair, bright smile, in her late twenties. Belsey called the company. They said she was on maternity leave. He said he wanted to send a present for the baby and the idiots gave him her home address.

Crouch Hill. Identical detached homes arranged in clusters of four to marginally offset the effect of an assembly line. The front gardens gave each occupant the opportunity for self-expression but few had ventured beyond a bird bath or some rhododendrons. Clean bricks, double-glazing. Christie's home had an empty driveway. A woman answered.

'Josie?'

'Yes.' She was pretty, a little pale with maternity. Glad of distraction.

'I need to talk to you. About Thomas Arnett. About the Bridge.' Her face fell. Belsey showed her the chrysalis card. She stared at it, at Belsey, then her eyes flicked to the road behind him.

'Who are you?'

'Someone who's concerned.'

'I'm not part of it any more. I've got nothing to do with them.'

'Then you're free to talk.'

'I can't.'

'Yes you can.'

'My husband will be back in a few minutes.'

'Then you better talk fast.' Belsey stepped past her, into a silent house. Nicely done up, slight smell of baby wipes. Josie looked around, uncertain how to manage this visit. She led him into the living room, didn't put the lights on. She picked up a few stray toys, moved a blanket from a sofa for him, perched on the second sofa. She had a view of the road in front. Daylight hit the side of her face. She wrapped herself in her cardigan, checked the clock on the DVD player.

'Why do you want to know about them?'

'All sorts of reasons. You've left?'

'Yes.'

'Why?'

'Well, it was a part of my life before I met Lawrence. Look, he never knew about any of it. I was in a bad place, now I'm in a good place.'

'How long were you involved?'

'Three years or so.'

'Did you know Chloe Burlington, Ian Harper—'

She raised a hand. 'We didn't use names. I can't talk about that.'

Belsey checked his impatience. She didn't want to look at him.

'Why is it called the Bridge?'

'Because it is – a bridge.' She blushed. Finally she fixed her eyes on him. 'For man. For humanity. That's the idea.'

'Who runs it?'

'Andreas Majorana. He's the founder. He founded all the groups.'

'Where are the other groups?'

'Abroad.'

'Abroad?'

'I think so.'

'Describe him.'

'I can't describe him in words. Not simply. He was an incredibly kind, patient man.'

'Was he white?'

'Yes.'

'Was he European?'

'I don't know. Not English, I don't think. But he didn't have a strong accent.'

'How old, approximately? Older than me? Younger than me?'

'About the same.'

'Do you know whereabouts he lived?'

'No.'

'Where is the group based?'

'Based?'

'Its offices, anything like that.'

'I don't know.'

'But you met.'

'We met all over. People's houses, centres with rooms they hired, or had loaned to them.'

'Give me an address. Any address.'

'I can't remember. It all feels so long ago.'

'This is going to take some time, isn't it. Maybe Lawrence can help speed things up. When he's back.'

Her face contorted. 'OK. There was one off Essex Road, a community centre. That's all I can remember. We met there a few times. I mean, it was the most frequent one.'

'How did you get involved?'

She hesitated, took a breath.

'I have epilepsy. I've had it since I was a teenager. It was becoming worse, with more frequent seizures. I was feeling very low. A friend had gone to a few sessions and she said it helped her with her emotions. Her skin had improved and she was generally feeling happier. Someone had come up to her in a café and invited her to a meeting, that was how she got involved. It was Andreas. She'd been crying. She'd just broken up with her boyfriend. He came up and spoke to her. Anyway, she said it was great, and I should try it. So I went.'

'What happened in the meeting?'

'We talked. We were all new. We talked about how we'd ended up there. Then Andreas spoke. He explained the importance of the journey we were beginning, that we had been chosen for a task. He said we could leave if we wanted, if we didn't want the responsibility. Our hearts would tell us if it was right.' She looked startled as she said this, as if experiencing the whole thing for the first time.

'Why didn't you leave?'

'Because of him.'

'Andreas.'

'Yes.'

'Is that his real name?'

'I don't know.'

Belsey was holding the Comfort CCTV stills. He spread them across the coffee table.

'Any of these him?'

She glanced, reluctantly. Shrugged. 'No.'

'Anyone else in the hierarchy that you can see here?'

'There was no hierarchy.'

Belsey sighed pointedly, gathered the pictures up.

'Give me something, Josie. Tell me about Andreas. Come on. Who is he? What's his background?'

'I . . . He'd had a terrible life, I think. He told us that he grew up around a lot of alcoholism, abuse, poverty. He started having visions of places and people. Later, when he was in the army, they tested him because they thought they could use his skills, but he ran away. He hated war, didn't want anything to do with it. So he spent years wandering and slowly met others who'd had contact with the secret, or who he could introduce to it, who were receptive. These people decided to work together.'

'Doing what?'

'Establishing the Foundation. Recruiting others, devising a system by which they could operate and grow without being harassed or exploited.'

'Did he ever ask you to break the law in any way?'

'No.' She looked offended.

'Are you aware of him having any relationships with people from the group?'

'It wasn't like that.'

'Are you sure?'

'Yes.'

'What about kids: were they involved?'

'Yes. There were kids.'

'That never struck you as odd?'

'People take their kids to church, don't they? To Sunday School. This was like school, an education. Because it's about developing abilities, you see. It's good to start young. Children have an unadulterated energy.'

'How many kids were you aware of?'

'Four or five in our group.'

'What ages?'

'All ages. It's not important.'

'What were their names?'

'I don't know. We didn't use names.'

'Last Friday, twenty-four people from the group met at the Comfort Hotel. What would that be about?'

'A meeting perhaps. A discussion, check-ups. News from other groups.'

'These other groups – the ones from abroad?'

Josie nodded.

'How many people are involved in the Bridge?'

'Several thousand, across the world.'

'Ever meet other groups?'

'No.'

'How many in your group, though?'

'Around thirty people.'

'And only Andreas told you about these other groups? The network. You'd never seen them.'

'No.'

'Josie, I think they're planning something that may lead to loss of life. What do you think that might be?'

She looked genuinely shocked. 'That's not right,' she said. 'I don't know where you've got that from—'

'Something significant has happened and people connected to the group are dying. I need to speak to someone who's still on the inside. People will be having doubts about it. Give me one name. Who'd talk to me?'

Josie shook her head. 'There are *no* names!'

Belsey sat back, studied her.

'How old are you?'

'Twenty-seven.'

'So in 2013 you were twenty-five. Bit old for an undergraduate.'

'I still had connections with the university,' she said quietly.

'No – I get it. You were searching for new recruits. You found Thomas Arnett, drew him in. Now he's in and you're out. How does that feel?'

Josie looked away.

'Did they tell you to prey on sad young men specifically?'

'I didn't prey on anyone.'

'You look for the vulnerable: students, young people away from their families for the first time. They're the ones to target, right?'

She shook her head, fell silent for a moment. Then she said: 'Is he OK?'

'Fuck knows. No, I very much doubt it. I reckon he's a few hours from dying, possibly in quite a horrible way. You should have seen the state of a body we pulled out of Epping Forest. Maybe that was Tom. Hard to tell, the way the face was left. I need to know where to look, where they're based. What their plan is.'

She picked up a child's bib from the seat beside her, folded it.

'Did you cut yourself off from your family?' Belsey asked.

'No.'

'How come?'

'He arranged it according to what was right for the individual. He said we should try to maintain our Earth lives if *possible*. Some of us.'

'Maintain your *Earth lives*?'

'Our level-one lives; our infancies, as he called them. They were a shell, a chrysalis. They could protect us on the journey, until the time was right.'

269

'Until the time was right for what?'

'The next stage.'

'What would that involve?'

'I never found out.'

'I guess the Earth lives help keep the money coming in as well. There are rich members, Josie – and a couple of them have been shedding cash like you wouldn't believe.'

'You don't get it.'

'I think you left because you knew something wasn't right.'

'I wasn't right.'

'How much money did you give them?'

'That's not relevant.'

'But you gave money.'

'Of course. Money is necessary. The richer help the poorer. Everyone's part of it. I thought I was involved in a ground-breaking experiment. I thought I was helping humanity. I . . . When I think about it, it doesn't make sense. I was a different person. You think I was mad. But I wasn't.'

'I don't think you were mad.'

'Lawrence would think I was mad.' She gazed towards the window, but wasn't looking through it any more. 'I didn't understand all of it. Everything is energy. I understood that. All atoms are energy. We think we're us, ourselves, but we're part of the universe. We waste so much energy – on useless things. That's why most people never develop their abilities. That made sense to me. War is a waste of planetary energy. I understood that bit too. And we tried to help people, in care homes, in prison. I saw men who had killed people become peaceful, kind. And then they would help others. There were so many kind people.'

'Did you go into prisons?'

'Once – Holloway. God.' She shook her head. 'If some people knew I'd done that . . . But I was good at it. In the early stages. I was told I had potential. And the seizures stopped.' She looked at Belsey. 'I could see things, when we did envisioning. My mother died when I was fifteen and I was able to see her and speak to her again.' Her voice was calm, as if recounting a dream. 'In the training I could often guess which card Andreas was looking at.'

'Really?'

'Yes.'

'Did he tell you this or did you see the card?'

She squinted at him. 'You're saying it was a trick. I suppose it might have been. But it made sense. I was never good at school, but I knew things – about people. If they were upset. And in my mind I'd always been good at seeing places, escaping.'

'Did they ever talk about how it ends? When their work is complete, or something stops them prematurely?'

'No. Is anyone going to find out about all this? About me?'

'I'm worried it's going to become public in a big way if I don't find Andreas fast,' Belsey pressed on, sensing weakness. 'He may be very wise and understanding – but I think he got filthy rich off this, Josie. I think maybe he knows it's ending, and that he can force good people to do bad things and cover his tracks.'

'That's not what the money was about.'

'What was it about?'

Another hesitation, then she looked at him with a new focus.

'To fund the new Research Centre.'

'Yeah, it funded something. Not a new research centre.'

'But I saw it.'

'You saw it?'

'Yes.'

'So where is it?'

'I don't know. We had to wear goggles – black-out goggles – to go there. To stop us seeing where it was.'

'You're kidding.'

'No.'

'In London?'

'Yes, definitely. It was close.'

'When you were inside, what could you see? What was outside the window?'

'There weren't any windows.'

'OK. No windows. What else? What was it like?'

'Big. With equipment.'

'What kind of equipment?'

'Computers, and things for measuring your skin temperature and voltage. There are special booths. The Foundation has this thing called Gateway. It's a training course with sound booths and isolation tanks. The booths are called CHEC units.' She paused for a moment, recalling the acronym. 'Controlled Holistic Environmental Chambers. You wear headphones and hear instructions, audio-guidance.'

'And the isolation tanks?'

'It's like any flotation tank. There's nothing so strange about it. You float in salt water.'

She caught his reaction.

'Do you think you could drown someone in there?' Belsey asked.

'In an isolation tank? I suppose so. If you really wanted to.' She looked puzzled. Harper's lungs. Jason Stanford wandering, wet, disorientated.

'And you think it was in London?' he said.

'Definitely. I think, maybe . . . maybe that's where Majorana is based. A couple of people thought that. You know, gossip.'

'Any idea which bit of London?'

She shook her head.

'How often did you go there?'

'Just once. It was new. I visited just before leaving.'

'Something happened there, didn't it – to make you leave?'

'No.'

'What happened there?'

'We had the experiences.' She looked at the DVD clock, at Belsey, imploring.

'The experiences.'

'Please . . .'

'Come on, Josie. What did the experiences involve?'

'I couldn't describe. Honestly, honestly – I wish I could. They were . . . I don't know how he did it. It was terrifying. And amazing, and . . . god. I don't know what they were.'

'Consume anything narcotic to engender these experiences?'

'I don't know what we consumed. There were drinks we had. Different ones. They were definitely part of it.'

'This occurred at the Research Centre.'

'Yes.'

'Where did you drive there from?'

'They picked me up from where I was living. Golders Green.'

'How long do you think you were driving for?'

'Maybe twenty minutes.'

'Into town?'

'I don't know. I thought so. I'm happy now,' she said. 'I'm in such a different place.'

'Good.'

'We just moved here. My family's nearby. And Lawrence, of course. I don't know. I was . . . It feels like so long ago. Really.'

'Call me if there's anything else,' Belsey said, getting to his feet. He tore a corner from one of the CCTV print-outs, wrote his number for her. She took it, but didn't look at it. He gathered the rest of the papers from the coffee table.

'I got carried away a bit. That's all.'

'I know.'

He left the house. A vehicle started moving as he stepped out: black, four-door, maybe a Saab. It turned the corner before he got a proper look.

35

BELSEY GOT BACK INTO THE Bentley and parked around the corner, waiting in case the Saab returned. He thought through what he'd heard. Josie Christie believed the Bridge had several thousand members across the world. He wasn't so sure. But there had been one international attendee at the Comfort Hotel. So what was the Dutch government doing getting involved?

He looked through the Comfort images he'd just shown Josie. There was the Europcar Toyota. But he'd never seen anyone get out of it. It was just watching. Lindy Voskuil remained in the car.

And she hadn't come up online in any departmental searches. So, working on something sensitive? Intelligence gathering? An elite department; one that didn't want its employees advertised.

It had to connect to Spier and the *Mail*'s mystery woman. Last Wednesday Dutch police picked her up near a research institute. Did that provoke an investigation that necessitated the skills of Lindy Voskuil? Did they have any idea what was going on? The mounting body count – its connection with the Chloe Burlington murder, with Amber Knight? Belsey could imagine the slow bureaucratic workings only too well. He was on his own.

A car pulled up outside Josie Christie's. Belsey tensed. It wasn't the Saab. A metallic-grey BMW. A man got out, took a case from the back seat. Lawrence.

She opened the door before he reached the threshold. Kissed him. Shut the door. The house sat there, ominously quiet; identical to the rest. But different. It contained someone who'd been picked out. It had the glow of possibilities. Someone had touched it with possibility.

Majorana.

Most organisations are a pyramid. But a pyramid needs each layer if it's going to stand up. For the Bridge Foundation, lines of power would have to lead upwards, through the mentors, the recruiters. A group is vulnerable where it touches the outside world. The moment to focus on was when the group met the outside, when truth crashed into someone's life and carried them off.

He thought about what Thomas Arnett's father had said: *He sounded OK. But not entirely himself.* People who came into contact with the Bridge changed. There was that fracture in their lives dividing a disappointing past from a future of infinite promise. He'd sat in meetings listening to gamblers, crackheads and alcoholics trace the same passage.

Where were members of the Bridge when the group first found them?

He knew how Thomas had been recruited: Josie Christie scouring campus.

Jason Stanford? Troubled for years, then around the end of 2013 he seemed to have put his demons to bed. Belsey googled, spent a bit of quality time with Jason. There was an interview online in which he spoke of a new focus. By coincidence, that was a few weeks after he'd been romantically linked to Amber. Gossip site Heatworld photographed him hand in hand with Amber, October 2013.

For Amber, 2013 was a good year. She'd finished a tour and shot a film. She'd recorded her award-winning album, *First Light*. Six months earlier she'd been in a bad place. The dark year, 2012, centred on the death of her father. She was photographed obliterated on the floor of a friend's bathroom. She threw a bottle at a photographer and was cautioned by the police. She picked up some scars.

And at some point she met Chloe. Did Chloe bring her in? It was possible he'd been seeing the power dynamic the wrong way around.

And Mark? Lost his job in the school lab. Didn't leave his room for weeks. Then he started going to the centre. '*Which centre?*' '*The one in Islington. It was a way of getting him out of the house. That helped.*'

What had Josie just said? Classes at a centre off Essex Road. Islington. Belsey reeled through his memories of a familiar patch of the city. He had a feeling he might even know the place. By the Marquess Estate. Not a bad spot to set up shop if you're looking to recruit damaged people.

The Marquess Estate was on a fault line, two of London's tectonic plates hitting each other hard. Essex Road was the poor side, away from the wealthy continent of Upper Street. It led to the estates: Packington, Barnsbury, Marquess. Marquess had a local community space in a hefty bit of red-brick Victoriana that had survived next to the council blocks. Belsey walked in, half expecting to interrupt a convocation of the Bridge.

It was cool inside, original tiles in the hallway, a noticeboard crowded with flyers for English lessons, Pilates, mother and toddler groups. Rooms for hire.

It also had CCTV. Belsey counted three cameras. That could be useful. He followed the ground-floor corridor past an unmanned canteen, counter shuttered, a table with tea and coffee and an honesty box. He wandered upstairs. There was a room with a mirror along one wall, a dance bar, a stack of torn mats. There were carpeted rehearsal rooms, one with a stand-up piano. A group of African women walked past.

'I'm looking for the manager,' Belsey said. 'Anyone in charge of this place?'

They pointed him towards an office at the end of the corridor. The office was locked. Belsey was considering his next move when a woman appeared.

'Can I help?' She looked hard and a little weary, in a tracksuit, short blonde hair. She held a bunch of keys and a pack of Silk Cut.

'Actually I had a specific question. There's a class I'm particularly interested in. Bridge something. Something Bridge. Does that ring a bell?'

It evidently did.

'How did you hear about it?' she asked, carefully.

'A friend recommended it.'

'We don't have that here any more.'

'That's a shame. When did you stop?'

'A couple of years ago. Who are you?'

He took a step towards her. 'I'm actually a private investigator. I'm interested in some individuals who attended the class and subsequently went missing.'

There was a flicker of guarded curiosity. 'Would you like to come to my office?'

The office was cramped, cluttered, one narrow window behind mesh. The manager cleared a stack of timetables from a chair so he could sit down.

'I'm Rebecca,' she said. 'I run this place.'

'Pleased to meet you. I'm Nick.'

'You're an investigator?'

'Yes. I have concerns about this group. I'm speaking to everyone who's had contact with them.'

'We hire rooms out. They ran a weekly class here for eighteen months or so. That's all.'

'Called what?'

'The classes were called something like Personal Potential Workshops.'

'But you knew the name, the Bridge.'

'Room-hire payment came from an account in the name of Bridge International. Something like that.'

'What did the classes involve?'

'I don't know.'

'Were they big?'

'None of the classes here are big. Maximum fifteen, twenty. They used Room 3. It's the medium-sized one. I never saw one of their classes in action. They had chairs, I think.'

'Who ran it?'

'All those kinds of details would have gone in the break-in.'

'The break-in?'

'I thought you might already know about that.'

'No.'

The manager raised her eyebrows. 'I assumed they'd done something like that again.'

'What happened?'

'Someone got into the office. Hence this.' She gestured at the bars over the office's single window. 'Not very friendly.'

'What did they do?'

'Took some computers. And files.'

'Files?'

'Yes. Membership files. Centre users. Personal details.'

'Did the police arrest anyone?'

'No.'

'But you think it connects to the Bridge.'

'Yes. Can you tell me what's going on?'

'I think the classes were a front for a group that was recruiting people from here. Here, and maybe other places.' She looked curious, not disbelieving. 'Did you mention your suspicions to the police when they investigated the burglary?'

'Yes.'

'And did the police speak to anyone from the group?'

'Yes.'

Belsey felt the old CID pleasure-centre light up. So the group were in the system. Majorana was in the system. He had history.

'But the police didn't charge anyone,' Belsey clarified.

'No. Not enough evidence.'

This was standard enough. A nicked community-centre PC not inspiring investigative dedication. Good old Met.

'So then you barred them.'

'No. We'd cancelled the classes a couple of weeks earlier. That was the thing, you see. They were switching off the security cameras – coming into the office and switching them off at the main control panel. I'm fairly sure it was them.'

'Why?'

'It had to be. It happened a few times before we figured out it coincided with their classes.'

'Why would they do that?'

'Anonymity, I suppose.' She shrugged. 'I don't know. Some of their workshops advertised themselves as dealing with drug rehabilitation, addiction treatment, abuse trauma. Even in here you can get some high-profile individuals coming in, or their kids.'

'See any high-profile individuals?'

'Not personally, but you learn not to look too closely.'

'Any idea where they were based?'

'No.'

'Did anybody mention a research centre of some kind?'

'A research centre? I never heard about anything like that. I really just processed the bookings. Why? What kind of research centre?'

'I don't know. Look, I'll level with you. I haven't got much to go on, but I believe this group has become progressively more dangerous.'

'Dangerous?'

'Yes. So please – do you remember *anything* about the individual running it?'

'Really, I never saw him. I don't have the emails any more or I'd show you. But the police might be able to help. They interviewed him, I think.'

'You think the guy running these sessions was interviewed by the police?'

'Yes. I specifically remember them telling me that. Because I was frustrated that nothing came of it.'

'Do you have a police reference number?'

'I guess I must do.' She went into her emails. Ten unbearable minutes later, Belsey had the police reference.

'So what exactly have they done now?' the manager asked.

36

BELSEY SAT IN ANDY PRICE'S Bentley with the reference number useless in his hand, like a record with nothing to play it on. An interview with the man setting up the Bridge. Andreas Majorana. With his date of birth, home address. Maybe his real name.

But he couldn't do anything without proper police back-up. With a warrant out on his name, the chances were nil.

Maybe he could call on some international support.

He tried Lindy Voskuil's mobile number again. No answer. Sifted through the notes he'd dumped on the back seat. He'd written her hotel down somewhere.

Five minutes later he was en route to the Park Grand, Kensington.

The hotel wasn't, in fact, particularly grand, shoehorned into a residential road behind Earls Court, the only modern building amongst the monotonous stucco of west London. The lobby was bright, plants reaching protective tendrils over scattered armchairs. A small, neat man on reception smiled as he approached with a thick sheath of notes under his arm.

'I believe you've got a Lindy Voskuil staying here,' Belsey said. The receptionist didn't need to check.

'Yes. Are you collecting her?'

Belsey wondered at this for a split second.

'Yes,' he said.

'She says she will meet you here.'

'When?'

The man checked a clock over his shoulder. Almost four o'clock. 'In a few minutes, sir. Want me to call her room?'

'No, that's OK.' Belsey went and stood amongst the armchairs. No one else present; no man for whom he could be mistaken. Then one walked in.

He was tall, bald, in a loose-fitting grey suit. He looked around, checked his watch. Belsey stepped back, turned his face, and when the man began towards the desk, he walked out and positioned himself across the road behind a delivery van, watching the hotel entrance.

The tall man emerged three minutes later with a woman in her fifties: short, copper-coloured hair, a green two-piece suit and raincoat over her arm. The receptionist accompanied them. All three looked up and down the street. They conferred, then Voskuil and her visitor set off west.

Belsey followed. They walked briskly, away from Earls Court to the back of Cromwell Road. To the tower block at 19 Collingham Place: the National Crime Agency HQ.

Belsey gave it thirty seconds, then went in after them.

The place had seen better days. The lobby was scuffed, one row of plastic seats bolted to the floor, one guard at a desk next to electronic gates. He stood up when Belsey entered. Unfamiliar faces are never very welcome in police HQs. Behind his desk was a room filled with parcels and post.

'You've got a parcel for DCI Ronald Jeremy,' Belsey said. The man studied him.

'Here?'

'That's right. It came here. Might say DCI Jeremy, National Cyber Crime Unit. It's a hard drive. Should be obvious.'

The guard went to check. Belsey took the visitors' book from the desk. Lindy Voskuil had been signed in by DCS David Walton. Europol Unit.

Belsey returned the book to the desk as the guard came back.

'I can't see it. When was it delivered?'

'Today. It might be with DCS Walton. He told me it was here.'

'OK.'

'Can you check? It's urgent.'

The guard scratched his head with a pen. He looked through a list of extensions stuck to the desk and eventually picked up the phone.

'DCS Walton? Reception here,' the guard said. 'There's a gentleman asking about a parcel . . . No, I don't know. He's here.'

'Let me speak to him,' Belsey said.

The guard passed the phone.

'I'm here about the Bridge Foundation. I'd like to speak to you and Lindy Voskuil.'

There was a pause, then Walton said: 'Who is this?'

'Someone you need to speak to.'

'Stay there.'

Walton appeared a moment later. Not the man who'd accompanied Voskuil: young, with a flush to his cheeks. He looked like someone who'd had a job at a merchant bank but felt they had to prove themselves, so joined the police. But he hadn't been cut out for the streets and ended up here. With him was Voskuil. She had a hard stare, smoker's lines around her mouth.

'What is this?' Walton demanded. 'Who are you?'

'You're investigating a group called the Bridge,' Belsey said. He turned to Voskuil. 'I'm guessing you're here in connection with the woman who was picked up near Spier. She was a member of this group. You were also at the Comfort Hotel when they met. Several members have died or been killed since that meeting, probably as a result of someone secretly filming it. Have you got information about who's running it? A man called Andreas Majorana?'

'What do you know about him?' she asked.

'Very little. But I've got something you need to chase up if you haven't found him yet.'

'What is it?'

'Can we talk?'

'Who are you?'

'I'd rather not give my name.'

Walton stared at him searchingly.

'Do you know about a possible attack?' Walton asked.

'I know all sorts of things. I collaborate better when offered a chair.'

'Maybe you should come up.'

They took a lift to the tenth floor, walked through open-plan offices. He was in an outpost of SOCA's International Crime Department: the UK Europol National Unit. They arrived at a conference room with a grey view of building works, an unused flip-chart, water bottles and loose papers in evidence bags scattered across a large, round table.

Two men waiting, seated at the table. One man in a short-sleeved white shirt, with a military-style buzz cut, the other the man who had collected Voskuil. He stood when Belsey entered. He had a slight stoop and mournful eyes. He glanced at Voskuil as if waiting for her to make an introduction.

'He knows about the group,' Voskuil said. The man put his hand out. Belsey shook it.

'Nick.'

'This is Superintendent Dreyer,' Voskuil said.

The buzz cut didn't get an introduction. He didn't get up. He studied Belsey closely, another Europol liaison officer, or maybe a more muscular arm of the Yard, Organised Crime or its satellite sections. Belsey took a seat, laid out the CCTV stills and DVLA records for the Comfort attendees, the files from the Bridge Foundation website; finally, Thomas's lecture notes. Walton leaned over, hungrily. *Do you know about a possible attack?* he'd asked. No – but Belsey smelled a middle-ranking investigator uncertain whether to take a specific worry higher. Half pumped with authority, half nervous about calling the shots.

'These people are connected to the Bridge Foundation?'

Before Belsey could answer the military-looking man sat up with a look of recognition.

'This is Nick Belsey,' he said. 'He's a disgraced police officer. There's a warrant on him.' He got out of his seat, went to a phone mounted on the wall of the conference room and called back-up. The others exchanged glances. Not great, Belsey thought. At the same time, it made him slightly less random. A disgraced police officer has more authority than a madman.

'Want me arrested?' Belsey asked. 'Or do you want to know why the woman was in Spier? She was trying to get into the Netherlands Institute for Radio Astronomy. Probably looking for proof, looking for Group 1, or some other crucial element of the Bridge.'

Walton looked between the buzz cut and Belsey.

'Have you been involved with the Bridge Foundation?' Voskuil asked.

'Not on the inside.'

'What do you know?'

'They're dangerous and we need to collaborate to stop them. It's led by a man going by the name of Andreas Majorana. They're training for the next, post-terrestrial phase of humanity. Which suggests, as well as being dangerous, they're deeply unhinged.' Then, to maintain some advantageous urgency given Walton's apparent concern, Belsey added: 'Have you contacted anti-terrorism?'

'We didn't want to be pre-emptive,' Walton said, quickly. 'To jump the gun, so to speak. But this . . .'

Walton and Voskuil sifted the CCTV stills, the details of attendees. A pair of thick-necked constables appeared in the conference-room doorway, hesitant.

'He has their names and addresses,' Voskuil said to Dreyer, gesturing at the research. Belsey continued.

'A man present, Ian Harper, secretly filmed the Comfort Hotel meeting. He was killed on Saturday. Word of the filming got to Majorana, I think. Another meeting was arranged on Saturday night at a research centre they have. I don't know where it is. I think Harper was drowned there, possibly in a flotation tank. His lungs were filled with salt water. Chloe Burlington was present. She was murdered on Monday night to stop her talking. A couple involved, John and Melissa Shaw, just killed themselves.'

'Is this true?' Voskuil glanced at Walton. 'The deaths?'

Walton looked to the UK officer for assistance.

'These are ongoing homicide investigations,' the anonymous man said. 'No one has suggested they connect. The suicides are fresh.'

The four of them turned back to Belsey.

'What about the rest?' Walton asked.

'Want to send the guards away?' Belsey said.

'Please,' Dreyer said to Walton.

Walton dismissed the two officers, shut the door. Took a seat. Belsey's antagonist shook his head, sat back down, glaring. 'How are you involved in this?' Walton asked.

'I was having a look into someone who's gone missing. It led me to the group. Simple as that. What about you?' Belsey said. There were nervous glances. They looked at his notes again as if assessing his value. 'Here I am, being generous. I can help, but I'm not going to do this one-way.'

Dreyer raised an eyebrow at Voskuil, which seemed to communicate that they had little to lose.

'The woman who was found near Spier is called Teresa Glynn,' Voskuil said. 'We traced her from travel tickets. She flew from London to Amsterdam on 4 May, and travelled north from there. She has told us very little. But from what we can discern her involvement with the Bridge Foundation dates back to 2011.'

Dreyer leaned forward in his seat. 'We believe she attended a seminar at the Holiday Inn in Swiss Cottage, in June that year. Do you know about this?'

'No. What does she say happened?'

'She claims she is involved in an experiment, chosen for her particular mental sensitivity.' The Dutchman spoke fluently but with care, as if his English might break if mishandled. 'Once involved with the group you receive instructions on everything from diet to clothing, what materials to wear, how to structure your sleep. Sometimes you will go several days without sleep. This is supposedly preparation for intergalactic travel.'

Walton smiled as if the embarrassment was his. 'It's nuts,' he said.

'What took you to the Comfort Hotel?' Belsey asked.

'There was a message on Teresa Glynn's phone regarding a meeting at the hotel,' Voskuil said.

'Do you know what it was about?'

'No.'

Belsey picked up one of the evidence bags. Inside he could see a flyer. It carried a photo of a man in a suit on a bench, head in hands. 'FACT: Depression causes the greatest disability for adults under 45. Find out what is stopping you breaking free. Learn to use your mind as it wants to be used.'

'These were all found in her home,' Voskuil said. 'Attendees of the seminar are then invited to entry-level workshops. In 2011 these were being run under the name Personal Potential Therapy. Here, individuals were supposedly tested for suitability for the advanced programme.'

'How many groups have you found?'

'We can only find evidence of the London group. We believe Majorana operates some form of pyramid scheme, financially. He is dependent on contributions from new recruits to maintain a flow of funds to Bridge projects, initially subsidising less well-off members as they become indoctrinated. This has increased in the last couple of years. Rapidly. Around September 2013 it seems the whole programme became a lot more secretive. Majorana's public website was taken down. We think there was a fundamental change in the operating strategy, possibly due to a partner coming in.'

Around the time of the break-in; the move from the hired room on the Marquess Estate.

As if to confirm his suspicions, Voskuil added: 'We believe a lot of money was put into converting somewhere new. Larger premises.'

'The Research Centre.'

'You know of this?'

'I spoke to someone who'd been involved, a woman called Josie Christie. She claims she was taken there blindfolded. It's in central London.'

Another exchange of glances.

'A research centre?' Dreyer said.

'She saw it?' Voskuil said.

'So she says. What else changed around that time?'

'The literature now refers more frequently to different levels, stages of initiation, ancient truths rediscovered,' Dreyer said. 'There is urgency. Earth is in a form of quarantine, a sick planet. Powers that benefit from this are stopping it healing; stopping mankind fulfilling its cosmic destiny. But soon the various Bridge groups will reunite, be free of the Earth.'

'It's a different MO,' Belsey said. 'The personnel's changed and so has the operating strategy.'

'Yes,' Voskuil said. 'We think so – that someone's come in, someone working with Majorana to run the group, maybe behind the scenes. There is now tighter security, more emphasis on raising money, the targeting of wealthy individuals. Plus increased suspicion of those they don't trust, people who are problematic for some reason.'

'Why would Majorana agree to that?'

'We don't know.'

Belsey tried to imagine. You find the truth, you're saving humanity, but somewhere along the line you need cash flow. Then you find there are indeed dark powers ranged against you, from concerned family members to HMRC, none fully swallowing the cosmic promise on offer.

'What makes you think they're planning something violent?' he asked.

'Well,' Walton said, 'if what you're saying is true they haven't exactly been very peace-loving in the last few days. Groups like this—' he looked disdainful '—they're clearly fruit loops. Who knows what they're going to do next.'

'They worship death,' Dreyer said. He nodded to the notes. 'Death and fire, the destruction of the Earth.'

'Do they?'

'You say there have been suicides.'

'Only two that I know of. Joint.'

Dreyer gave a deep sigh, furrowed his brow, glancing across the CCTV stills as if they were already a memorial.

'We believe the Comfort meeting involved rehearsals for an attack,' Voskuil said. 'Or at least a mass suicide, a demonstration.'

'The cult going public,' Walton elaborated. 'Going out with a bang.'

'Why do you think that?' Belsey asked.

'In their communications, there is increasing reference to something called eclosis. Have you heard of that?'

'It's how a chrysalis becomes a butterfly.'

'Well, I believe in this context it refers to whatever spectacular end they have planned.'

'Really? I think it's about becoming enlightened,' Belsey said. 'Shedding your earthly identity. That's what they're into.'

Walton looked unconvinced. They had something else, Belsey could tell. They were hesitating.

'Come on,' he said. 'What is it?'

It was Walton who gave in. 'An hour after the meeting in Finchley we intercepted a call from a known associate of Teresa Glynn. A man, warning a family member to avoid central London on Saturday.'

'Tomorrow.'

'Yes.'

'It could have been about traffic,' Belsey said. 'Central London's a nightmare on Saturdays.'

'Maybe,' Walton said, with a sigh. But the room had become a little cold with reality. 'Only he gave a specific time.'

'Go on.'

'Between twelve and two p.m.'

'Not rush hour.'

'No.'

'I don't think they're like that,' Belsey said.

'Where are they all then?'

'I don't know.'

Dreyer cut in. 'We think that members of the group have congregated somewhere. They haven't travelled far. They are in London, maybe at this Research Centre you've mentioned.'

Belsey sat back. His phone buzzed with a text. It wasn't a number he had stored. Then he saw the message: 'This is Josie. You visited me today. Please call this number asap.'

He got to his feet, handed Walton the crime reference number from the Marquess Community Centre. 'This is one of the places they recruited from. In September 2013 they broke in and removed all traces of their presence. I think Majorana was interviewed as part of the investigation. He'll be on record if you get the file. Excuse me for a second, I have to make a call.'

37

HE STEPPED OUT TO THE corridor under their watchful stares, dialled the number. Josie answered immediately, whispering, terrified.

'Nick?'

'What's happened, Josie?'

'You led them to me.'

'Where are you? I'll get you somewhere safe.'

'Don't say anything else on the phone, please. I need to show you something.'

'Where are you?'

'Is your phone safe?'

'Yes.'

'Meet me at 201 Scrubs Lane, as soon as possible. In Acton. Please. Please make sure they don't follow you.'

Belsey moved through the open-plan office to the stairs, out through reception and back to his car. Scrubs Lane – a long way from her home. Maybe that was the point. She sounded genuinely terrified. He drove fast, throwing in late turns with no signals, sudden bursts of speed, keeping an eye on his mirrors until he was sure he was alone.

She'd sent him to a stretch of dilapidation between Wormwood Scrubs and St Mary's Catholic Cemetery – a long row of terraces that became a threadbare industrial estate as you drove north, with piles of tyres, a rickety van selling bacon rolls and three hand car washes.

Number 201 Scrubs Lane was derelict, a former garage stripped to its crumbling bricks. Belsey parked. He wondered if she'd made a mistake. Then he began to wonder what he'd been called to. The units either side were shuttered. A mound of sand and a cement mixer in front of the garage suggested someone had intentions. No sign of any builders, though. No one in sight. He climbed out of the Bentley and picked up a rusted length of engine pipe from the rubble, stepped past the sand into the dank interior.

'Josie?'

'Nick.'

Her voice came from beyond what had been a second doorway, now a crude gap amidst bricks. Belsey walked through. A bag came down over his head.

He lashed out, dropped the pipe, reached up to the bag and his arms were pulled back. Two hands on each arm. He could hear a third person close by. He checked his instinct to struggle. One of his few rules of survival: if you're the only one who can't see, stop fighting. There was a ripping sound and then his wrists were bound with gaffer tape. His phone was taken out of his pocket. He was marched to the back of the building, then they were outside again and he was forced into the back of a van, down to the floor.

The engine started a moment later. Someone kept a heavy, booted foot on his head. It meant there were rear seats of some kind. A minibus or maybe a modified Transit. His hood had a distinct smell of hairstyling wax. He reckoned a pillowcase. No mouth gag. A used pillowcase and gaffer tape around the wrists: amateurs using whatever came to hand. Where were they going?

The van lurched right onto Scrubs Lane. He tried to keep a sense of direction. They were driving south, past the cemetery; then they turned left. After another few minutes he thought he could hear the Westway beside them. So they were heading into town. He wondered whether Josie Christie was OK. He listened whenever they stopped at lights or junctions as if parts of London might announce themselves. Eventually they slowed, dropped to the speed of residential roads. He heard a radio outside – the hysterical pitch of football commentary – then it was gone. They made a final turn and stopped.

Nothing happened for thirty seconds. Then the van's back door was thrown open and he was bundled fast across what was definitely cobblestones, led up four stone steps. He was indoors. There was a sound of a tap running, or a bath of some kind. But he wasn't stopping. The hands on either arm dragged him through successive rooms, one door after another, to somewhere darker, then down concrete stairs.

The temperature dropped. He smelt salt water.

They pushed him through a final doorway and his toes hit a box on the floor.

'Sit down,' a man said. Not a voice he recognised: middle-aged, middle-class. Belsey eased himself down. He heard the rip of duct tape again. His ankles were bound. That was a blow. The edge of the pillowcase was lifted up just enough to expose his mouth. He felt a finger at his mouth, then a pill forced in. He wedged the pill between his teeth and bottom lip. The neck of a plastic bottle touched his mouth. He accepted the water, made a show of swallowing. The hood dropped back down. He held the pill between his front teeth to stop it dissolving.

'Get some sleep,' a woman said. Belsey listened. Maybe four pairs of feet marching out? Then a door being locked.

He spat out the pill then shuffled in each direction. He couldn't get far. There were shelves, boxes. A store cupboard. He felt along the wall, found a corner, a rough edge of brick. He sawed the tape against the brick, steadily, silently, until his upper arms were aching. He couldn't tell if he was doing anything. Then it began to give. After ten minutes he could force his hands a little further apart, stretching the tape. After another five it snapped.

That felt good.

He lifted the pillowcase. Found his lighter, sparked it. The room was approximately ten feet by ten. Shelves of cleaning products, light bulbs, tea lights in metal holders, bags of Epsom salt, tubs of chlorine. Stacks of towels in plastic wrap, black robes: the kind he'd seen Stanford wearing.

Was this it, then – the Research Centre?

The lack of a gag suggested they were relatively confident of his isolation. He untaped his ankles, but kept the loose tape attached, ready to wrap back around them. If he heard steps he could revert to hostage mode in ten or fifteen seconds.

Belsey found the pill he'd spat out on the ground. Pale blue, oval-shaped: marked APO 7.5. Zopiclone, a sleeping pill; easily available. He pocketed it and went over to the door.

Through the keyhole, he could just make out a large space, faintly lit from a corridor beyond. It contained what looked like chest tombs, alongside white pods big enough for an individual. He could smell lavender. Aromatherapy oils? He looked at the towels, the robes, thought of his journey from the van, over cobblestones, up four steps. That sound of a tap; maybe not a tap after all. He knew where he'd heard it now. It was a water feature. He was in the Retreat Spa. Was that possible?

He listened for movement outside. After several moments' silence, he tried, very gently, pushing the door. Locked tight. Were they waiting to kill him? Killed in a boutique spa. Luxurious. Holistic.

Belsey shook a tea light from its holder and crimped the metal into something resembling a blade. Slipped it into his back pocket. He swept the candle beneath the shelves. There was a blue aerosol can of

WD40 on the floor. He checked it sprayed, then placed it inside his jacket.

He sat back down in the corner, wrapped the loose tape around his ankles. The pillowcase was ready, over his head. He practised rejoining his wrists so that it looked like they were still bound.

Then he waited.

38

BELSEY HEARD A KEY TURN in the lock several hours later. He'd been deep asleep, long enough to leave his muscles stiff. He wondered if some of the Zopiclone had got into his system after all. There was just enough time to pull the pillowcase fully down and put his hands behind his back, pressing his wrists together.

He was shaken by the shoulder, lifted to his feet.

'Take this off me,' he said. And, after there was no reply: 'I can't breathe.'

'You can breathe fine.' It was a different man, older. Someone cut the tape between his ankles so he could walk.

'Where are we going?' He wanted to hear voices, discern numbers, scraps of identity. You never knew what would give you leverage. They didn't play along. He listened for the number of footsteps. More than two people, possibly four again. He was careful not to break the superficial bindings around his wrists as they moved him back up two flights of stairs, into the brightness of what he was sure was the reception. The water feature trickled. The can of WD40 felt bulky and conspicuous in his jacket.

He could hear what sounded like a four-litre engine growling as they left the building and the air became fresher. They crossed the cobblestones towards it. There was a step up to the back seats.

'Lie down.'

He lay down on the seats. An SUV, he imagined. The upholstery smelt new. A heavy blanket was thrown over him. But the general situation was positive, relatively speaking. He wasn't in the boot. That would have been the obvious place to put him. He wasn't in the boot with his throat cut. He had room to manoeuvre here.

Doors slammed closed. Three people: two up front, one beside him, pushing Belsey's legs up into a foetal position to make room. They drove fast, out of the residential area, back into the sound of main roads. Hit traffic. No one was talking. Belsey sensed nerves. Kidnappers were at their most vulnerable out and about with a hostage. Eventually someone turned on the radio: 9 a.m. news. He had thought it was earlier. Unrest in Ukraine, car bomb in Nigeria. Sirens pealed out, close enough to spook his co-passengers. The car slowed. Someone turned the radio off. A phone rang and was answered brusquely.

'Turn left,' the man who'd answered the phone said. They turned. There was something odd about the way they were driving. Approaching lights and junctions the driver slowed well in advance. Which was foolish – made you more conspicuous, not less. Then Belsey realised: they were in convoy.

The same phone rang again and they pulled over. The driver got out, climbed back in; after another thirty seconds' driving they sped up a steep gradient onto a faster road. A flyover. The Westway again.

Belsey eased his hands free behind him.

So, possible minimum of two cars: he could be up against six or seven individuals, possibly eight, heading somewhere fast. He didn't want to get there.

'Stop moving,' the man beside him said. They nudged into the fast lane. Belsey felt a lorry buffeting them. They must have been up to 50mph, which would do the job. The car moved back into lane. A klaxon blared. Belsey eased his hands to his front. He found the crimped metal in his back pocket, moved it to his right hand.

The seat bounced. Belsey froze. But his guard was leaning forward to begin a debate.

'Let me speak to them.'

'We don't have time.'

Belsey took the pillowcase off. He sat up, threw the blanket over the driver's head, stabbed his back-seat companion in the face. The man was middle-aged, unshaven. Belsey went for the jugular, ended up ripping out half his cheek as the car swerved. Blood hit the back window. The front passenger grabbed the wheel then produced a lock knife from his jacket with the other hand. Belsey sprayed him in the eyes with lubricating oil. They careered into the central reservation, Belsey wedging himself against the front seats to soften the blow. A vehicle slammed into the back of them and they came to a stop facing the wrong way.

The three men bailed, injured and staggering, but finding a burst of energy. They ran to a black Vauxhall Zafira that had pulled onto the hard shoulder ahead. It tore off once they were inside, doors flapping. Belsey looked around. He was in a Jeep Cherokee, beige interior bloodstained. Outside: the elevated dual carriageway of the Westway – a steep drop down towards trees, the rooftops of an estate, a pub he didn't recognise.

A minor pile-up had occurred behind him, a collision of three or four cars. Police would be on the scene soon enough. The driver of the Ford Focus that had crashed into the back of them climbed out, pale with shock, wife and kids silent in the car. He looked at the blood on Belsey, then the remains of tape on his wrists and ankles.

'Where exactly are we?' Belsey said.

But the driver had been distracted by the boot of the Cherokee, smashed open. Inside were three bulletproof Kevlar vests, a box of olive-green military biohazard suits, respirator masks. Belsey picked up a mask, then he closed the boot as best he could, got in the front of the Cherokee, checked the car was still working. The engine purred. A fallen Nokia was ringing in the footwell. He picked it up, answered it.

'You've just made a really stupid mistake,' someone said.

Belsey hung up, pocketed the phone, put his foot down.

When he had half a mile between himself and the crash site, he reached for the radio. The presenter, a chirpy-sounding woman, was debating the 'celebrity story of the morning', whether a video posted online by Amber Knight was genuine.

'Has she snapped for good this time?' the presenter asked, laughing. She played a clip. It sounded like Amber: calm, young, sincere. Only she wasn't Amber any more. This was, she began, '*a message for anyone in the world who cares about me.*' And the first thing they should know was her new name. Stella Polaris. '*Latin*', she said, '*for pole star.*' Then it got really interesting:

> *By the end of today you will have heard of the Bridge Foundation, and probably read a lot about how I'm involved with it. Given what society is like, there will probably be a lot of anger at our actions, an attempt to ridicule us, and finally an attempt to portray us as evil. This is in a world where crimes and genocides are taking place every day and no one cares. Those in power will spread more lies through a media that has reduced the consciousness of the population to a bare minimum. I ask you to use your own minds, and decide for yourselves what you think.*
>
> *Whatever happens now, let it serve as a beacon for those whose hearts are not already ashes.*

He took the exit at the next junction, then the ramp onto the eastbound carriageway, and drove back towards the Retreat.

39

IT WAS A BEAUTIFUL DAY to enter a new epoch of life on earth. Sun out, sky blue. Belsey tore the rest of the tape off his wrists and ankles as he drove.

He left the Westway at Edgware Road, cruised into Marylebone. Parked on Montagu Place and approached the Retreat Spa with caution. Its front doors were open. No one on the desk.

The water feature was still going, the only movement in the place. A cover for a massage table lay on the floor. Around it were loose papers fallen from the reception desk.

Belsey tried to retrace his steps.

He wandered in, looking for a way down. Through exercise rooms, massage rooms, studios. Blankets and pillows lay tangled on the floor. People had been sleeping here. He smelt sweat.

He found stairs up, not stairs down.

But he'd been taken down.

Belsey tried every room, until he saw a camera above an anonymous metal door, currently propped open with a fire extinguisher, a code pad beside it. 'STAFF ONLY'.

It led to fire stairs. Here was his down option – down to a neon-lit basement corridor, bare but for motion sensors every few metres or so, ending abruptly at two large, panelled mahogany doors.

Belsey stopped at the doors, listened. He tried a black, iron handle and it turned. He opened the door slowly and stepped into the Research Centre.

Green exit lights cast a dim glow across a space the size of a community hall, double-height, with a balcony looking down over forty plastic seats that had been arranged in neat rows. Circular charts of the night sky covered the walls at either end. A line of writing stretched across the top of each wall, in a script he'd never seen before, involving triangles and parallel lines.

Beyond a dividing shutter was a separate area with a combination of fitness equipment and clinical-looking apparatus. Along the right-hand wall were eight computer monitors. Stacked hard drives had been locked inside two wire-mesh cages in the corner.

Belsey entered a smaller side room with benches and lockers, a single bin overflowing with clothes, shoes and empty mineral-water bottles.

Where had they gone?

In a fourth room at the back he found the isolation chambers. These were the chest tombs he'd seen: squat, black boxes. Opposite them, in white plastic pods, were individual flotation tanks, dry now. He wondered which one Ian Harper had died in.

Beyond the tanks was the door to the storeroom they'd locked him in. Beside it were double doors, an emergency-exit bar across them.

He returned to the smaller side room and the bin, took the bin bag out and emptied it across the floor. Beneath the clothes and water bottles was an oddly familiar detritus: wraps for powdered drugs, squares cut out from a body-building magazine. With these were vials, and inside the vials were the soggy remains of blotter acid tabs. He couldn't remember the last time he'd done someone for possession of acid. Where did the Bridge score? Then, out of the daze, the truth began to emerge.

Belsey found the Nokia from the Cherokee in his pocket, got a signal at the very back, near the storeroom. Lee Chester answered.

'Who's this?'

'It's Nick,' Belsey said. 'What exactly were you supplying to Mark Doughty?'

'Everything. Why? Speed, MDMA. You name it.'

'And a lot of acid.'

'Right, yeah.'

'How much did he buy last time?'

'Acid? Fifty tabs, two bottles of liquid. Hundred pills as well.'

'How long's he been ordering that kind of selection?'

'I don't know – five years now? Every month or so. Never this much before.'

'Can you imagine him as a leader of something?'

'A leader? He's mental. He's a danger to himself, Nicky. Have you found him?'

'Not exactly.'

'Well, he's still about. I heard he was getting fake passports off Kieran Banks.'

'How many?'

'A couple.'

'Know if he got hold of them?'

'No idea, mate.'

'Who was the other passport for?'

'Haven't the foggiest.'

Belsey heard movement. The mahogany doors opened. The main lights came on, bright halogen bulbs blinking across the ceiling. Belsey hung up, turned.

Mark stood at the end of the main meeting room. He wore a dark suit, white shirt open at the neck, black hair in a short ponytail. He saw Belsey through the door of the side room and froze. Belsey dialled 999 with his thumb, slipped the phone into his jacket. Emergency services would put a trace on it. If they had a tag on this phone they might even send someone fast.

The bright light was unnerving. With the house lights up, you could see signs of wear. The plastic chairs looked cheap, the wiring at the back of the isolation chambers exposed. Limescale crusted the edges of the flotation tanks.

Mark tore his eyes from Belsey and surveyed the space like a host at the end of a party that has enchanted everyone but himself. At his feet was a canister of petrol. He nodded at Belsey as if conceding defeat, sat down on a plastic chair in the back row.

'So this is yours,' Belsey said, stepping past the fitness equipment and through the open shutter into the main room. 'Your show, Andreas. Classy alias, by the way.' Mark nodded. Belsey looked around, nodded too. 'Not bad.' He checked his watch. 'Where's the rest of them? What's next?'

'I didn't want it to end this way.' Mark's voice was calm and surprisingly soft. He fixed his pale eyes on Belsey.

'How else was it going to end?'

There was no answer to this, it seemed. Mark's eyes flickered over the screens, the charts, as if seeing things he might have done better.

'You had a good thing going,' Belsey said. 'You were helping people. Then you started killing them. That tends to spoil things.'

'I wasn't involved in the death of Chloe Burlington,' Mark said. He sounded sincere.

'No? What about Ian Harper? He was going to ruin everything, wasn't he? Make it all public?'

'I don't believe I've done anything that needs hiding.'

'He was drowned here.'

'Not at my hands. There are other people involved. They've made us rich,' he said, drily. 'They must be appeased.'

'Sure. Police are on their way,' Belsey said. 'You can convince them of that.'

Mark nodded. He ran a hand through his hair, stared down at his shoes, then up at Belsey again.

'You could join us.' He said it casually, as if inviting Belsey to an impromptu dinner.

'I might have been tempted. I feel I missed the best times though.'

'Not at all. They're just beginning.'

'What's the plan?'

'You're more than a detective, Nick. You know that. You were always looking for something more.'

'Was I?' Belsey checked that his phone had connected. It had signal. The call was still live. He wondered if the call operator was hearing this. 'You know a lot about me, it seems.'

'There are ways of knowing someone.'

'Perceptual Augmentation.'

Mark raised his eyebrows, impressed. 'Amongst other techniques.'

'Is that how you got to know Amber? Is she good enough at mind-reading to know what a horn you have for her? That you have a shrine to her in your bedroom?'

The light in Mark's eyes changed. A more human anger lit them now. Belsey caught a glimpse of the rage behind it all, a glimpse of Queen's Crescent, the life before the Bridge, a life stunted, plans frustrated.

'I *do* know you,' Mark said.

'Great.'

'I know that in fifteen years of CID you've never felt like you've solved anything.'

He let this settle in. Belsey watched him: a guru, like any conman, feeling for the pressure points.

'I've had my moments, Mark.'

But Mark didn't blink. He had recovered his poise. 'Trying to solve death,' he said. 'Bring justice to the world.' He smiled. 'You.'

'I can see the funny side. You've built an incredible thing here. You've got a lot of people high on your own frustration. I respect that. But it's over now and you've left people with a steep come-down. It's a long-winded way of getting laid, that's all I'm saying. It's a waste of life. John and Melissa Shaw . . .'

'You know what's a waste? Throwing away hope when it's offered to you.'

'I think all you really want is Amber and if you can't have her you don't give a fuck what happens, on this planet or any other.'

Mark looked away, shook his head. Belsey watched his face to test the truth of his assertion. What he saw was resolve.

'Have you never killed anyone?' Mark asked, turning back towards him.

'No.'

'Sure?'

'Yes.'

Mark nodded. 'Remote viewing is an incredible thing,' he said, eventually. 'Whether you believe in it or not.'

'I bet.'

'You can follow someone's life back through the years, see the energy being accumulated. It's like tracing a river to its source. Do you know where I get to when I trace yours?'

'Where?'

'A flat in south London. It's not your flat. A woman's. She's not breathing.' Belsey stared at him. Mark's gaze had become distant. 'It's November,' he said.

'Go on.'

'It's difficult getting her downstairs on your own. Into your car.'

'What the fuck are you up to?'

Now Mark closed his eyes. 'King's College Hospital. You think if she dies it will all be over. Then you will have to rethink everything. Maybe it's a shame you never did.'

He rolled his neck, opened his eyes. 'Moments like that are an obstruction. They stand out.'

'How do you know about this?'

'It's hard for some people to accept that their past actions remain inscribed. They think time has washed the guilt from them. But it's those people who become the strongest, who are forced to dive down, to reclaim their own hearts.' He sighed, tensed his hands. Closed his eyes again. 'You think about the girl so much because she was a door. Her death was an offer to you. No wonder you've never been able to talk about it. Sometimes we can't share something because we need it for ourselves. We haven't finished using it.'

'Nice trick,' Belsey said, but his voice had turned weak and unfamiliar. 'This is bullshit.'

'It was the week your father died. You've tried to think about why these things happen. How energy is exchanged. When you took his money, the money he'd hidden, you were taking on his energy, transforming it into the drugs that killed the girl. That's a chain. You could endure it, she couldn't. Hence you're in A&E and you want to run. You don't even wait with her. Because you need to keep your job; keep policing. And where did you think that would take you?' He opened his eyes. His pupils were needle-sharp amidst a pained, pale blue. 'That's what I'm saying – it took you here.'

'How do you know about all this?' Belsey said.

'You can't shut a door like that. Light comes through. It keeps you awake at night.' Then Mark leaned forward, like a salesman ready to close. 'But you can convert it.'

'Melanie Crews didn't die.'

'Not that night, no. I know you tried. She wanted more than she was ever going to get. That's usually the problem, isn't it? But you don't need me to tell you about your past. I see your future. I wish you could see it too. You will achieve things I have failed to achieve.' Mark stood up, petrol canister loose in his left hand. 'Still don't believe me?'

'No.'

'Want to see something? Want to see Melanie Crews?' He walked past the room divider. Belsey remained where he was, tracked him as he passed into the final room, with the tombs and flotation tanks. Mark pushed the lever across the emergency doors, there was a metallic clunk and he ran. A second later Belsey saw the yellow flames spreading across the floor.

40

HE MADE IT UPSTAIRS, THROUGH the spa and out to the Cherokee. There was already black smoke pouring out of the place. He called the fire brigade, then slumped in the driver's seat, stunned, thinking of a bad forty-eight hours thirteen years ago. Melanie Crews.

The sound of approaching sirens jolted him back to the present. Walton and the Dutch must be wondering where he'd got to. Belsey found the number for UK Europol and got put through.

'Where've you been?' Walton asked.

'In a store cupboard.'

'Great, we've got a situation on our hands. Over the past six hours, we've had several leads on people from this group. Some have tried to flee the country, a couple of others have already fled and been picked up visiting various radio telescopes in Europe, like that Spier girl. To be honest, I don't think they know what's going on either – it doesn't seem like a co-ordinated thing. Counter Terrorism are on their way in now. We've got the break-in report you requested.'

'I know who it is,' Belsey said. 'He's called Mark Doughty. I don't know if there's much we can do now.' He looked at the thickening smoke and saw King's College Hospital A&E. Melanie Crews' skin, her cracked lips and pleading eyes.

'Mark Doughty? Is he known to police?'

'I'm not sure.'

'Can you come in?'

'I'm coming in. Where else am I going to go?'

Belsey hung up. He felt numb. He drove. The Aylesbury Estate, he thought. Helping her down the stairs. That week, with the funeral, the stash. A cold winter. *You don't even wait with her. Because you need to keep your job; keep policing.* But he had wanted to wait. It wasn't his idea to leave the hospital. It was his boss's instructions.

Detective Sergeant Bullseye McGovern.

He stopped at the side of Harley Street.

No wonder you can't talk about it. But one person didn't have to be told.

He thought back to Mark's defence: *There are other people involved. They've made us rich. They must be appeased.*

The change in the group, described by the Dutch – someone new had come in. Someone working with Majorana behind the scenes. Tighter security, more emphasis on raising money. More suspicion. Right after the Marquess centre break-in.

Belsey started the car again. By the time he reached Cromwell Road, things had begun to make a lot more sense.

He stopped outside the Europol HQ, walked straight in, jumped the barrier.

'Hey!' the guard called. Belsey sprinted up the stairs to the conference room. It was crowded now. New faces. Everyone turned.

'How did you get in?' Walton asked.

'Show me the break-in report,' Belsey said.

'We've got people looking for Mark Doughty, the man you mentioned.'

'The report.'

Walton lifted it from the conference table and passed it over. 'Islington Police Station, 12/09/2013'. Damage to the community-centre security camera, to the office window. No forensics report. No record of the manager's suspicions; no suggestion that anyone had been interviewed. Attending officer: DI Geoffrey McGovern.

Belsey could see it as if he'd been there: McGovern interviewing Mark Doughty in Islington police station. *Tell me again what they pay? Really? Who?* The question that had been troubling him: why would Majorana allow someone else to come in on his project? It was because he had no choice. *OK, let's say we come to an arrangement . . .*

He saw that initial encounter by the Mayfair crime scene. McGovern hustled his way onto the investigations he wanted to be involved in. Ones that might implicate him if not steered. Belsey looked at his wrists, still a little reddened from the tape, thought of Shaun White, less fortunate, taped to his chair. *Good old Bullseye. Geoff knows how to get them talking.* He also knew the *Sun on Sunday* crew.

Belsey looked up. They were all staring at him.

'What is it?' Walton said.

'This is what he does.'

'What do you mean?'

'Geoff McGovern. I used to work with him.'

'What does he do?'

'Fucks things up with his greed.'

'I don't follow.'

'He's a DI on the Homicide team now. But he used to be in Islington CID. He got involved with the group when he interviewed Mark Doughty about a break-in in 2013. That's why it wasn't pursued. He got involved, saw a way of making some money. A guy called Ian Harper went to the *Sun* with a story about the group. Geoff got tipped off – he has friends at the paper. Harper filmed a group meeting at the Comfort Hotel in Finchley and the next day Geoff drowned him in a flotation tank in front of several cult members. I think he persuaded other individuals present to dispose of the body. Some of them handled all this better than others. Chloe Burlington didn't handle it well. I reckon he confronted her and things got out of hand. I think Geoff might have had low-level surveillance on individuals he didn't trust. He's a paranoid bastard. See if he was using police resources to monitor Chloe Burlington.'

'He's a Homicide detective?'

'That's right.'

Silence. As people were digesting this, the wall-mounted phone rang. Someone picked up, motioned to Walton. He took the receiver, spoke for a few seconds then hung up and grabbed his jacket.

'They've arrested a man at a house connected to Doughty – Herbert Street, Kentish Town.'

'That's his home,' Belsey said. 'His mum's place.'

'He was apprehended a few minutes ago.'

Everyone seemed to rise at once.

41

IT WAS SIRENS ALL THE way to Kentish Town. Belsey rode the slipstream. Herbert Street was already blocked with vehicles. He abandoned the SUV and ran.

Mrs Doughty's front door had been smashed in. A crowd filled the living room, uniformed and plain-clothed. The international contingent joined it, Walton and Voskuil and some Counter Terrorism officers. A man lay face down on the floor. All the furniture around him was upended, slashed. Yellow stuffing and paper money covered the carpet. Maureen Doughty sat in the corner with several grand in twenty-pound notes on her lap.

The crowd parted to reveal Stefan Keydel on the carpet, hands cuffed behind his back. The Sisco investigator's right hand was wrapped in a blood-soaked T-shirt.

'Sit him up,' Belsey said.

Keydel winced as they lifted him. He saw Belsey.

'Tell them who I am,' he said.

'What are you doing here?'

'The Addison Lee account – this is the address for it. Mark Doughty. He just stabbed me through the fucking hand.'

'He was here?'

'Yes. I've got bank statements for him as well. You might want to have a look, fast. He's bought flight tickets.'

Walton found the statements, bloodstained beside the coffee table. A pair of paramedics walked in. Belsey looked at the paper money, the furniture. He walked over to Maureen Doughty in the corner.

'What did Mark say?'

'He's gone now.'

'Gone for good.'

She nodded once.

'He took the knives,' Keydel said, as a constable uncuffed him. A paramedic tentatively unwound the T-shirt. 'He stabbed me and ran.'

Belsey went to the kitchen, saw the drawer out: no sharp knives. One of the constables was talking quietly on his radio, eyes fixed on Belsey. Belsey moved past him to the stairs. He heard the discussion amongst the senior officers in the living room.

'There's payment to British Airways,' Walton said.

'Flying tonight.'

'Get those details to Border Control.'

The rucksack containing Amber's clothes and travel kit had gone from Mark's room. Belsey took a final look at the books and papers, the psychotic library, the bottle of perfume.

Bride.

Officers were coming up the stairs, stalking him around the house. Belsey pushed past them, back to the living room.

'It's Saturday,' he said.

'That's right,' Walton said.

'It's Amber Knight's wedding.'

'OK.' People looked at him curiously.

'Is it happening?'

'Why?'

'How many flight tickets are there?' he asked.

'Two,' Voskuil said. 'And a night booked at the Dorchester Hotel, tonight.'

'Why book a London hotel if he's flying out?' Walton asked.

'To get access to it,' Belsey said. He turned to Keydel. 'How long ago was Mark here?'

'About ten minutes.'

'Get an armed-response unit to the Dorchester.'

'We're going to have to ask you to stay with us, sir,' one of the constables said.

'Not just yet, lads.'

42

HE RAN TO THE CHEROKEE and tore into central London, stopping a block away from the hotel. Fans and paparazzi crowded the streets either side of the Dorchester's main entrance, corralled behind barriers. At the entrance itself were police, doormen and private security in fluorescent tabards. No parking allowed: chauffeured cars circled the place like vultures.

No way in.

But you couldn't defend it all. The hotel building spread over a square kilometre; some of its bars and restaurants had their own entrances. Belsey started around the perimeter. Twenty metres down Park Lane, he found China Tang. A couple of extra security guards stood coldly by the doors. They eyed Belsey as he approached, looking for cameras or any other pap kit, but didn't move to block him. A maitre d' appeared fast, against a backdrop of dark wood and art-deco glass.

'Booking in the name of Belsey.' The man bent over the reservations book. Belsey moved past, weaving between restaurant tables to the double doors that led into the hotel.

The maitre d' called out as they slammed shut behind him. Belsey found himself in a long, opulent, salmon-coloured room, with people taking high tea amongst pillars and flowers. A man in coat-tails played a grand piano. Belsey turned left, past the piano, past staff in red waistcoats all nodding and smiling at him. At the far end was another set of double doors, where the private security started again. He knew where he'd find the wedding.

'Sir!' a man behind him shouted, unmistakably in his direction. Belsey checked his options. He saw a girl in a pink costume walking fast, a promo girl, with a bag full of bottles of Bride. She disappeared through a small, unmarked door.

'Excuse me, sir—'

Belsey followed her through the doorway. On the other side was a long unlit corridor with palm trees in pots. He dragged a pot in front of the door. The door slammed against it. The promo girl turned.

'Where's the wedding?' Belsey asked. She pointed ahead, glanced at the obstructed door. 'Let's go quickly,' he said. He accompanied her swiftly around the next corner into a cramped little room filled with bags and coats. A second young woman in pink was checking her phone. She wore a tray with a neck-strap, like a cigarette-girl, but loaded with perfume. At the sight of Belsey she put her phone away guiltily. There was a second door with a full-length mirror on its back. Belsey opened it and walked into the wedding.

Five hundred expensively dressed guests filled the ballroom, beneath chandeliers and purple drapes, amongst ice sculptures of the bride and groom, and pyramids of champagne flutes. Belsey was beside the stage. A band played a jazz version of one of Amber's hits. A few guests danced; most clustered around the alcohol, the trays of miniature hamburgers, the famous.

Belsey entered the crowd, took a glass of champagne, scanned the faces around him. He saw security appearing behind him, through the door he'd used, moved deeper in. A few metres away, beside one of the ice sculptures, he saw Karen with a man in white; Amber's new husband, looking tanned and pleased. Then they moved apart and Belsey saw Amber. She shone out, her face and arms caught in an explosion of satin and crystal. She looked unreal, bejewelled and dazed.

She looked drugged.

Her entourage stayed close by, monitoring her face for any re-emergence of Stella Polaris. A couple of feet behind them, loitering beside a table of desserts, stood Mark Doughty.

He stared at Belsey. Belsey raised his glass. No response. Belsey took a step forward. Mark reached inside his jacket and brought out a carving knife.

Belsey carried on towards him. Karen turned. She clocked Belsey, stared in disbelief.

'Oh my god,' she said, searching for security. 'It's him!' She pointed at Belsey. Two more security guards approached fast. Belsey continued towards Mark, who stepped forward and grabbed Amber. He got a hand around the top of her right arm, gripped the knife in his left. The tip of the blade brushed her cheek. It took guests a second to respond, then someone screamed.

The crowd rippled backwards, away from the couple. Plates fell. The music lurched to a halt. Then you could hear the crackle of the guards' radios. Mark tried to move Amber towards the door.

Amber stumbled. A man launched himself at the pair and got caught in an awkward tangle of limbs. There were more screams. Someone else rushed to help, then rushed back fast. By the time Belsey could see what was going on there was blood. The man who'd tried to intervene was on his knees, holding his arm. Amber had bright blood splashed across her dress and face. Mark pressed his lips to her ear.

Pockets of the crowd stampeded towards the exits. Mark started again, trying to manoeuvre Amber onwards. A wall of twenty thugs in fluorescent yellow stood between him and the door.

'Mark,' Belsey said, feeling more likely than the hired muscle to steer this to a peaceful conclusion. Security looked at him, contemplating this dubious negotiator. 'Put the knife down, Mark, and they'll let you both go.'

The guards considered this. Mark considered this. Then they all turned, as an unintelligible roar came from the main doors. Armed police crashed in, black caps, bulky Kevlar, waving baton guns and G36 assault rifles and roaring 'Get down!' and 'Put the knife down!' They saw the blood and the lead officer fired his Taser. Mark fell, twitching, to the ground.

They moved for Amber. She backed away. This caused some confusion. Wedding guests approached her. Amber picked up the knife, climbed onto the stage, then, when people approached the stage, she clambered up onto a speaker cabinet. Blood ran down her neck to her dress. All eyes were on her now.

Belsey slipped out.

He walked through the hotel, past the police back-up and security, the waiters and guests, onto Park Lane. The armed-response vans had blocked traffic. He stretched his arms and breathed. Someone barrelled into him.

Belsey hit the floor hard. His head smacked the side of a car. He was turned face down, nose pressed into the pavement, arms wrenched behind him, wrists cuffed tight.

They lifted him to his feet and threw him into the back of a police van.

43

BELSEY SPENT TEN MINUTES GETTING his wind back. His head throbbed and he'd taken a knock to his right knee. He was dazed. Eventually he had breath, then he slowed his breathing and relaxed. Through his half-open eyes he watched the light flicker through the van's window. He could feel every bump in the road. This is what a corpse feels like, Belsey thought, transported in its coffin. Like a child in a pram. No decisions to make. After twenty minutes he wondered where they were going. He couldn't hear any voices or police radios. No one in the back with him.

He smelled whisky.

Belsey hauled himself upright. McGovern sat alone up front. No grille separating them. It was an officer transportation van. They were on a motorway.

'Geoff.'

'Nick.'

'What's going on?'

No answer. McGovern kept his eyes on the road, jaw tense. There was a half-bottle of Bell's beside the handbrake.

'Is Mark alive?' McGovern asked, after a moment.

'He was the last time I saw him.'

'Amber?'

'I hope so.' Then Belsey clocked a road sign.

'Heathrow?'

McGovern reached into his jacket, placed Belsey's passport on the passenger seat.

'You've got two hours to be out of the country.'

'There's a warrant on me. I'll be on the list.'

'You might find you're not.'

'You took me off?'

'People slip through the cracks. While the cracks last.' McGovern checked the dashboard clock. 'Which I reckon will be eight or nine hours. By which time you're going to be very far away, aren't you.'

'You fucking beauty.'

McGovern remained expressionless. Belsey climbed awkwardly through to the passenger seat. 'Take the cuffs off.'

'You've got to be joking.' McGovern negotiated the junction with the M25 and continued south towards the airport.

'Are you flying as well?' Belsey asked. No response. 'How much did you make?'

'Not enough for the shit I've had to deal with.'

He was on a mission now, Belsey saw. Up against it. Bullseye with a last-ditch plan.

'You told him about Melanie Crews,' Belsey said.

'That's right.'

'So he could mind-fuck me.'

'Thought it might shut you up.'

'What else did you tell him?'

'Nothing much. He was a psycho bastard.'

'He was all right until you showed up.'

'Sure, raking in thirty or forty quid a week. I should have left him to it. What a fucking shower.' McGovern shook his head, unsettled.

'Awful for you.'

'This is the second time today I've tried to give you an airport transfer rather than a knife in the face. You might want to show a bit of gratitude.'

'Those amateurs were taking me to the airport?'

'I don't know why I bother sometimes.'

'Give me a swig.'

McGovern took one hand from the wheel, poured some whisky into Belsey's mouth. Someone in an adjacent car stared. McGovern stuck two fingers up, floored the accelerator. Belsey laughed.

'Last time we were at Heathrow together we were picking up Kevin Sanders,' Belsey said.

'The Colonel himself.' McGovern took another swig, didn't offer it.

'He couldn't get off the plane. Do you remember? Twenty-five stone of him. Totally obliterated.'

'Not the man I'd send on a recce to Barbados,' McGovern said.

'Red as a postbox. With his suitcase full of those painted coconuts.'

'The Chief made him strip to see the tan lines.'

Belsey laughed. 'And there's no tan lines. He's burnt all over.' He remembered it now, the Chief's nasal disdain. *Did I say you were to go fucking native, Kevin?* 'Where did Kevin Sanders end up?' Belsey asked.

'Fuck knows.' McGovern slowed as they approached the junction for Terminals 2 and 3. Long-haul. Chain hotels dotted the landscape. 'Where do you think you'll go?' McGovern asked.

'Mexico.'

'Good.'

'They've got a saying there. "*Más sabe el diablo por viejo que por diablo.*" "The devil knows more from being old than from being the devil."'

'What's that meant to mean?'

'I don't know. I'm going to ask them.'

Belsey eased the pressure off his wrists and settled back in his seat. The air-traffic control tower appeared ahead, then the airport's multi-storey car park. He breathed, enjoying the sight of a plane soaring away from the horizon. It struck him as gleeful, a fuck-you to the surface of the Earth; to England, the M25, the Premier Inn. Its vapour trail caught the afternoon sunlight so that, for a moment, it looked as if the sky had been ripped open to reveal another sky behind, the real one, which was golden.